Distant DESIRES

by

Cambria Hebert

DISTANT DESIRES

Published by: Cambria Hebert Books, LLC

CAMBRIA
HEBERT

your key to escape.

http://www.cambriahebert.com

Interior design and typesetting by Sharon Kay
Cover design by MAE I DESIGN
Edited by Cassie McCown

ISBN: 978-1-938857-52-2

Other books by Cambria Hebert

Heven and Hell Series

Before
Masquerade
Between
Charade
Bewitched
Tirade
Beneath
Renegade
Heven & Hell Anthology

Death Escorts

Recalled
Charmed

Take It Off

Torch
Tease
Tempt
Text
Tipsy
Tricks
Tattoo
Tryst

Distant DESIRES

Part One

the abduction

It smelled like stale smoke and beer inside the overcrowded bar. Music that was popular about a decade ago and overplayed so much I wanted to scratch out my eardrums pressed in around me. Between it and the smell, I felt like I might suffocate.

Even though my shift was over, the place was busy enough that I would likely be asked to stay later, to help close down. Normally, I wouldn't even ask. I would just keep working. But tonight this place was getting to me.

My feet hurt, my head hurt, and if one more guy asked me if I moonlighted as a stripper, I was going to waste a good bottle of beer smashing it over his head.

Stupid college town.

Actually, it didn't even matter that there was a college in this town. It would still be stupid without it.

Born and raised in this tiny town in Maryland, I grew up with the right to say that. I wasn't sure of the population, but I knew it was minimal. We had a tiny mall where half the stores were closed because there just wasn't enough business to support them. The entire town breathed a sigh of relief when a big-box store moved in because, for once, no one would have to drive an hour just to get to one.

There was absolutely nothing to do here, which was probably why this bar was always crowded. When people were bored, they tended to drink. Not to mention the start of fall semester last week and the fact RoundRock was a block from the university made this place a popular watering hole.

Not that anyone here was drinking water.

I stopped at the end of the bar and waited for one of the two bartenders to make his way to where I stood. It was Matt. He'd been tending bar here since before I started. He was tall, blond, and looked like he was destined to become a doctor.

He wasn't going to become a doctor.

He played guitar, did shots under the bar when no one was looking, and drove a motorcycle even when it was raining.

Sometimes I teased him and said the reason he kept himself so clean-shaven and preppy-looking was because he didn't want anyone to know exactly how much trouble he was.

He never disagreed, so I knew I was right.

"You look like shit, Soph," he said, leaning across the bar to grin at me.

"You look like a life-sized Ken doll."

His grin grew even wider, revealing a small chip in the corner of his right front tooth. "Wanna be my Barbie?"

A squeamish feeling burst in my middle, but I ignored it. Matt wasn't interested in me. He never had been and he never would be. He was just a charmer who didn't realize the kind of effect he had on women.

Well, no. He did know. It's the reason he made such great tips.

He just didn't know I was also totally taken by his charm. It was something I never let him see. I wasn't about to turn into one of those giggling little ninnies that sat at the bar for hours, just waiting for him to smile my way.

Instead, I dished it right back. We'd fallen into a sort of friendship that way, sort of like I was the annoying kid sister he put up with because he had to.

In a way, it was a better deal than dating him. I actually knew him better and saw him more than any girl who went out with him. He wasn't the kind of guy to stick with the same lady very long. There were too many fish in the pond, waiting to be hooked by him.

"As tempting as it is, I think I'll pass," I shouted over yet another annoying song.

He placed a hand over his heart like he was wounded. I knew he was anything but. "Get out of here. Get some rest," he said.

"You sure?" I asked, glancing around the room again. "We're busy."

"I can handle it," he said, pulling a couple longnecks out of the cooler and sliding them down the bar to a set of waiting hands.

"Okay," I replied, untying my apron and tossing it on the shelf behind the bar. "I'll see ya later."

"Sophie," he called as I turned away.

My dark ponytail swung over my shoulder when I spun back around. "Yeah?"

"You sure you're okay?" Concern lit his caramel-colored stare.

He had the most beautiful hazel eyes. Sometimes they were green and sometimes, like tonight, they were the color of warm caramel drizzled over a sundae.

Ooh, ice cream sounded good.

"Yeah, I'm fine," I said. "I just have a headache."

Matt nodded and ran a hand through his already messy hair.

"Thanks for covering for me."

He winked at me, causing that fluttery sensation to reassert itself in my belly, before turning away to flirt with a blonde at the end of the bar.

I shook my head and left through the back, wondering how many numbers he would leave with tonight.

The rush of crisp autumn air against my skin was refreshing, and I took a deep breath, rolling my head on my shoulders to stretch out the knotted muscles.

The sky looked like liquid ink, dotted with a smattering of stars across the dark canvas. Mountains rose up out of the earth to jut into the night like great fortresses. When I was little, I always felt protected here because it seemed the peaks formed a shield around this town, carving out a little piece of safety in an ever-changing world.

Maybe that was why I never moved away. It wasn't like I hadn't thought about it a million times before.

Even after I graduated high school and the opportunity to go away to college presented itself, I still chose to stay, instead attending the same university that many of the bar patrons inside did.

I realized I would likely always be a small town girl, but I was okay with that.

The gravel under my feet crunched as I walked across the parking lot toward my used Jeep Wrangler. It was an older model, white with a black ragtop that was slightly frayed around the edges. The seats inside were some kind of vinyl material, black to match the top. It didn't have air-conditioning and the controls were as basic as they got.

But it had new tires, working heat, and four-wheel drive. Those things were a must, considering the cold temperatures, snow, and mountainous terrain that was Frostburg, Maryland.

The ragtop was currently down, and I knew it was going to be a cold ride home, but I didn't care. Soon enough, I was going to have to strap on the top and leave it that way through the entire winter. I wanted at least a few more rides with the wind in my hair and the tingly feeling I got in my cheeks from the biting cold.

I tossed my bag onto the floorboard of the passenger seat and slid the key into the ignition. The radio blasted out of the speakers, and I jumped, immediately reaching over and shutting it off.

You'd think by now I would come to expect that. Whenever the top was down, I had to turn the music up really loud to hear it over the ripping wind.

But tonight was a no-music kind of night. Besides the headache that throbbed just behind my eyes and the tension coiled in my neck, I just wasn't interested in music tonight. I wanted to hear the rumble of the engine, feel every bump and jolt this old Jeep made over the road, and let the wind carry away every thought, care, and sound that came close.

It wasn't like I had anything to really be stressed about. My life was pretty good. I was a college student, had my own tiny apartment, a job, and friends. My parents were still married and lived just fifteen minutes down the road.

I wasn't trying to get away from anything specific. But sometimes a girl just wanted the open road, the silence, and nothing but the cleansing wind.

Before pulling out of the parking lot, I tightened the band holding my ponytail and pulled a Frostburg State hoodie out of the back and wrapped it around my body.

I took the long way home, driving down several roads I didn't have to, but choosing to because I liked cruising around. There were still people here and there on the sidewalks of Frostburg, their laughter floating into the open Jeep as I drove. On the side of Main Street was a popular coffee bar (it was popular because it was the *only* coffee bar besides the gas station) that looked like an old church. It sat on a little hill with cement steps rising out of the sidewalk to carry you up to a small green space dotted with outdoor tables. A group of college kids were exiting the arched door and laughing as the light turned green and I hit the gas.

After a while of just driving around, I glanced at the dash and sighed. It was after midnight. I had class at eight a.m. Time to go home.

My apartment was on the second floor of an old house that was converted into several apartments for college students. It was small, with only one bedroom, a tiny kitchen, a bath, and a living room. The rent was cheap and it wasn't too far from campus, so I considered it a good find. Only one other apartment in the house was rented, though, so I don't think many people agreed with me.

It stood down a narrow, single-lane road, kind of off the beaten path. True, it didn't take long to reach everything from my place, but it felt miles away from all the "nightlife" of the small town.

My headlights illuminated the single lane as I turned down it, gravel crunching beneath my tires. I imagined this used to be an old farmhouse, and the people who once lived here grew wildflowers along the roadsides. Big winding trees reached up into the sky and russet-colored leaves threatened to fall overhead and land in the seat beside me.

This road stretched about two miles before it gave way to the area where the house sat. The entire two miles were lined with long grasses, trees, and a wide view of the sky.

My foot pressed the brake and the Jeep obeyed, slowing a bit. I lifted my face upward, gazing into night. The stars were easily seen here because there weren't so many lights like all the other streets.

Beneath my hands, the Jeep stuttered. "What the hell?" I muttered and looked down at the gauges.

The headlights blinked out, shrouding everything in darkness as the entire vehicle shut down.

I wasn't going very fast, thankfully, so I just steered to the side of the road and braked, throwing the shifter into park. From there, I turned the key and nothing happened.

I knew I wasn't out of gas. I'd just filled up yesterday at the Sheetz near school. It hadn't been making any odd noises while I was driving, and I wasn't late on my oil change. Okay, maybe I was a little late on the oil change. Surely that wouldn't just make the thing shut off.

The headache behind my eyes decided to remind me it was there and pierced me with a sharp stinging pain. I sighed wearily.

I was only about a mile from my place. I'd just walk home and then call my dad in the morning. He'd know who to call to get someone out here to look at it.

After fishing my bag off the floor, I climbed out, not bothering to lock the doors. There was no point when it didn't even have a roof. Besides, there was nothing of value inside to steal, and unless they planned to carry the car away, I doubted anyone would be taking it.

I pulled the hoodie a little tighter around me as I walked and reached up to pull the band out of my hair, letting the dark-brown strands fall around my shoulders. Using the tips of my fingers, I massaged my scalp as I trudged down the road.

The sound of a plane flying overhead filled the night, and I pulled out my cell to shoot a text to my dad so he would see it first thing in the morning.

But the battery was dead.

Odd… I just charged at work.

I stuffed the useless phone into my pocket, muttering about how I couldn't afford to go buy a new one. Suddenly, an odd feeling washed over my body, something that seemed to penetrate below the surface of my skin and make my insides vibrate.

I noticed then that the sound of the airplane overhead wasn't fading away…

It was growing louder.

And it was unlike any other plane I'd heard before.

The ground underfoot began to vibrate, and I thought vaguely of an earthquake, but we didn't have those in this area. The sound overhead was like one of those annoying bug zappers, the kind that screeched when it caught its prey. It grated down my spine like nails on a chalkboard, and I recoiled.

My feet stopped hiking and I looked up, desperate to know from where that awful sound was coming.

My mouth ran dry.

My hair fell down my back and tickled my butt as my head tilted up to stare at the source of the sound.

I was seeing things.

The headache was causing me to hallucinate.

I was tired. Maybe I was coming down with something.

I blinked and swallowed hard. The little bit of saliva my mouth produced scraped down the back of my throat like jagged pieces of glass.

There was a giant disk floating overhead.

Like, for real.

If I had to describe it, I would say it looked a lot like a Frisbee, a silver one that seemed to hover high in the air without any help. It was much larger than me, blocking out my view of the sky and the moon.

As I stared, a few pulses of blue light blinked on and raced around the edge, like a little car on a track. There was a sound of metal scraping against metal as something in the center of the disk began to open, revealing a dark hole in the center.

"What. The. Fuck?" I said, staring at that black void. Fear skittered up my spine and snapped me back to reality.

I took off running, propelling my feet across the ground as fast as I could. As I ran, I glanced over my shoulder, swiping the wayward hair out of my eyes.

It was gone.

I practically tripped as I lurched to a stop.

I turned completely around, staring up at the empty sky. There was no little light. No bug-zapping sound. No giant Frisbee floating alone in the night.

I was insane.

Absolutely crazy.

I could never tell anyone about this. About the night Sophie Perez thought she saw a… a… spaceship.

A laugh burst from my chest.

I'd been watching too many reruns of the *X-files* on TV.

Then something behind me lit up, literally casting a light so bright it caused my body to create a shadow that stretched across the ground like I was suddenly seven feet tall.

My back stiffened.

It was eerily quiet—no sounds of an approaching car, not even the sound of the rustling wind. But the light couldn't be denied. It illuminated the green of the grass so everything appeared electrified, like a major thunderstorm ready to attack.

Slowly, I pivoted, the silence of the night causing an odd sense of panic to claw its way up the back of my throat.

The light was coming from overhead. Several yards away, it shone in a wide beam from the sky, revealing the road like a giant spotlight.

It was coming from that disk.

I blinked hard, but when I looked again, the image was still there.

It hovered in the air silently, no blue moving light, no annoying sound. If I weren't seeing it, I would have sworn nothing was there.

My breathing was ragged. My heart squeezed with great effort as it stuttered from the intensity of its beating. The light blinked out and barely two seconds later it reappeared.

This time it didn't just light the road.

There was something else. *Someone* else.

I opened my mouth to scream, only no sound came out. I lifted my leg to run, but it didn't obey. I was frozen where I stood. The only thing about me that worked was my brain, and right now I wished it didn't.

I'm going to die.

I'm going to die a horrible death and no one will ever know.

The silhouette in the center of the light began walking toward me. Sort of. It was more like it floated over the ground, hovering just over the gravel, gliding gracefully through the air.

I willed my body to move, to get the hell away. Still, my stupid body betrayed me.

I was a prisoner inside my own skin.

As the thing moved, so did the light and the disk overhead. Simultaneously, they all approached as one, drawing closer and closer until I was sincerely afraid I was going to pee my pants.

The being was wearing a silver robe with an oversized hood that shrouded its face. They weren't much taller than me, so I would guess them to be about five-eight or so. Of course, maybe if they were actually standing on the ground, they would be shorter.

I tried to call out, to beg for my life.

My voice didn't work.

It was as if everything around that disk was completely frozen in time.

The creature stopped before me, saying nothing, but I could feel the penetrating stare behind the shadows of the hood. Silently, it reached out its arm, the silky material of the robe draping toward the ground like a waterfall.

I tried to recoil, but it was no use.

Eerily long fingers with oversized knuckles reached for me. The skin that covered them was ultra pale and so smooth it looked like polished stone.

Two fingers wrapped around the skin just above my elbow. I imagined they would be icy cold, but they weren't. This thing's touch was much warmer than me. Even through my hoodie, I could feel the heat.

The next thing I knew, the sweatshirt around me was gone. Ripped away and out of sight. I felt myself swallow as fear flooded my limbs.

The fingers once again found the skin above my elbow. They were intensely hot.

It moved so achingly slow, trailing those too-long fingers down the curve of my elbow, down the sensitive flesh of the inside of my arm. If I had control of my body, I would have shuddered.

Then the fingers threaded through mine, a possessive action. This being seemed to claim my hand.

You can't have that! my mind screamed.

"Yes." The creature in the robe spoke aloud. "You are mine."

A single tug on our joined hands set my body in motion. I spilled forward even as my insides recoiled.

The light grew brighter, so bright I had to shut my eyes.

I felt something wrap around my body and support my weight because I no longer could. A feeling of lightness came over me, and then my feet no longer touched the ground.

I forced my eyes open, looking up toward the sky. That black hole in the bottom of the disk was back. It was an unwelcoming void in the center of the neon light. My robed kidnapper and I were being towed upward, like it was a giant spider and I was now tangled in its web.

I had no idea what was waiting up there for me.

But I knew it couldn't be good.

the pleasure

I had to be dreaming.

I mean, seriously. This shit just couldn't be real.

Did I really just get beamed up into a spaceship?

I was going to wake up in a few minutes in my own bed and laugh my ass off because this was all just a crazy dream.

I really wanted to wake up.

I wanted to wake up *now*.

Slowly, I opened my eyes, expecting to find myself in bed but wincing from the neon light I'd shut my eyes against in the first place.

There was no neon light, but I wasn't in bed either. The room was lit with a soft blue hue. It was a calming sort of light—that is if one could be calm at a time like this. The *person* who brought me up here was standing very close at my side, but I didn't look at them. I wasn't ready. Instead, I took in everything else.

It was a large open space, very sterile in appearance. The floors were white, spotlessly clean, and the walls were the color of brushed nickel and curved with the shape of the ship. The soft-blue was supplied from what looked like some sort of rope lighting that circled the perimeter of the ceiling and spiraled inward toward the center to reveal a simple teardrop-shaped hanging pendant. The teardrop was made of glass, reminding me of a giant water drop, and in the center was a light, again in soft blue, but it didn't look like a bulb. It floated in the center of the glass, not connected to anything.

Along the far wall were sleek white cabinets, seamless in design. There were no pictures on the walls, no furniture, and no clutter.

I was afraid, so afraid I was almost numb, yet the longer I stood here, the more at ease I became. There were no torture instruments in sight. No evil scientists, no scary men hovering with shackles and chains. No laser beams threatening to singe off my hair…

What? You get beamed into a spaceship and your imagination would run wild too.

If anything, the lack of these items made me curious. Why else would I be beamed up here if they didn't want to dissect me like some kind of frog?

Gathering courage and taking a deep breath, I turned slowly to look at the person standing shrouded in a silver robe.

"I can't see you," I said, my voice shaky and low. My entire body trembled with uncertainty and fear. "Remove your hood."

"No." The voice was deep and low, so I assumed it was a male.

"Why?"

"What I look like isn't important."

Seemed pretty important to me, but I was afraid to challenge him. He had a major advantage here. "Then what is important?"

"You need to understand."

"Understand what?" I glanced down at the floor. He didn't appear to be hovering, but I couldn't be sure because the silver robe he wore pooled onto the floor, hiding his feet.

"You will not be hurt while you are here." His voice was exotic, thick with an accent, but not hard to understand. I found myself wishing he would say more just so I could hear the lilt in his tone.

Sexy voice aside, did he really think I was just going to believe what he said? I'm sure every killer told his victim not to be afraid just before he slit her throat.

"Why am I here?" I asked, taking a small step away from him.

He made no move to close the gap I put between us.

"We are here to gather information."

"We?" I asked, panicked, and looked around for more robe-wearing creepers.

"They are here, but not in this room," he replied.

"Are they like you?"

"Yes."

"Who are you?" I asked. "*What* are you?"

"Will you help us?"

"You didn't answer my question." I pointed out.

Silence was the only response I received.

"You can't just beam a girl up into a… a spaceship and expect her not to ask questions." I crossed my arms over my chest. Then I paused. "Is this a spaceship?"

"We prefer the term hovercraft."

I rolled my eyes. Like there was a difference.

"Answering questions is a waste of time. When we

are finished here, your memory will be wiped anyway."

Panic twisted my belly. What the hell were they going to do to me that would need to be wiped from my brain?

"I want to go home."

"And you will. But first, we would like the opportunity to study you. To learn about your kind."

"Umm, no."

Again, I was met with silence.

"I don't have a choice, do I?" I asked after a few minutes. My voice sounded small to my own ears.

"It will not hurt. You may find it pleasurable. Your kind likes pleasure, yes?"

"As opposed to pain? Yeah."

"Let us begin," he said, moving forward.

I leapt back. "I didn't say yes."

"Come," his voice commanded. "Submit and then you will be delivered safely home."

"And if I don't?" I said, raising my chin.

More silence.

I wasn't too fond of his kind of silence because it left my over-creative mind to fill in the gaps of conversation.

He moved farther into the room, stopping in front of the wall of cabinets and opening a door. Inside was all kind of controls; it reminded me of a giant computer. He pressed a button and the silent hum of action filled the space.

The center of the floor opened up and something started to rise. It was a white platform, and in the center was something that looked like some kind of dentist chair.

I thought about running, but where would I go? There was no door in sight, and even if there was, weren't we in the sky? Was I going to jump out with no parachute, no means of survival?

"What the hell is that for?" I asked, terrified.

"Sit," he commanded.

"No."

He lifted those long white fingers and made a small gesture. My body moved; I was completely powerless to stop it. I glided forward until my knees hit the chair. It was made of buttery-soft white leather.

A sharp ripping sound and a draft of warm air brushing over my skin made me look down. With barely any effort at all, my jeans and low-cut top were yanked away.

"Hey," I cried, moving to cover what I could of myself.

"I like the way your kind is shaped," he said, the hardness to his tone gone and the lilting accent returned.

I was wearing nothing but lacey black panties and bra, and I had no doubt he could see exactly how I was shaped.

"Sit down."

I did, because refusing seemed kind of stupid at this point. He'd just make me. At least this way I could pretend I had some kind of control here.

The softness of the leather against my bare skin wasn't unpleasant. If anything, it felt sinful. I found my limbs relaxing against it, and I studied the soft glow the blue lighting cast over my skin.

"I will begin." He came forward, and I watched him warily, still not trusting a word he said. A small tray of instruments appeared beside me and on it was a needle and several tubes.

"Hell no," I said, starting to get up.

"It will not hurt," he said, lifting his hand and pinning me to the chair with some unseen force.

He grasped my arm in his hand and I couldn't help but notice how smooth and pale his fingers were. The knuckles were over-exaggerated and wide and he had no fingernails.

A needle pricked my skin and I gasped, watching as a tube filled quickly with my blood. And then he filled another.

When that was done, the needle was removed and he placed two very warm fingers against the entry wound. My skin tingled and warmed beneath his touch, like I stepped in front of a window that was letting in warm sunlight.

Seconds later, he pulled away and I looked down. There was no evidence of the needle drawing my blood. He had healed me.

Another robed figure appeared and took away the tray, along with my blood. I watched until they were out of sight.

"I will examine you now," he said. "It will not hurt."

True to his word, it didn't hurt, and he seemed genuinely curious about my body, my heart, my pulse. He spoke very little and moved with fluid grace. The heat from his hands, the softness of the leather beneath me, and the soft-blue glow to the room lulled me into a sense of security.

Maybe he was telling the truth. Maybe he really was just curious about the human body. After a while, he walked away, toward those cabinets once more, opening yet another door to press some more buttons. Something beneath the chair hummed to life and it began to vibrate softly.

Even my fear couldn't disguise the rush of pleasure throughout my limbs. My eyes slid closed momentarily as the muscles in my back were soothingly kneaded with gentle motion. When I opened them again, he was standing over me, peering down from inside the oversized hood. I hadn't realized he was there, and I jerked in surprise.

His large hand covered my bare shoulder and settled me. His fingers squeezed lightly as if testing the elasticity of my skin. I thought he would pull away once I stilled.

He didn't.

Instead, his fingers probed my collarbone and against my neck. My breath caught and tension coiled inside me. What was he doing?

A finger slid beneath my bra strap, pulling it over my shoulder and exposing the top of my breast. Even though I couldn't see his eyes, I felt his stare.

I shivered.

Slowly, his fingers trailed down my chest and across the tops of my creamy breasts.

"What the hell are you doing?" I gasped.

"Is it true?" he said after a while. "That pleasure can be achieved with touch?" His fingers dipped below the lace of the bra and teased the flesh of my breast.

"Yes," I said, partly a sigh.

"I want to see."

I stiffened, my eyes shooting up to him.

But then his large hand covered my breast, his fingers squeezing gently until I was cupped in his palm. Damn if it didn't feel good.

His hand was incredibly warm. Almost like a hot stone massaging my flesh. Of its own accord, my nipple tightened into a hard bud, puckering against him. He yanked away the fabric of the bra to stare down at the formed pebble. Without saying a word, he reached out and touched it, curling a finger around the outside and then pinching.

I gasped, my back arching on its own.

He stilled and I felt his stare. I looked up at him, knowing desire was written in my eyes.

Did he see it? Did he understand?

He must have because his hands grew bolder.

A small scalpel appeared in his hands, but before I could even be afraid, he sliced through the front of the bra and discarded it, leaving my chest completely exposed. Both my nipples hardened into fine points, and the fullness of my breasts began to ache with need.

He leaned closer, taking both breasts in his hands and pinching the nipples, rolling them around between his forefingers. I squirmed a little in the chair, and he squeezed harder. I thought it might hurt. It felt incredible. He played with the hard pink tips for a while, tugging and pulling, pinching and squeezing, until my breath came in short gasps.

When he seemed to tire of that area, he grabbed both swollen globes and pushed them together, rubbing the centers against one another to create friction that made me squeeze my thighs closed.

One of his hands left me, and I heard him rustling around for something, but I didn't bother looking because his other hand was still moving over my breast.

Then his hand grasped it, pulled upward, and gathered it together. Something fastened over it, holding it in place. My eyes shot open and I looked down. It was some sort of clear cup that had a long clear tube coming out of the center.

I watched as he flicked a switch and it began to suck. It was like a low-powered vacuum, pulling the already sensitive skin upward.

I groaned out loud. God, the pressure was so freaking delicious. I arched up into it as my breast was sucked with the gentleness of air. Then he pressed another button and the chair, which was in a sitting position, began to recline.

My head and shoulders lowered as my feet came up to the same level. His large warm hands grabbed my ankles and laid my legs out across the chair so my knees were not bent.

When I was completely stretched across the vibrating, warm leather, he stood over me again, taking the uncovered breast in his hand and placing an identical cup over it. Another push of a button and it began suckling at my skin as well.

Holy shit, I should be creeped out by this, right?

But oh. My. God. The sensations shooting from my breasts down into my crotch were unlike anything I'd ever experienced.

His hands grasped my waist, traveling over my navel and probing gently at my belly button. His warm finger dipped into the little circle and then pulled out to trail down to the waistband of my panties. I thought he was going to tear away the fabric. In fact, I hoped he did.

The insistent pleasure being delivered into my chest was making my vagina throb with need.

But his hands kept going. They traveled down between my legs so he could grip the insides of my thighs. His palms were so large that they completely covered the delicate flesh.

Moving to the foot of the chair, he popped a little latch and the bottom section of the chair separated.

After making sure one of my legs was on each side, he pulled it apart, making me completely open and vulnerable to him.

I shuddered with fear but also with lust. I'd never been treated this way before. I'd never had anyone so intent on studying my body and seeing what made it hum.

I heard him pick up the scalpel, and I glanced down. My entire body began to quiver. He made short work of my panties, and then I was completely naked. I felt the juices of my center drip down onto the leather.

He stared at that part of me, placing a hand on each thigh and pushing my legs wide so I was completely open. Several minutes later, I felt a single finger probe at the short curls at the apex of my thighs. He seemed fascinated that I had hair down there.

He twirled his fingers in the coarse curls and then glided down the crease where my thigh met my torso. I shuddered because he was so incredibly close to my opening. I knew when he realized I was oozing juices because he paused.

Next thing I knew, his finger dipped into me. It was a gentle swipe, quick, but I still shuddered from the contact. My thighs moved to close, to squeeze at the sensation, but he stopped me, pressing them wide once more.

"This spot is sensitive, yes?" he asked.

"Yes," I said, my voice low and hoarse.

The pressure on the cups over my breasts increased just slightly, and I moaned.

His finger plunged into me, dipping so far in I felt him scrape my inner walls. I let out a little cry and then bit down on my lip. He pulled out and then swirled his saturated, slick finger around my opening. The tip of it rubbed against my clit and my legs jerked upward.

He flicked at it again. My body reacted the same. Over and over he touched it, cajoling the already swollen bud into a desperate fervor. And then he pulled away.

But not completely.

He went back to sliding his finger into my opening.

"More," I begged, unable to keep quiet anymore.

"More what?" he asked.

"Use more than one finger."

Two fingers filled me and stretched my walls. It'd been a while since I had sex and I felt tight. The stretching action was beyond welcome, like it was way overdue. His fingers began a circular motion, spinning around inside me.

I made little sounds of pleasure because holding them in was impossible. And then his free hand found my clit and pressed down, creating a sweet pressure.

My inner muscles clenched around his fingers as I searched for sweet release.

It was so slick between my legs he moved with ease, slipping out of my hole and making me cry out, but even as I protested, his fingers moved up and down my slit, slipping down into the base of my butt crack and then back up to penetrate my hole again.

"Don't stop," I whispered as he pumped his fingers farther inside. His palm settled over my clit, pressing down as his fingers splayed out over my lower belly. Just when I thought I couldn't take any more, the two fingers inside me curled forward and pleasure burst through me like a bomb demolishing an entire building.

I shouted with the release, my body arching up off the table as I cried out, and every part of me shook. He kept pumping his fingers, coaxing out more and more pleasure until I collapsed against the leather, boneless and drained.

Seconds ticked by. He withdrew his fingers. I glanced down, noting the way they glistened from my orgasm. I felt the penetrating gaze from beneath the hood, and then he took his drenched fingers and wiped them on the inside of my thigh. I shuddered. Every single part of me was uber sensitive from what I'd just experience.

The sucking motion on my breasts stopped and the cups disappeared. I was so utterly relaxed that I didn't even care I was completely naked and shaking on a table in the center of the room.

I was pretty sure… No, I was totally sure I had never felt so completely satisfied, ever.

"First part of experiment is over," he said, standing over me.

"I want to see your face."

"Next time," he said, wrapping his fingers around my wrist.

"Next time?"

"I'm not done with you yet," he said. His other hand wrapped around the top of my head.

A little thrill raced over me with his promise.

Then I remembered what other promise he made. He said I wouldn't remember this.

I didn't want to forget the kind of world-rocking pleasure I just experienced.

"Please," I said, touching the hand on my head. "Don't make me forget. I want to remember."

His fingers went lax against my forehead as I held on to his wrist. Bright neon light flooded the room, and I squeezed my eyes shut, turning away my head. The next thing I knew, I was being laid on something hard and cold, something that wasn't nearly as comfortable as the leather chair.

I opened my eyes.

I was back on my street, my Jeep just feet away. I was dressed in my jeans and shirt. I looked up at the sky, expecting to see something hovering overhead.

The only thing I saw were stars.

No ship. No aliens. Nothing.

I stood up. My legs felt wobbly at first as I moved forward. *What the hell just happened to me?* Maybe I was hallucinating. Maybe someone slipped something in my soda at the bar.

I walked toward the Jeep, the seam of my jeans rubbing against my crotch. I paused. Where the hell were my underwear? And why did I feel so wet and stretched down there?

On impulse, I looked beneath my T-shirt. I wasn't wearing my bra, either.

It was real.

I remembered. He didn't take away the memory.

What's more… He said he'd be back.

the craving

I couldn't concentrate. It was like my body still hummed from that night.

I still looked the same. I still talked and walked the same. But everything was different.

Aliens existed. They knew about us, our planet… and they were curious. Instead of being freaked out like I probably should be, I was curious. Now more than ever, I wanted to see the face he kept hidden. I wanted to know where he came from, why he was here, and why he chose me.

Maybe it was stupid of me, but I wasn't even frightened. I didn't feel threatened by him. By any of them. Was I being blinded by lust? Was I literally letting my libido think for me? I had been scared when I was first taken onto the ship.

And then he started touching me. His curiosity drew out my desire, and my reaction to the things he did seemed to propel him further. I'd never experienced anything like that before. Could I even call it sex?

It was pretty one-sided. The only part of him that entered me was his fingers. It was like he was solely intent on pleasing me and only me. Usually, with guys, it was about their pleasure. There would be a little kissing, a little fondling here and there, and then they would jump right to the part where they were sticking their cock inside me. It wasn't that I didn't enjoy sex with guys; it was just that I never really felt like they tried to please *me*.

But that night… oh, that night had been nothing but pleasure. He seemed to know exactly where to stroke, when to apply pressure, and when to take it away. His gaze was often times penetrating, and I think I understood why. He was intent on my reactions. He wanted to know exactly what I liked.

I couldn't be scared when someone's sole purpose was to see what satisfied me most.

It had been over a week since that night, but I still thought about it almost constantly. At night, I would look up into the sky and wonder if he would actually come back like he said. I waited for him. I craved him. I wanted more.

A sharp thud in front of me caused me to jerk suddenly and press a hand to my chest. The noise of the bar pressed in on me, flooding back, reminding me I was supposed to be working.

"Soph," Matt said from the other side of the bar. "Are you okay?"

I glanced up into his concerned face. Tonight his eyes looked green. "Yeah, of course. I guess I was just daydreaming."

He smirked. "Well, it must have been a good daydream 'cause you've been standing there for five minutes."

"Shit," I said and put the beers and martini on my serving tray.

"Who's the guy?" Jess said, sidling up beside me.

"What?"

She grinned. "The guy? A girl doesn't daydream like that unless there's a guy."

I felt Matt's stare, and my cheeks heated. "There's no guy."

Jess made a sound like she didn't believe me. "Sure there's not."

I shrugged. “Nope.” And then I went off to deliver the drinks.

I kept my head focused on work the rest of the night. Every time I found myself gazing out the window, up at the sky, I would yank back my thoughts and tell myself to stop it.

I was being ridiculous. Maybe I was losing my mind.

I mean, aliens? That was outrageous. Maybe it *had* been a really realistic dream. The odds of something like that actually happening were like zero.

Maybe I was sexually frustrated and that dream was my body’s way of getting what it wanted. If that were the case, then my body had some pretty freaky fantasies.

By the time my shift was over and the bar was emptying out, I wanted to go home and go to bed. I was exhausted, mentally and physically. After putting away all my stuff and tallying up my tips, I put away my apron and grabbed my bag from behind the bar.

“Hey,” Matt said, coming up behind me as I was stepping around the counter.

“Ugh, busy night,” I said.

"Tell me about it."

I smiled at him over my shoulder. "You probably have a pocket full of phone numbers."

He shrugged. "You seeing someone?"

I wrinkled my nose. *Why would he be asking me that?* "No."

His eyes narrowed on my face like he thought I was lying. "I want to know, Sophie."

"I told you," I said, spinning all the way around to face him. "I'm not seeing anyone."

"Jess seems to think otherwise."

"Jess doesn't know me."

"You've been distracted lately."

"And you think the only reason could be a guy?" I said, annoyed. Never mind that he was sort of right.

He plowed a hand through his hair and sighed. "Sophie." His tone held a hint of warning.

"What does it matter anyway?" I asked. "It isn't like I haven't dated guys before."

"I just don't want you to get hurt is all."

There he went with his big brother attitude again. "I'm not going to get hurt, Matt. I'm fine."

"You can call me anytime. You know that, right?"

"I'm sure the girl of the night wouldn't be too happy with your kid sister interrupting her date." I said the words kind of bitterly, surprised at the way I sounded.

I needed to get the hell out of here. I was losing my ever-loving mind. I spun on my sneakers to rush away, but he caught my arm and towed me back behind the row of shelving beside the bar where we kept extra napkins and stuff.

"Kid sister?" he asked, pinning me with a stare.

I shrugged. "Isn't that how you think of me? Why you're getting all bent out of shape because you think I'm dating some guy who hasn't come to sit at the bar for you to scope out?"

Most all the guys I've dated in the past have all ended up at the bar, waiting for me to finish my shift. Matt always plied them with beer to loosen their lips so he could ask them a ton of questions. It was so annoying.

His hand slapped the shelving right beside my head and he stepped forward, pinning me against the wood and crowding my personal space. My heart began to thud in my chest; it became hard to breathe.

"I do *not* think of you as my *sister*," he growled, leaning in. The green of his eyes was deep tonight, like the moss covering the bark of a tree. It was probably because he was wearing a hunter-green polo shirt with his jeans.

"Oh," I muttered. His words actually stung a little. I knew he wasn't interested in me—like in the way a guy liked a girl—but I still always felt kind of special to him because I thought he saw me as a little sister.

I took a deep breath. Even hurt, I was still affected by his nearness. Even after a full shift in a rowdy bar, he smelled good. Like he hadn't even broken a sweat making drinks and slinging beer all night. He was clean and spicy, a deep scent that tantalized my thoughts and scrambled any words I might have said.

"You think of me as a brother?" he said, lifting his eyebrows.

Of course I didn't. Hell, I considered it a good thing he was an only child because I would have felt sorry for any sister he might have had. That poor girl would have been tormented for life with such an enticing sibling.

"I thought we were friends," I said, indirectly answering the question.

His body language relaxed, making me realize how tense he'd been before. The change in his posture brought him a little closer. I looked up to see if anyone was watching us, but I couldn't see over his broad shoulder.

"We are friends," he said softly, dragging the pad of his thumb down the side of my cheek.

I felt like my insides were filled with quicksand and I was being slowly dragged in, being buried by that single, innocent touch.

He pulled his hand away and my eyes inadvertently followed. "Hey," he said, tipping up my chin so he could look into my face. "If you need me, you call. I'll drop whatever I'm doing and be there."

I couldn't say anything. My tongue felt thick and my throat felt swollen. Instead, I nodded. Before pulling away completely, Matt tugged the end of my ponytail and gave me a lopsided smile.

I stood there for long seconds, even after he went back behind the bar, before I could move. *What just happened?* Why did it feel like something between Matt and me just shifted?

I really was losing my damn mind.

First, I think I'm abducted by aliens, and now, I'm imagining Matt was implying some kind of interest in me beyond friendship.

I rushed out of the bar and into the parking lot at the side of the building. I sucked in lungfuls of cold air and let it burn my chest and clear the fog clouding my head.

I tore the band out of my hair and let the dark strands fall down around my shoulders, then hopped into the Jeep, throwing it in reverse and pulling out onto the two-lane road. The wind pushed at my hair, and I welcomed the strands against my cheeks and eyes.

I needed a distraction. A distraction from myself.

Maybe I was just sleep deprived. I'd been up and down every night the past week, looking out the window. A hot shower and bed was exactly what I needed. Maybe I would just sleep in and skip class in the morning. Surely I'd feel better, less confused.

As I drove, I couldn't help but think about Matt, the way he touched my cheek earlier, the way he declared I was not his sister.

Was he trying to play me? Play me like he played all the women who sat at the bar, all the women he took out on dates and likely never called?

I wasn't going to be a victim to his charm. I knew better. But damn, why did he have to look at me like that?

My headlights speared the empty road as I headed toward my apartment. Usually, I enjoyed the drive home from work, the cold air, the night sky, the long grass illuminated in the yellow glow from the Jeep. Not tonight. Tonight, I didn't pay attention to any of it. Tonight, I only wanted to go home.

Beneath me, the Jeep stuttered. I pressed the gas all the way to the floor. Still, the car didn't obey. It shut down right there in the center of the one-lane road, slowly rolling to a halt.

I pulled out my phone to look at the time. It was dead too.

It was just like last time. Like last week. The minute I was returned from the spaceship, my phone was working once more and so was my Jeep.

The last words he said while I was up there… in his ship echoed through the deepest recesses of my mind. *I'm not done with you yet.*

A jolt of anticipation shot through me like a lightning bolt in a rainstorm. I tilted back my head and looked up as bright light filled the darkness overhead.

the satisfaction

I was brought aboard the hovercraft again. This time he didn't come below to get me; I was drawn up alone.

He was waiting for me, still hidden in the folds of the silver robe, still keeping his face from my eyes. Part of me whispered that I should be afraid, that they could be back to do something awful to me, something they'd been planning this entire time.

The other part of me was secretly thrilled. I wanted more; I wondered what new kind of pleasure he would introduce me to.

"You came back," I said, not moving from the spot I was delivered to.

"We are not done," he said, his accent washing over my body and making me tremble. It was like I was one of Pavlov's dogs, but instead of being conditioned for food by the sound of a bell, I was conditioned for sexual pleasure by the sound of his exotic voice.

"I don't understand," I said.

"You're very healthy for your species," he replied. "A good candidate."

"A candidate for what?"

"For more research," he said.

A heavy feeling dropped into my lower abdomen, and the place between my legs began to throb. I resisted the urge to squirm under the idea of more "research."

"Come," he said, stepping aside and gesturing toward the center of the craft. The leather chair was already raised from the floor. It was cast in a blue-ish tone from the lighting overhead.

I didn't obey immediately. I just stood there as he approached the chair. When he realized I wasn't following, he flicked his hand toward me and an invisible force towed me closer.

"Remove your clothes," he told me.

I swallowed.

"The pleasure you felt last time, I will deliver more."

I pulled off my clothes. I could tell you I did it because I was scared of what he would do if I refused, but that would be a lie. I wanted to undress; I wanted more.

When I was completely naked, I slid into the chair. The little massaging vibration was already on and so was the heat. I relaxed against it like I was at the spa. Strangely, I wasn't embarrassed to be completely nude, completely exposed. If anything, it turned me on more.

He came to the side of the chair. The hood fell down low as he tilted his head down. "It intrigues me how your kind feels so much pleasure."

"You don't?" I asked.

"No. Our bodies are made differently than yours." He reached with those overly long, marble-like fingers and wrapped them around my breast.

Instantly, my nipple hardened.

"For example, a touch like this would not affect someone like me."

I moaned a little because he squeezed gently, the heat from his hand penetrating my skin. He plucked at my nipple like he was playing a guitar, and my flesh started to quiver and hum. My breast throbbed with so much need I couldn't help it. I reached up and grabbed it, squeezing firmly and making a sound of relief.

His hand left my breast and traveled down my ribs, climbing over my hipbone and around to my thigh. “Roll over,” he instructed.

I stilled and glanced up.

“Onto your belly,” he said.

Slowly, I did as he bid, rolling so my chest and belly pressed against the chair. The massaging motion of the chair tingled my already sensitive breasts. He adjusted my legs and unlatched the chair, spreading my thighs wide.

I felt both his hands on my butt cheeks, like he was tracing their shape and palming the fullness. His fingers crept up to wrap around the small of my back and then drag up my sides to tease the rounded part of my breasts sticking out from beneath me.

After he fondled what he could of my breasts, he dragged his fingers across my back and kneaded the muscles there, making my entire body feel like Jell-O. If I had been tense before about this position, it was impossible now.

I felt him move between my legs and then his fingers pulled away only to probe between them. I was already drenched, already worked up and wanting release. A single finger dipped into my crotch from behind, sinking deep into me and making me groan against the chair.

My ass arched upward, giving him better access and hoping he would take it. Agonizingly slow, he pulled out his finger, running it over my slit and spreading my juices all over my vagina. And then he pulled his finger back through the silky fluid pouring from me, dragging upward and circling around my other hole. I shied away, lowering a little back down onto the chair, but he didn't pull away. He used the slickness of my juices to slide up and down my crack, just barely teasing my tight, puckered ass. I began to relax because the sensation of being touched there was rather erotic, and then he slid away, delving not one, but two fingers back inside me.

I cried out and pushed my bottom toward him and rocked my hips. He moved his fingers inside me, occasionally pulling out to play with my clit.

I began to shake, my lower half trembling so badly that I began to whimper for release. He pulled his hands away completely and ordered me to flip over. I did so, pushing my vagina toward him, begging for more.

He pressed a button and the chair moved, spreading my legs even wider apart. Then from below, something rose upward, a short silver pole. On it hung several odd-looking tools.

He picked up one shaped like a thick rod with a bumpy texture all over it. It was silver and the blue lighting reflected off of it, making it glow. He came forward and poised it at my entrance. In one sweeping motion, he jammed it inside me, twisting it slightly so I felt the full effect of the bumps. I arched upward, unable to hold still as pleasure exploded within me. He rocked the toy back and forth, keeping it deep, and the orgasm ripped over me like a tidal wave in a flood.

I cried out, unable to remain silent as wave after wave of bliss stole over me.

When my body began to quiet, I heard a low sound and I looked up. The clear cups he placed on my breasts last time were descending from the ceiling. My breasts were already swollen and throbbing for attention. The orgasm only seemed to make them hurt more. I bit down on my lip and closed my eyes as the cups were placed over my flesh, and then he flipped the switch, turning on the suction.

A growl ripped from the back of my throat and my thighs pressed together. It felt so good. Like my body was just so overcome with ecstasy I couldn't even think.

Hands grasped my thighs and pushed them open once more as the gentle sucking motion continued on my breasts. I glanced down to see him selecting yet another of his instruments off the pole. This one was attached to a long cord and was slightly more intimidating than the last. It was also shaped like a rod, but the end branched off into several smaller balls. I wasn't sure it would fit inside me and, if it did, how it would feel.

He seemed to sense my hesitation because he didn't just impale me with it right there. Instead, he held it up against my folds and hit a little button. The circular heads on the tip all began to move. It was like being massaged by four things at once.

I melted against the seat as he moved it around the inside of my thighs, pressing against my clit, my hole, and then dragging it down between my ass cheeks.

I moaned because I'd never been so thoroughly touched like this.

And then he started to probe me. The massaging heads slipping inside me one by one until the entire instrument was massaging my inner walls. The muscles of my vagina spasmed around the toy, and he glided it farther inside.

I grabbed onto the chair at my sides because tension was building inside me once more. My body was coasting to the top of a hill, poised to barrel over a cliff and into oblivion.

He must have hit another button because a low hum filled the room. The toy moved within me, thrusting as it massaged. I splintered apart into a million pieces. My eyesight blacked out as I rode the wave of the most intense orgasm I'd ever known.

I even imagined the feeling of hot seed pouring into me and my body drinking it up like I was dry as the desert. Even after my body came down from its high, the tool kept working, pushing around inside me, creating little aftershocks of pleasure that rippled through me.

When at last the tool withdrew, I looked down to see it glisten with the evidence of my orgasm, and then it was put away out of sight.

I expected him to be finished, but he wasn't. He stepped up and sank two long fingers into me, feeling along my inner wall. I moaned and my eyes slipped closed.

The suction on my breasts stopped and the cups were taken away. His fingers pulled out of me, flicking over my clit one last time and making me shudder.

"It is done," he spoke, his accent thick.

All I could do was smile. Oh yes, I was done all right.

I probably wouldn't be able to walk for a week. I felt like a newborn calf, with trembling legs I knew wouldn't support me.

The chair reclined a little farther and the bottom portion came back together, closing my legs. I had no desire to get up. I was totally languid, in between sleep and bliss.

In my blissed-out state, I reached for the man in the robe, catching the sleeve of the silky fabric and tugging him a little closer. I let my hand slip down so it grasped his. "Show me your face," I prompted.

He glanced down at where I held his hand, keeping his head bowed forward. "No."

"Please. I want to see you."

"What I look like does not matter."

He tugged his hand away from mine and then walked away. As he went, he said, "Rest. Then I will deliver you home."

I didn't see him again.

the realization

I felt dirty.

Satisfied yet dirty. It seemed wrong to enjoy what he did to me aboard his hovercraft, but it was like my body had a mind of its own. I couldn't stop it from enjoying the teasing pleasure, the rippling orgasms that stole over me under the ministrations of the creature in the robe.

The first time it happened, I walked around for almost a week, craving more, in a state of half belief it had even been real. I won't lie; it was thrilling. To be pleasured like that, for someone to only want to watch my reaction to the things they did to me.

No longer did I doubt what happened was real.

It was. I wouldn't be able to make that shit up even if I wanted to.

I'd dare say it was some women's fantasy. I'd never really fantasized about my idea of "perfect" sex… until now. It seemed it was all I could think about. The fact I felt dirty was very revealing.

There was no denying everything that happened to me on that ship was incredible. I couldn't even lie to myself and say I didn't enjoy it. I totally enjoyed it.

But I wanted it to stop.

I didn't want them to come back for me.

Even as I admitted that to myself, my body protested. A yearning for more satisfaction crawled over me, the muscles of my lower abdomen contracting. If he came back, I would surrender. I would submit to him without hesitation. I would lie out on that white leather chair and spread my legs in anticipation.

But it was wrong.

It went against everything in my head. Everything I felt in my heart.

Yes, I supposed what I experienced up there was close to physical perfection, but that was the problem. I realized my idea of perfect sex went beyond the physical. True, I enjoyed being pleasured by that otherworldly being, but it was too one-sided.

I wanted emotion. I wanted the sizzle of chemistry between two people. I wanted to feel a man over me, his weight pressing me down against a mattress. I wanted to feel the softness of his lips, the pressure of his tongue as it tangled with mine.

I couldn't get that from a being who refused to show his face.

He said it didn't matter what he looked like. But it mattered to me. How could someone make me feel so much, make my body hum like he did, and not care at all?

I was curious about him and it didn't seem fair. I literally gave him limitless access to my body, inside and out, but he wouldn't even let me see him.

I wondered if he would come back. If perhaps that's why he said it didn't matter. Maybe he got all the knowledge, all the answers he needed about me, about the human body. He didn't tell me he would be back, not like that first time.

After I rested for a short while and redressed, he sent me safely back down to my Jeep, where it started up with no problems and I drove home. Never mind that my insides still tingled. Never mind that when I went to bed that night, I dreamed about him, about the way he touched and stroked my skin.

I woke up flushed and breathing hard, my body yearning for someone it didn't even know.

But…

My body *did* know him. My body knew him better than I ever would.

Sadness cloaked me, refusing to be cast aside. It was almost as if I walked around with a permanent raincloud over my head and it stormed on me daily.

I went to work and delivered drinks, flirted, and smiled for tips. I went to class and took notes, did the required reading, and daydreamed through the lectures. I ate. I visited my parents. Life went on, and I tried not to think about those two nights up in the sky.

Weeks passed and I told myself to be glad because it was what I wanted. I didn't want to feel dirty and used.

But I did feel abandoned.

I just finished another endless shift at the bar on a busy Friday night. I was exhausted, my feet hurt, and my limbs felt rubbery from all the walking and lifting of drink-laden trays. I wanted to climb in bed and sleep for a week, but I knew I wouldn't. *I couldn't.* I dreamed about him almost nightly.

I dreamed about a being whose name I didn't know. Whose face I'd never seen.

Sometimes in sleep I would hear his voice and his accent would wash over me with a feeling of rightness. A feeling of home.

I shook my head, trying to shake the thoughts. They were only dreams. It was only natural to have bizarre dreams and feelings after literally being sucked up into a spaceship.

He'd probably brainwashed me.

I should have let him make me forget. It would have been easier.

How was I supposed to walk around knowing there was life out there? How was I supposed to look up into the onyx sky and not wonder where he was? How long would I wonder about his face until I stopped caring what he looked like?

"Sophie," a voice called from behind, and I turned to see Matt jogging up behind me.

"Did I leave something inside?" I asked him.

"No. I wanted to talk to you."

"Oh," I replied, turning fully around to face him. It was the first time he'd ever followed me outside to talk.

"Is something wrong?" I had a moment's worry about my job and wondered if maybe I hadn't been performing as well as I used to.

"I want to know what's up with you." He pushed a hand through his hair, making it stand out all over his head.

"What do you mean? Have I been doing a bad job at work?"

He made a frustrated sound. "You've been fine at work."

"Then…?" My voice trailed away, trying to figure out what he was really asking me.

"You're quieter, distracted, and sometimes when I look at you, it seems like you're a million miles away. Are you in some kind of trouble?"

"No," I said softly. "I'm not in trouble."

He studied me for long moments and sighed. "There really is a guy, isn't there?"

My gaze locked on his. "I told you there is no guy."

Technically, I wasn't lying.

I could tell he didn't believe me. I could see the doubt bloom in his eyes and in his posture. Then his gaze softened. His hazel eyes swept over my face like he was taking in every curve and line.

Matt took a step forward, closing the distance between us. His thumb was soft as he trailed it down the side of my cheek. "You know how special you are, right?" he whispered.

I stuttered a little, his words and tone completely taking me off guard.

His eyes roamed my face once more, his thumb still brushing against my skin. "You're the kind of girl a guy would be proud to be with. You shouldn't be someone's secret."

My insides flipped a little and it was hard to breathe. "You think I'm having a secret relationship?"

He shrugged. "People talk."

"People talk about me?" I asked, surprised. I was like the least interesting person I knew. This was definitely a small town, but people must really be desperate if they were making up some kind of secret relationship for me.

The pad of his thumb traced the edge of my lower lip, and his gaze dropped to where he touched.

"Matt?" I whispered, not sure what was happening.

His hand curled around the base of my neck and drew me closer. “I don’t like the idea of you with someone else,” he whispered, warm breath brushing over my lips. “I don’t like that faraway look in your eyes every night when you think of him.”

“I’m not—” I started to protest, to tell him he was wrong. But my words were silenced.

By his kiss.

I imagined being kissed by Matt a million times. I wondered what it would feel like to have his hands on me, to feel his tongue stroke over mine.

It was better than I anticipated.

His fingers pressed into the back of my neck, delving into my hair and pulling me closer. His lips covered mine totally as he rubbed them over mine like he was a piece of sandpaper and I was wood that needed smoothing.

He brought up his other hand so he could cup my jaw, and I clenched onto his wrists with both my hands, anchoring myself to him in case my body tried to melt into the ground.

He tasted faintly of beer, and his tongue was warm. Matt licked into my mouth, coaxing me open like the sun to a newly bloomed flower. Gently, he titled my head backward so he had deeper access to my mouth as he swept in, completely stealing my senses.

He slanted his mouth one way and then changed course and went the other. He kissed me from different angles without even breaking contact. My God, he was skilled in kissing. If it were an Olympic sport, he'd have the most medals.

When at last he pulled back, it was merely a fraction of an inch, just enough so he could open his eyes and let our gazes collide. He smiled slightly, dropping not one, but two more butterfly kisses to my swollen mouth before completely stepping away.

I brought two fingers to my lips and stared at him in shock. Sure, I'd imagined kissing him, but I never thought it would actually happen.

"You kissed me." Yes, I totally realized I was pointing out the obvious, but my brain just wasn't working the way it should.

His lips tilted up. "You liked it." He grinned like he was insanely proud of himself.

"You weren't in any hurry to pull away." I pointed out, recovering some of my wits.

"Nope," he drawled.

"Why did you do that?" I asked. Then I narrowed my eyes. "I'm not one of those hootchie mamas that come sit at the bar just to get whatever crumbs you're willing to toss their way."

"You wound me," he said, holding a hand over his heart.

I rolled my eyes. I wasn't going to fall for his charm. I spun away toward the Jeep. This conversation would only twist me around more than I already was.

"Soph," he said. My name sounded more like a sigh when he spoke. I felt his warm hand wrap around my wrist. But for some reason, it just wasn't warm enough. I wanted heat. Heat that seared me to the core.

Matt backed me up against the Jeep, letting me feel the hardness of his chest against mine. "I know what you think of me. What kind of rep I have."

"You disagree?" I arched a brow.

"No." He shook his head. "I'm a total player. But not with you. Never with you."

"Why are you saying this now? We've known each other for years."

"Because I wasn't ready. *You* weren't ready."

"But now you are?" I asked, taking a deep breath and feeling my breasts brush against him.

"I feel like I'm losing you, Soph. I don't want to lose you."

I wasn't sure those were the words I wanted to hear. "I have to go," I whispered, pushing against his shoulders.

He stepped back but took hold of my hand.

"You have options, Sophie," Matt said. "Think about it. Think about me."

My pulse hammered in my veins as I started up the Jeep and put it in reverse. Matt didn't say anything else, but he stood there until I turned out onto the street.

I slowed to a stop just yards down the street, a red light bringing the Jeep to a halt. His words replayed in my head and then finally sank in.

Matt said he wanted me. He kissed me. Once more, I touched my lips, as if trying to re-feel his kiss. It was something I always wanted but never thought would happen. And I just drove away.

I drove away and didn't look back.

Several weeks ago, if Matt had kissed me, if he'd talked to me like that, I would have jumped him right then and there. Likely, I would have made a fool out of myself jumping for joy.

But not now. Now I was more shocked than excited. My mind and body weren't screaming, *Oh yes!*

Why?

My eyes drifted heavenward, toward the black night sky, searching for something. For someone.

Surely, *he* wasn't the reason.

Was he?

the visit

I called in sick to work.

For three days in a row.

I managed to drag myself to class during the day, but I was exhausted, had no appetite, and felt dehydrated.

By the time my classes were over, I would drag my lethargic ass home and fall into bed, wanting nothing more than to sleep half my life away. The idea of going to work and waiting tables made me literally want to cry.

So I didn't go. I called and told them I was sick. I wasn't sure I was, but since I was staying in bed, it didn't feel like such a stretch.

On the third night, I was dozing in bed when a loud pounding at my door made me jerk awake. With a groan, I pulled myself up and went to the door, jerking it open.

Matt stood on the other side of the threshold, wearing a black polo shirt and a pair of jeans. "Are you really sick?" he demanded.

That zapped some of the sluggishness from my body. "What?" I asked, straightening my posture.

"You haven't been to work since I kissed you," he said, pushing past me and letting himself into my place. It wasn't like he hadn't been here before so he knew his way around.

"It doesn't have anything to do with that." I protested, shutting the door behind us even as part of me wondered if maybe it did. I was beginning to think maybe there was something seriously wrong with me. Like the man in the ship did something to me and I was just now feeling the effects. Why else would I be so exhausted, so thirsty, so confused about my feelings for Matt (and for the man whose face I'd never seen) all the time?

He stared at me for long seconds and then sighed. "You don't look so good, Soph." Two great strides brought him before me. He pressed the back of his hand to my forehead as if feeling for a temperature.

"You feel warm," he murmured. "Have you been running a fever?"

Surprised, I touched my forehead. It felt normal to me. "I don't think so."

"You been to the doctor?"

"No."

"You need to go."

I nodded. I didn't feel like arguing with him. Besides, he was probably right. But what was I supposed to say at the clinic? *Yes, I need to be seen because I was abducted by an alien in a spaceship, and I've never seen his face.*

Hello, padded walls and straightjacket!

"Come here," Matt said, pulling me against his chest and wrapping his arms around me. My head fit perfectly against his shoulder. I shut my eyes. This was what I'd been missing before. The reason I felt so dirty when I was with… Well, I didn't know what to call him because he never told me his name.

If Matt and I were to be intimate, I would be able to feel him. I would be able to connect to him, the same way I was connecting to him right now.

A low curse slipped from his lips. I pulled back and looked up. "What's wrong?"

"I'm supposed to be at work."

I glanced at the clock. It was after five. I hadn't realized it was so late. "What are you doing here, then?"

"When I showed up and they told me you called off again, I couldn't stand it. I had to know if you were avoiding me."

"I'm not avoiding you, Matt."

He pressed a soft kiss to my forehead. I liked it. "I wish I could stay."

"It's okay. I'm just going to go back to sleep."

"Can I call you later?" he asked, releasing me and moving to the door.

"Sure."

He made a sound in the back of his throat and then appeared before me. Grabbing my chin, he swooped down and pressed a solid kiss on my lips.

"You're going to get sick," I said when he pulled away.

"You're worth the risk," he said and winked.

When he was gone, I sank down into the couch with a sigh. Part of me was still in shock that Matt was interested in me. I wondered if he was serious or if this was some sort of phase. What if he was only interested because he thought I was interested in someone else? The whole *the grass is always greener on the other side.*

He did say he wanted me to know I had options.

But I didn't. I hadn't seen the man in the robe for over a month. Besides, he'd never been an option to begin with. I'd been a plaything. An experiment.

A little pang of hurt pierced my chest and a hollow feeling filled my chest. Unshed tears blurred my vision. I lay down and curled up on my side, tucking my hand beneath my chin.

I'd feel better after I got some sleep. The several hours I managed earlier this afternoon just hadn't been enough. Sleep overcame me and I awoke several hours later with a foggy head and sluggish limbs, the inside of my mouth felt bone dry, and I tried to swallow to dampen my throat, but there was no moisture to be swallowed. My tongue poked out to run along my lower lip, which felt brittle and cracked.

Why was I so thirsty? I pushed up off the cushions to glance at the clock, wondering how long I'd been asleep. Surely a long time for my body to get so arid. But it hadn't been a long time. It was just after eight in the evening.

If I didn't know any better, I would have thought I was drunk the way I staggered into the kitchen for some water. It seemed like a giant effort just to lift my foot off the ground to take a simple step. "What the hell is wrong with me?" I wondered out loud.

Just as I reached the kitchen doorway, I stumbled, the effort of walking becoming too much for my weary body. I fell to the ground like a ragdoll. My body made a thudding sound against the linoleum. My cheek lay against the smooth, cool surface of the floor, and my eyes sought out the tiny window above the sink.

Stars twinkled in a cloudless sky. It made me smile. And it made that awful hollow sensation fill my chest again.

I closed my eyes against the feeling.

Even with my lids closed, the light in here suddenly seemed terribly bright. *Odd,* I thought. *I didn't turn on any lights.* It was so bright I lifted my hand to shield against it, but my exhausted arm didn't obey.

I blinked, trying to figure out why the kitchen was so bright. Neon light filtered in through the tiny window and illuminated the darkened apartment. Several things happened at once. The light went out, the hollow feeling inside me dissipated, and someone lifted me off the ground to cradle me against their chest.

Rolling my head to the side and blinking upward, I caught the familiar sight of a silver robe. Something inside me leapt and I felt my lips curl into a smile.

But then I remembered I shouldn't smile at him. He was the reason I was like this. He'd done something to me and now I was terribly sick.

"What did you do to me?" I asked, my voice sounding weak to my ears.

He didn't say anything, but shifted my weight in his arms, pulling me just a little bit closer. He'd never held me like this before. I'd never felt the hardness of his body before. I hadn't realized how strong he seemed. He acted as if I weighed nothing at all.

Even in my weakened and sickly state, I knew I might not get an opportunity like this ever again. I didn't know why he was here, but something inside me whispered he probably wasn't supposed to be.

My fingers spider-climbed up the front of his robe, slowly, as if I were moving unintentionally. He didn't act like he noticed so I kept moving, creeping upward toward that damned hood that shielded his face.

He stood utterly still, almost as if he wasn't even breathing, as my fingers curled around the edge of the hood. The fabric was silky and cool against my fingers as I bunched it in my grip. I hesitated one second before going forward, ready to pull it back and reveal his face.

He jerked away, turning his head and pulling the material from my fingertips just out of reach, denying me the sight I so desperately wanted to see.

"You said you wouldn't hurt me," I whispered. He hadn't kept that promise and he knew it. It seemed the very least he could do was let me look at him.

Slowly, he turned his head toward me once more, tipping his chin down so he still was completely in the shadows of his clothing. Without hesitation, I grasped the fabric again and tugged it back, anxious.

The entire hood didn't slide away as I hoped, but I kept peeling it back anyway. My breath caught when the sight of the smoothest, palest skin I'd ever seen caught my eye. It was absolutely flawless. It appeared as if he didn't have any pores at all. I kept tugging, desperate now to see more.

My fingers dipped farther beneath the fabric and came into contact with his cheekbone, brushing against it and making me gasp out loud. Both of us stilled. He felt like the smoothest stone that sat for days in the summer sun. The heat that radiated from him and into me was unlike anything I'd felt before.

There were just no words to describe it. I could say it was like getting a hot stone massage, but from the inside out. I could say I imagined this was the feeling cats got when they lay in the rays of the sun in front of a window.

But I wouldn't say that.

Because this felt better.

One touch (especially an accidental one) just wasn't enough.

Forgetting completely about actually seeing him, I delved forward again, letting the pads of my fingers stroke over him once more.

I actually purred. Like a vibrating sound rumbled in my chest and broke free of my throat. It seemed to bounce around the room like an echo, an echo I hoped never faded away.

He made a startled sound and jerked away again. But not before I could catch the edge of the silver hood and reveal a glimpse of his face.

His eye.

I froze, feeling like the wind had been robbed from my lungs. Unable to stop him, quickly he jerked the hood back up and cheated me of the view.

I hadn't expected it.

Not at all.

I honestly thought he'd be hideous. He'd be grotesque and frightening. I thought there was a reason he kept himself hidden.

He wasn't at all frightening.

He was achingly beautiful.

His eye was almond shaped, almost like the curious wide eye of a cat. It was rimmed in onyx lashes that were impossibly long and thick. They were so dark it almost looked like he wore eyeliner because it defined the shape and color so well it couldn't possibly be natural.

And the color…

They were purple. A deep violet hue that likely only existed outside the realm of this planet, a shade that reminded me of the purest twilight, the color just between dusk and darkness before the stars outshined it and made it appear black. I could search forever and never find a color that could compare. It had depth and lightness to it, like a gem that reflected the light of a thousand bulbs. And in the very center were silver specks—like his eyes were their very own universe and contained their own twinkling stars.

I was lost.

I was falling.

If only a single glimpse at just one eye did this to me, then what kind of power would his full gaze ignite?

"You're coming with me," he said, penetrating the total devastation he'd caused within me.

I didn't argue. I'd beg to go.

I no longer felt completely exhausted. I no longer felt foggy, confused, and dry. It was like I'd been crawling through the desert and blissfully found a fountain of the purest drinking water.

I was revitalized. Rejuvenated. Recharged like a once-drained battery.

But beyond that there was something else.

I now felt tethered to him. Claimed. Possessed.

I was his.

the truth

I had to see his face.

It pounded through my bloodstream with the insistence of a heartbeat. Now that I'd seen a glimpse of the beauty he kept concealed, wondering would never be enough. I had to see.

He brought me into his hovercraft. One minute we were in my kitchen and the next we were in the sterile environment of his ship. He stood in the center of the bare space, not making a move to put me down.

I wasn't a small person, standing at five-feet-seven and roughly one hundred and fifty pounds. My curves were well-defined from all the walking on campus and waitressing I did on an almost daily basis. But even at this height and this weight, he held me up like it was no effort at all. He wasn't much taller than me, but he made me feel small.

Beneath the robe he wore, I could feel how hard his body was. Almost like he was carved out of marble. There was nothing at all soft about him, and I would bet obscene amounts of money (if I had it) that he likely had no body fat at all.

I glanced up at him, my cheek brushing against the silky robe, trying my hardest to look beneath the hood. He'd turned away his face so it was nearly impossible. I reached up to touch him again, to slip my fingers inside the fabric, and it jolted him into movement.

He carried me across the ship, toward the back section where I'd not been before. There was an oval-shaped white couch made of the same buttery soft leather as the chair I usually lay in and a chrome coffee table in front of it.

I was placed on the couch and he swiftly moved away. My eyes followed him as he went to the wall of cabinets and opened one, producing a tall, clear bottle, which he offered me.

"What is that?" I asked suspiciously.

"Water," he replied. "Are you thirsty?"

"God, yes." I took the bottle from him and let the cool water flow down my parched throat and coat my insides with moisture. When half the bottle was drained, I remembered my manners and pulled it away to wipe my mouth with the back of my hand. "Thank you."

"Drink the rest," he told me.

I did because it felt so wonderful to finally feel that my thirst was quenched. I glanced at the empty bottle and tilted my head. "Are you sure this is water?"

"I'm quite certain," he replied, and I swear I caught a hint of humor in his tone.

"Well, I've been dying of thirst for days, and this is the first bottle of water that actually made me feel less thirsty."

"It's from my planet."

Panic clawed its way up the back of my throat. "I just drank alien water?"

"Alien water?" he asked.

"Oh my God, am I going to die now?" I burst out, leaping to my feet.

He moved swiftly, gracefully. Both hands clasped around my shoulders, his very long fingers engulfing my frame. "You will not die," he commanded. If my body were capable of obeying such a command, I had no doubt I would live forever.

I shivered.

"I do not understand why your people must call us aliens," he said, gently pushing me back onto the couch.

"Such an idiotic term."

A laugh bubbled up my throat. "So what is the more politically correct term for you, then?"

From beneath the hood, I saw his head tilt as if he were contemplating my words. My fingers itched to pull away that fabric, to reveal everything I wanted to see.

"Well, on my planet, I'm a human just like you. We call ourselves Sapiens. As in *homo sapien.* A being who breathes and eats and lives."

I guess it made sense. He really didn't look like an alien. I always pictured aliens as being short and green with oversized black eyes. He talked and moved just like I did. Who was I to say there weren't other types of humans beyond Earth?

"What's your planet called?"

"Sapia." The way the word rolled off his tongue spoke volumes of the love he felt for his home.

"I don't understand why you're here. Why I'm here."

"You've been ill lately," he said, completely ignoring my question.

"Not really," I argued. "Just tired mostly."

"And thirsty," he added.

I nodded and the fear I was feeling at home rose up inside me. I glanced at him, not wanting to think he did something awful to me, but the truth was he could have. "What did you do to me?" I whispered. I was so afraid of the answer.

"How do you feel right now?" he asked, once again ignoring my direct question.

"I actually feel better." *You make me feel better.* I didn't say those words out loud, though. They made me uncomfortable just drifting through my head, let alone speaking them.

He turned and walked across the ship to another of the cabinets. From inside, he withdrew something that fit in the palm of his hand and came back toward me, bypassing the chrome table. The hem of his robe brushed over my bare feet, caressing the tops with its lightweight, cool fabric.

He lowered himself onto the tabletop. It was the first time I'd ever seen him sit. His knees stretched the fabric of the robe, causing me to realize how very long his legs were. In his lap, he rested the object, some sort of white-looking box.

"What is that?" I asked.

"I need to do something."

I pressed a little deeper into the couch. "What?"

"Let me see your hand," he said, reaching between us.

I hesitated.

"I will not hurt you," he vowed.

I believed him.

My fingers slid into his palm easily, and even though I couldn't see for sure, I knew he was looking at where our bodies joined. This little current of energy raced through him and into me, making my fingers jerk and his grip tighten. My eyes fluttered closed for long seconds because touching him was incredible. He made me feel alive; he amplified everything I felt from the way my lungs expanded with breath to the direction in which blood flowed through my veins.

Slowly, he tugged my hand closer to him, turning it so the palm lay face up, the back of my hand cradled in his. Using his pointer finger and thumb, he dragged his touch down each of my fingers, straightening them out and causing little tingles of awareness to race over my skin. I couldn't help but remember the other times he'd touched me and how awesome it had been.

When he was finished, he took my middle finger and held it firmly, lifting the white box and pressing a button on the side. A small needle popped out of the top and a little screen lit up.

Before I could protest, he poked the pad of my finger with the needle, the sharp sting barely registering in my brain. Blood welled to the surface, threatening to drip onto the pristine floor. Before that could happen, he used what looked like a slip of absorbent paper (also attached to the white box) and soaked it up.

The paper and needle were drawn back inside and the screen blinked like it was doing something.

"What's going on?" I asked.

"We're waiting," he said, placing the box beside him on the table and completely ignoring it. "You're bleeding," he said, drawing my attention back to my finger.

"Well, you're the one who caused it." I pointed out.

The pads of his fingers caressed the inside of my wrist, and this tight feeling knotted in my stomach, making me want to squirm around. He lifted my hand, staring intently at my bleeding finger.

"May I?" he asked.

I nodded, unable to make a sound.

He bent so he was hunched around my finger and lowered his covered head. I stared at the back of the fabric, tempted to rip it away.

But the temptation died quickly. My hand was lifted into the private space of his hood, and the feeling of something incredibly warm and smooth wrapped around the tip of my finger.

I gasped, holding the bit of air inside me, unable to take or release any more breaths. He was kissing it. Heat burst through me, turning everything beneath my skin to liquid. This feeling of peace washed over me; this feeling of complete stillness relaxed my bones.

After long seconds of contact, he pulled away my finger, returning it to me. I glanced down. The injury was completely gone.

"What is your name?" I whispered, willing him to not ignore this one question.

"Tarek."

It was an exotic name. One that held great strength, like I knew he did.

"Tarek," I whispered, trying it out as my hand still burned from his kiss. "Tarek, please show me your face."

"I'd like to try something," he said, his voice very low.

I nodded. I'd give him anything. It was as if he'd cast a spell upon me, and I would never be able to deny him.

"Close your eyes."

I closed them.

"Do not open them," he commanded.

I sat poised on the edge of the couch, keeping my eyes closed as my body began to tremble. His fingers brushed against my cheeks, stroking outward toward my ears. And then I felt his incredible heat grow nearer. Like I was right beside the direct flame of a candle. But I wasn't afraid of being burned. I welcomed it.

One of his hands slipped along my jaw, cupping my face, cradling it against him.

He moved closer, so close I felt his breath fan out across my lips.

"Please," I begged on a whisper.

His kiss was hesitant at first, like he wasn't sure what to do. I slid forward just a little bit, bringing our lips more firmly together. A heavy fog draped over me, pushing out everything but him. His lips were hot, just like the rest of him, and it was exactly like having that first sip of hot coffee on a cold winter's morning. I felt his touch all the way to my core. He branded me from the inside out.

Tentatively, he moved across my mouth, rubbing his lips into mine, caressing my flesh with his, tasting my flavor like I was some kind of fine wine.

In my lap, my hands fisted. If I looked down, I knew my knuckles would be white. I wanted nothing more than to grab him, to hold him to me until every part of our bodies fused together. But I didn't. I let him lead.

I wasn't sure, but I felt like this was something for him, that this kind of contact was rare.

Up until this point, I stayed still. I didn't attack him as my body demanded. But I couldn't anymore. I parted my lips and moved, kissing him back, returning the sensation.

He sucked in a breath and stilled. The hand once cupping my jaw had fallen to the base of my neck and it tightened, spasming against my skin. The edges of the hood he wore brushed against my forehead and temples. Ever so slowly, I reached up, trailing the pad of my thumb over his cheekbone and then drawing back so I was no longer beneath his hood.

I opened my eyes and wasn't surprised to see that everything was blurry. My entire body felt off kilter from that innocent kiss we shared. After blinking several times, my vision began to come into focus.

Using both hands, I grasped the edges of the hood.

"Tarek, show me."

He didn't protest or jerk away. He leaned slightly closer.

Anticipation curled along my nerve endings and parts of my body started to tremble. I tugged the fabric, ready to reveal the complete face of the man who made me feel more than anyone I'd ever met.

Beside us, a beeping sound pierced the bubble of intensity that hovered around us.

Tarek jerked up and looked to the side.

I tried to pull him back, but his attention was now focused on that little machine. He picked it up, pressing another button and looking at the screen, which was lit up with a red light. I didn't understand what it said.

My hands fell into my lap as the energy around us shifted. "What is it?"

He leaned back and then stood, pacing just a few steps away. "It worked," he said, more to himself than to anyone else.

I stared at the wall of his back, waiting for some kind of explanation.

He never turned around. He just stood there staring down at that stupid little machine like it was something incredible.

Frustrated, I got up and walked around to where he stood, looking down.

"What worked?"

"The experiment," he replied, still looking at the blinking screen in his grip.

I grabbed his arm, my fingers tightening around him. "What experiment?" I demanded. My pulse hammered inside me, causing fear to skitter around, spreading panic in its wake. *What did he do to me?*

He glanced up sharply, and I caught a flash of violet in the shadows of his hood.

"You're pregnant," he said, his voice filled with awe. "My child grows within you."

Part Two

the impossible

I was hallucinating.

Either that or I was completely bat-shit crazy.

I stood there for a long time, waiting for him to laugh. For a teasing chuckle to float out from beneath that silver hood he wore.

But no laugh came.

My child grows within you.

I know he only said it once, but I heard those words over and over again. *It couldn't be.* Even as I thought the words, my hand fluttered over my flat stomach and settled there. I felt the same. It was impossible to believe there was a baby… *this faceless man's baby* inside me.

"Ummm," I said, wishing I could look into his eyes. "I don't know how things happen on your planet, but on Earth, you have to have sex to get pregnant."

"And what exactly is sex on Earth?" he asked like he was merely asking about the weather.

I might be a college student, but in that moment, I was transported back to middle school when all the girls were herded into the gym for a "health" class that detailed exactly how girls would get pregnant if they didn't practice abstinence.

It was embarrassing then, and it was embarrassing now.

Clearly, it didn't matter how old I got. Talking about inserting part A into part B wasn't something I would ever be comfortable with.

Suddenly, I was thankful I couldn't see his face. And I sort of wished he couldn't see mine. It was likely beet red.

He remained silent throughout my trip back to adolescence. I figured that meant he really wanted an answer. Hell, maybe sex meant something else to his people.

"Sex is when a man puts his penis inside a woman's vagina."

Oh my God, I just said that out loud.

"And that's all?"

"Well, no," I said, hedging.

A sound pierced my inner squirming. My eyes flashed up toward him where he stood just feet from me. He was laughing.

He was laughing at me.

Goose bumps broke out across my arms and legs. It was only a laugh, but it affected me in ways I didn't think possible.

Back when I was fifteen, my mom took me and my best friend to see our first concert. I still remember what it was like to stand there near the stage with the music pounding around me, drowning out even the roar of the crowd. It vibrated my insides and made me feel all shaky. And then the headliner started to sing. It had been incredible. Unforgettable.

That's what Tarek's laugh was like.

"I know what sex is," he said, a smile in his voice. His accent made me want to hang on his every word. Even when he was poking fun at me.

"Then why the hell did you just ask me?" I said, scowling.

He chuckled lightly and again, goose bumps raced across my flesh. I rubbed at my arms, trying to calm the sensation.

"Are you cold?" he asked, his light tone disappearing instantly.

I wasn't even able to answer because he moved quickly across the room and pulled out a white blanket. Instantly, he was before me, so close the heat from his body warmed my front. He spread his arms out wide, unfolding the blanket.

He had long, graceful arms—I could tell despite the robe he wore. "That's some wingspan you've got there," I said.

"I assume that's a joke?" he asked, wrapping the blanket around me and pulling it closed at my chest. "Because I do not have wings."

"You have long arms," I explained, unable to come up with anything snazzier because his closeness was affecting me so.

"They're actually average among Sapiens," he remarked and pointed me back to the sofa I'd leapt up from when he announced I was pregnant.

"Sit down," he said.

I did because a knot formed in my stomach as the thought of me actually being pregnant rushed back.

"If you know what sex is, then you must know I can't possibly be pregnant."

Tarek sat on the couch beside me, spreading his arms out along the backrest, literally draping himself on the leather. I was beginning to get very angry that I was having this conversation with a man whose face I couldn't see.

"The last time you were here, while I was pleasuring you, I placed some of my semen inside you."

What. The. Fuck?

"You artificially inseminated me!" I burst out, pissed and grossed out all at once.

"I told you I wanted to do an experiment."

"A *baby* is not an experiment!" I yelled. Horror struck me. Horror and disbelief. It couldn't be. There was no way I got pregnant that way. My body wouldn't betray me like that.

Oh yes, it would, a little voice sang. *Your body desires him and you know it.*

I moved to jump up from the couch. The blanket tangled around my legs, and I pitched sideways. Tarek moved quickly, showing more grace than I could ever possess. His arms swept around me, stopping my fall and holding me steady.

I hung there for long seconds, suspended between the floor and his body, his arms literally my only support. And then he curled them in.

Like a fisherman reeling in a line, he dragged me closer until we were mere inches apart.

The heat from his fingers seared through the back of my shirt. I wondered if his handprint would permanently scar my skin. He used his body almost like a shield, guiding me back down onto the couch, this time sitting much closer to me.

"I know this is a lot, but try not to overreact."

I laughed.

His hand lay between us. I could feel his fingers against my thigh. Without thought, I reached forward, linking our fingers together and drawing his hand into my lap. "Don't you think I should at least be allowed to see your face?"

I sensed his hesitation. But instead of trying to convince him, I waited for a reply.

"I don't look like you."

"No one else looks like me either," I said.

"That's true," Tarek agreed, but it didn't sound like he was speaking to me. Then he spoke out, "I mean the people of your planet. I don't look like your version of humans."

"Then what do you look like?" I asked.

"Like a Sapien." He shrugged his shoulders as he said the words.

"Show me," I said.

Tarek untangled our fingers and withdrew his hand. Slowly, he reached up and grasped the edges of the hood. Then he paused.

I groaned out loud.

This guy was going to kill me!

"I'm afraid I won't please you," he said softly.

The words pierced my heart. He thought I was going to think he was ugly. He didn't realize how those words made him so very similar to me and every human I knew.

He was vulnerable and self-conscious, just like the rest of us.

The fact he even cared at all what I thought of him took away some of my shock and panic.

"Try me," I said equally as soft.

You could have heard a pin drop through the silence that encompassed the room.

The silver silky hood fell back, lying against his neck, the folds of the fabric bunched in a way that created a loose frame for everything above his neck.

He was right. He looked nothing like the human's here on Earth.

Tarek was better.

In those first moments my eyes fully took in his face, I felt as though a violent hurricane ripped through my body, scattering pieces of myself beneath the skin that bound me together. Looking upon him was so intensely shattering I knew even once I was put back together, I would never be the same.

The oxygen in my lungs evaporated, but if my body missed the air, it gave no indication.

From the brief view I got of his eye, I knew he was going to be beautiful, gorgeous even. But he was absolutely devastating.

Like the rest of him, his face was long, but the length of it was balanced by the strong angle of his jaw. His cheekbones were high and narrow, his nose perfectly straight and austere. His skin was absolutely poreless. A creamy pale color, as if it had never seen the sun. There were no wrinkles, no creases, nothing to mar his sleek perfection. I was pretty sure he didn't grow facial hair because there was just no way a razor would give him that close of a shave.

His mouth was shaped like a bow, his lips not overly full, but certainly enough there to give definition. The pink undertone of his mouth might have been feminine—on anyone else. On him, it was seductive, captivating… and it created a yearning deep inside me.

Even in all his facial glory, nothing could compare to his eyes.

They were wide and almond shaped, fringed with the kind of lashes women would kill for. The perfect frame for a stunning picture. They were still the color of a velvet night sky before it went completely dark. A rich, deep purple with flecks of silver near the center, stars amongst a galaxy. Glitter in the dark.

One might think the wide stare he bestowed upon me would be childlike and innocent, but it wasn't. He held the kind of wisdom in his gaze that made me shudder. Maybe it was the silver against the amethyst that afforded him the appearance of unwavering steel at his core. Or maybe it was the way he carried himself, sturdy, strong, and sure.

When I was able to tear my eyes away from his, I glanced upward. My fingers flexed, wanting to glide through the deep-brown hair that effortlessly crowned his head. It was boy band hair. You know the kind of hair that probably took five hours to make look so natural. The kind that seemed to have a mind of its own, a rebellion to look nothing but enticing. The rich brown should have been too dark for the paleness of his skin, but it wasn't. It was the perfect contrast.

I truly couldn't imagine anyone looking as superior as him. Ever. Yet he seemed to imply he was average-looking for his race. There could never be anything average about him.

I was unable to speak; I could only stare. After very long moments, he ducked his head and reached for the hood, meaning to conceal his face once more.

"No," I said quickly, reaching out to stop him. "Please don't."

He lowered his hands.

"I've never seen anyone like you before," I whispered.

"I know," he said, the corner of his mouth lifting.

"You're absolutely beautiful." My voice was breathless, my lungs still trying to inhale properly.

Tarek's lips parted as surprise registered on his face. "I thought—"

I shook my head, cutting off his words. "Whatever you thought was wrong."

Quietness enveloped the room, but neither of us looked away. I studied his face like it was a painting I could stare at for days and still not have explored all the color. He let me gaze at him, openly accepting my stare and not shying away from it at all. He seemed content to say nothing, even though we had so much to talk about.

Everything inside me felt jittery and fragile. The pieces of me that had yet to shatter threatened to at any moment. I remembered what it was like to have his hands on me. To have him bring pleasure to my body like no one had ever before.

"Why?" I asked, still looking at his face. "Why did you… touch me?"

"It's known that a human female body is more likely to accept a man's seed when she is pleasured, when she is relaxed. It opens her body more freely."

I couldn't argue. My body had been open. *Way* open.

I pushed away the memory of pleasure and stood. "I'm not pregnant."

"Yes. You are."

I paced the floor like a caged animal and then turned to spear him with a look. "Here on Earth, you can't just impregnate a woman without her consent. A lot of people would call that rape."

He got a sour look on his face. "As you already pointed out, we technically did not have sex. I remained covered the entire time. I did not push myself on you in any way."

"No, you just injected me with a baby!" I yelled.

"Your kind is very emotional," he said without heat, "especially when your hormones are out of balance."

His calm demeanor irritated me. "I don't believe you."

"The exhaustion, the dehydration, lack of appetite—those are all symptoms of a Sapien pregnancy."

"I'm not a Sapien," I growled.

"No, but I am."

the reason

I was speechless, completely unable to speak or feel. If what he was saying was true, what was I going to do? How would I work, finish school, and take care of a baby? I drove a Wrangler, for God's sake. I couldn't strap a baby in the back of that! My parents were going to be livid. I was going to be unwed, alone and pregnant. What's worse, I could never tell who the baby's father really was because everyone would think I was insane.

People were going to talk. Rumors in my little town would soar.

Tears filled my eyes, threatening to spill over. "You have no idea what you've done to me." The first of the tears leaked from my eye, rolling down my cheek and curving under my jaw. More followed. I didn't attempt to wipe them away. They weren't going to stop.

It was like I was looking through a wet windowpane as I stared at Tarek. His image was slightly blurry, but I could still make out his features. It was so wrong that he did this to me and I still thought he was absolutely gorgeous. It was so wrong that even now my body craved him.

His eyes widened, alarm filling them as more tears rained down my cheeks. It was clear he had no idea what to do. I was glad he didn't try to comfort me. He wouldn't be able to anyway.

"I didn't think it would work," he said after a long time.

I tilted my head to the side, finally wiping away the wetness on my face. "Then, why?"

"Our planet is aging. The females on Sapia are not conceiving, and without repopulation, my planet will die."

"But I'm not one of you. This baby…" I swallowed past the words. "It's a hybrid, not fully yours."

"I'd rather have half of my planet left than none at all."

My shoulders sagged.

"Some of us were sent out to try and find a way to help repopulate our world. Up until now, no pregnancies have taken. Most of us had lost hope. We were beginning to think perhaps our race was meant to die out."

"Then why did it work?" *Why me?*

"I'm not certain," he said, but I heard the hesitation in his tone.

"But you have an idea."

"It is unfounded."

Sometimes the way he spoke made me want to giggle. He was formal, or maybe he was just very intelligent. I was so used to slang and texting that it seemed odd to hear words like "unfounded."

"Tell me anyway," I asked, staring at him through drying eyes.

"I think your body was more accepting of my seed because you felt pleasure at my hands."

My cheeks heated and I ducked my eyes. I couldn't deny that I fiercely enjoyed every second I spent with him touching me.

"Don't," he said, his tone sort of cold and commanding.

I glanced up. He moved across the floor, closing the distance between us until I felt the heat off his body like I was standing before a bonfire on a chilled fall night. His long fingers nudged at my chin, tilting up my face so I could meet his violet eyes.

I stopped breathing. All the embarrassment I was feeling vanished as I sank into the depths of his gaze. It was almost hypnotizing, the way he made me feel. He could likely issue any command and I would obey, no matter how insane it might be.

"I'm pretty sure you need to breathe," he spoke. The words were thick with accent and his lips curved up into a full smile.

I filled my chest with oxygen, still unable to look away.

"Don't be embarrassed," he spoke, reminding me we'd been having a conversation. "The pleasure you displayed, that you so boldly felt… I never thought possible."

My head jerked back slightly, unintentionally pulling away from his touch. He didn't know pleasure was possible? That was odd. "I don't understand."

"Sapiens are very much like humans in many ways, but in other ways, we are very different."

"Are you saying you don't find pleasure in sex?" I couldn't believe I was having this conversation. On a hovercraft. In space. With an uber-hot alien.

"Sapiens don't find pleasure in most anything. Our planet is colder than earth, more serious. You are a race governed by emotion and feeling. At my home, we prefer to live a simpler life. A life less governed by gratification."

"That must suck."

The corner of his mouth tipped up. "Yes, I suppose it does… suck."

I laughed. The term seemed out of place on his tongue.

His eyes drank me in like I was something he'd never seen before, something he was fascinated by. Maybe it was the amethyst hue or perhaps the way he made me feel like I was gazing up at the most brilliant of night skies, but no one had ever looked at me that way.

It was like he looked *into* me. Like he saw things that even I didn't know. It was as if he'd made some amazing discovery that no one had ever stumbled upon…

And that discovery was me.

Exhilaration bubbled up inside me, fizzing up like a shaken liter of soda. Just the hint of air, the suggestion of release, and everything inside would explode out of me. He made me feel bold, inspired… *exclusive.*

"Then, why?" I asked. "Why would the Sapiens live that way? Why not change?"

An almost sad look crossed his features. His sadness penetrated me, made me feel hollow. I couldn't imagine a life without any kind of pleasure or enjoyment. How lonely he must be.

"The elders who govern my planet do not like change. They uphold tradition and respect."

"Getting enjoyment out of life isn't a bad thing."

"We wouldn't know how to attain it anyway," he whispered, gazing away. It made me wonder about the failed attempts at pleasure. It made me wonder what kind of hidden trials there had been.

"I could show you," I said, my voice turning breathless.

The silver flecks in his eyes seemed to glisten when he looked at me once more.

"And how would you show me?" he murmured.

The exhilaration that burned through my veins caused me to lift my hands and place them, palms down, on his shoulders. His pupils dilated slightly, and a little shudder moved through me because he was like my own personal sauna. My skin greedily soaked up his heat.

"In order to know pleasure," I whispered, dragging my hands across his wide stature and down his covered arms, "you must feel."

He swallowed thickly, the Adam's apple in his neck jerking with the effort.

I felt his hunger. Perhaps I always had. Maybe that's why when he touched me before, I enjoyed it so much, because I knew he liked it. He wanted me to purr in satisfaction, to show him a side of human nature he thought was unattainable... He hadn't realized I could make him feel the same.

Oh, and I was going to.

I was going to give back to him every ounce of bliss he gave to me.

For the first time in Tarek's life, I was going to show him what it was to feel.

I glanced up at him through lowered lashes, my fingers trailing across his chest, fondling for the zipper that held the robe around his body. "Will you let me show you?"

He swallowed again, his eyes looking at where I was caressing him atop the silky material. Tarek's eyes met mine and he nodded.

the lesson

I was shaking.

The zipper on the robe slid down with ease. My arm lowered as far as it could reach. It wasn't low enough. I wanted his clothing gone. I wanted to see him entirely. I ached to touch wherever my fingers chose to drift.

I glanced at him, then lowered, bending my knees so I slid down his chest, descending the zipper as I went until I was almost on my knees. Tarek stood still, his arms at his sides, and I enjoyed his stillness. I enjoyed being the one in charge.

Slowly, I stood back up, letting my front graze his chest as I moved. The edges of the robe were parted only slightly, revealing more of that marble-like skin, perfectly pale and taut. I held his eyes, fighting the urge to get lost in their depths as my fingers slipped beneath the fabric and pushed it over his shoulders.

The robe landed soundless at our feet, curling around both of us like it was purposely tying us together. I didn't mind. Being this close to him was a high. Like a rush of lazy adrenaline filling my limbs and causing the area between my legs to throb with desire.

His body was unbelievable. His skin was pure, like the way fresh fallen snow appeared as it blanketed the ground. His arms were long and sinewy, the muscle corded beneath his skin, affording him the look of being crafted from steel. There wasn't a single mark on him. No hair, no birthmarks, no moles. He didn't boast any little wrinkles from the sun or show any kind of wear and tear from everyday life.

His chest, dear God his chest, it was broad and strong. If I wasn't standing so close, I would have sworn it was carved out of granite. His pecs were so defined my palms itched to fill themselves with them. In the center of each perfectly formed muscle were symmetrical nipples. The skin around them was slightly darker, drawing even more attention to the area, and the center was puckered with hard little pebbles.

Without thought, I leaned in and sucked one into my mouth.

I heard his breath catch, but then my own mind and body overruled my ears. It was so incredibly easy to roll that little round stone in my moist, eager mouth. I opened my lips wider, sucking more of his chest into my mouth, creating a gentle tugging sensation against his skin.

If ice were hot, this was exactly what it would feel like. His skin glided over my tongue, almost melting in my mouth, slipping across my lips, sliding against my teeth. It was taunting to say the least.

Before pulling away, I tugged at him with my teeth, nipping at him and noting the once pale and flawless skin was slightly flushed from my ministrations. I lifted my head momentarily and Tarek looked at me, this hazy expression upon his features.

I smiled and lowered my head to his other nipple, giving it the same treatment.

The ridges of his abs were unmistakable and spanned the entire length of his waist, giving way to a V-cut at his hip where even more remarkable skin was on display. Tarek was wearing nothing beneath the robe, and the thought of him being so close to naked all those times I'd been here with him caused my body to shudder.

What would it be like to have his rock-hard body over me? Would his cock be as solid as the rest of him?

Would he spear me from the inside until I could only gasp?

God, I hoped so.

But I was going to take my time. I was going to show him exactly what he'd been missing all these years.

I licked his abs like he was some delicious lollipop and I wanted to get to the treasure in the center. I knew I was affecting him because as I licked, his abs would contract, quivering under me and making me even bolder.

I grasped his hips, tightening my fingers around him and letting my nails dig into his flesh just slightly. Slowly, I pushed him backward, his feet obeying my command. When the backs of his legs hit the sofa, gently I pushed him down onto the white leather.

I fitted myself between his legs and looked down, taking in the cock between them. It stood straight out, straining against the skin and jerking with every breath he took. Like the rest of him, his member was very long, but unlike his arms, he was not sinewy. He was thick and meaty, a primed sword ready for battle. I was pretty sure if I wrapped my finger and thumb around the base that the tips would barely meet.

Little thrills shot through me. I wasn't sure my body would open wide enough for Tarek, but I sure as hell wanted to try.

The area around his wood was completely hairless, smooth, and unlined. His balls seemed larger than any I'd ever seen, and they weren't wrinkled like that of a human male. I was pretty sure if he stood, they would hang heavily against his thighs, like trophies of manliness, a promise to deliver copious amounts of hot seed into my wet and waiting pussy.

The bottom of my stomach dropped as I realized just how heady it was to look upon him. I'd barely touched him, yet I knew if he even grazed me with an accidental touch, I would explode into an orgasm unlike any I'd ever known.

The desire in this room, the raw passion, was undeniable. It made it hard to think, to see…

"Can you feel that?" I asked him, unable to tear my eyes away from his waiting cock.

He made a sound that was a cross between a denial and agreement. That's okay. I wanted to work for it.

I dropped to my knees before him, letting my shoulders brush against the inside of his knees. Using my palms, I spread his legs to grant myself more access and then I dragged my nails down the insides of his thighs.

A slight tremor moved beneath his skin, and I smiled.

He was not unaffected by me.

Eager to explore him, I wrapped my hand around the base of his penis and squeezed. His head fell back against the couch, and I hunched over him, slowly sucking his swollen length between my lips.

His entire body stilled, shock seemed to ripple around the room. I withdrew slowly, pulling my lips up the sides of his dick, delivering a little bit of pressure. Before lifting my head, I sucked the very tip of him, twirling my tongue over the small hole at the top.

I looked up. “Do you like this?”

He lifted his head and looked at me. “Don’t stop.”

I smiled. “I wasn’t going to.”

After that, I wasn’t as slow. I slid my mouth down over him, sliding until he hit the back of my throat. Even then, I pushed a little more, just because I loved the way he felt against me. My mouth worked him with eagerness, pumping up and down along his rigid length, leaving his cock moist and throbbing. Every so often, I pulled back completely and nipped down the outside of his dick with my teeth.

Little sounds erupted from the back of his throat, and his hands fisted at his sides.

Wanting to give him even more pleasure, I gripped the base and held him firmly, lifting him so I could dive down and suck one of his sacks into my mouth.

He mumbled something I couldn't understand and his hips surged upward, pushing himself farther into my mouth.

Releasing his cock, I grabbed his inner thighs and lavished attention on his boys, sucking and licking until his legs were shaking with the need for release.

Momentarily, I lifted my head, wanting to see his face. He rolled the back of his head along the couch and glanced at me, his eyes almost glowing the most brilliant shade of purple. My lips parted with surprise as I studied the glittering color.

"I…" he said, his words faltering. His hips rotated upward, seeking something he probably didn't know he needed.

I smiled and grasped his hands, placing them on my shoulders. “Hold on,” I whispered and took him into my mouth once more.

I pumped him quickly. Letting my lips close around him, keeping the pressure steady as I milked his cock for every last ounce of pleasure I could. I knew he was going to erupt when his fingers dug into my skin. I made a little purring sound in the back of my throat and it vibrated the tip, which was buried against my throat.

His shout came quickly, suddenly. His cock jerked almost violently. Hot liquid filled my mouth, and, yeah, I drank it down because I wanted every last drop of satisfaction he gave me. Even after his moans quieted and his fingers went slack against my shoulders, I sucked him gently, not quite willing to lift my head.

My underwear was drenched with arousal. My knees were trembling and my breasts ached to the point of pain. He’d barely touched me, yet I was so ready for sex that I almost stood and sank down over top of him to quench my thirst for his oversized cock.

When I finally released his member, I laid it gently against his thigh. It wasn’t quite as hard as it had been, but it was nowhere near flaccid. In fact, just looking at its firmness caused me to want to ride him all over again.

I sat back a little, remaining between his legs. My tongue darted out to feel the swollen flesh of my lips. Tarek stared down at me with wonder in his face.

"Did you feel?" I asked him, my voice hoarse.

"Is that what it's like for you?" he asked, his voice low.

"When you touched me, yes."

"I… No one's ever taken me in their mouth before," he said.

I smiled, feeling quite full of myself.

"It was incredible. It was like my mind just emptied."

I nodded, totally understanding. I knew what it was like to have your body and senses take over. My legs were actually wobbly when I stood. Desire hammered through my bloodstream like a drug, making me drunk, making me feel high. I grabbed the robe that lay abandoned on the floor and carried it over to sit beside Tarek on the couch. I used it to drape over us both, totally thrilled that we shared the same cover.

"Your blanket is there," he pointed out, motioning to the blanket he gave me earlier.

"But this is yours."

He looked at me like he didn't understand.

"I want this because it smells like you. Because it was wrapped around you. It makes me feel near you," I replied honestly, my words making me feel completely vulnerable.

"I'm sitting right here," he pointed out.

"I know."

Something in his eyes shifted, like a star shooting through the sky. And then it was gone. I knew we had things to talk about, things I needed to yell at him for, a scary reality looming. But I wasn't ready yet. I wanted to sit here in this safe cocoon of denial, just him and me and nothing else.

Tarek's heat drew nearer when his hand slid up the bareness of my calf. I looked up at him, wondering if his touch was intentional.

It was.

"It's your turn," he said as his palm covered my inner thigh. "I want to taste you."

He slid out from beneath the silver material, unabashedly naked, and sank before me beside the couch. He took my ankles and guided me around, positioning my feet at the edge of the couch. My knees were bent and my core accessible to his touch.

Tarek's palms slid beneath my buttocks and into the waistband of the sleep shorts I was wearing, swiftly pulling them down my legs and bringing my lacy panties with them. He tossed them aside and then ripped the robe away, leaving me completely exposed.

I was half reclined against the back cushions as Tarek tugged me so my bottom rested on the edge of the seat. With my knees bent and my legs open, I knew he had uninhibited access to the most secret place on my entire body. Yet I wasn't embarrassed. I didn't feel my face flame with shyness. I'd seen the way he looked at me before, with wonder and amazement. I wasn't sure what his past experiences were like, but I did know in his eyes I was beautiful. He enjoyed my reactions, my rawness. He enjoyed seeing emotion ripple through my limbs and burst off my tongue.

I'd give him that. I'd let him see the kind of power he wielded over me. It was the headiest aphrodisiac I'd ever known: surrender.

His fingers tangled in the short curls above my slit. I wasn't one of those girls that shaved themselves bare. I didn't care what the women said on hair removal commercials or in magazines. That shit itched when it grew back. There wasn't anything worse than carrying a tray of drinks around in a bar with this itch that couldn't be scratched.

"I've never seen this before," Tarek said, his voice drifting up between my legs.

I began to reconsider my previous statement. Shaving down there might turn me into the Itchy and Scratchy show, but I would endure it if he liked it.

"So wild and imperfect," he murmured, stroking the curls again.

I was torn between mad lust and being offended. Yeah, I surrendered to him, but I didn't really want to be called imperfect. My legs began to close, the self-consciousness I hadn't felt before rearing its ugly head.

Tarek's long arm reached around me, draping over my hips to pin me in place. "I think I said that wrong." He looked up. All I could see were the perfectly messy hair and his incredible eyes. Eyes that were sparkling with merriment.

For a man who seemed fairly cold and detached when I first met him, he was sure starting to show signs of life beneath his flawless exterior.

Ah, the power of a blow job.

"You think so?" I arched a brow at him.

The way his eyes gathered at the corners, I knew he was smiling. I pushed up onto my elbows so I wouldn't miss it.

His teeth were straight, white and utterly perfect. It wasn't a surprise. But the way my heart stuttered when he turned on the full wattage of his smile was. There was such sincerity in his smile that it could only be honest. It transformed his face from untouchable beauty to an absurdly handsome man full of ornery charm.

"You are imperfect," he said, repeating the exact thing he shouldn't. "But that's what makes you beautiful."

Oh, good save.

"Sapien females are all incredibly beautiful, fragile, and all *the same*." He finished with clear boredom.

"You're more open, more vocal, certainly more clumsy and loud."

"Hey," I warned, unable to produce any heat to go along with it. I simply couldn't be mad.

"Untamed." He finished like he was thoroughly proud of that description.

Untamed.

I liked that.

And really, didn't it mean I didn't always have to comb my hair? A girl could get onboard that kind of crazy train.

His fingers delved into the short, wiry curls once more. "I like this," he said, staring down at me intently. My body shuddered under his touch, even though there wasn't really anything erotic to it, other than the place he was soo close to.

I made a sound, acknowledging his words. Without meaning to, my hips rocked upward, giving him even greater access. His fingers slid down, one on each side of my clit, blazing a path down the sensitive skin around my opening. By the way his fingers glided, I knew I was still dripping wet and I hoped he realized it meant I was intensely enjoying his attention.

His free hand splayed across my inner thigh, the hotness of his palm searing my skin, and I groaned. My body melted back against the leather of the sofa, and my eyes slipped closed. His fingers moved inward and I felt him pulling gently at my folds, almost like he was teasing them open.

I squirmed a little, wanting even more.

"This," he said, flicking over my swollen clit, "is the area that drives you the most wild."

"Yes," I whimpered as he languidly rolled it between his fingers.

I felt the first sizzle of release. I was so far gone that I knew it wouldn't take much, but before I could completely tumble over the peak, he pulled back. My eyes shot open with desperation and I lifted my head.

The image of his dark head dipping between my creamy thighs was the last thing I saw before my vision went dark.

He rendered me sightless.

He likely rendered me deaf as well.

It was as if he robbed my body of the majority of its senses and put all their power into his touch.

His tongue tasted me tentatively at first, licking just a little, then pulling away. I wondered if he was sampling my flavor on his tongue before deciding if he liked it. As he pondered, one of his incredibly long fingers delved inside me, slipping right in, burying in the center of my body. He twisted his finger around, caressing my inner walls before curling his finger in a come hither motion and making my back arch with delight.

And then his mouth was on me again, this time no kind of hesitation in his actions. His tongue was as long as the rest of him, and he used it incredibly well. He started down below my opening and licked up, like I was a melting ice cream cone on a summer day. Upward his tongue would drag, applying the perfect amount of pressure that made me writhe. When Tarek arrived at my clit, his lips closed around it, tugging the engorged flesh into his mouth and sucking gently.

I felt my mouth open as my entire body went rigid. The orgasm was so intense my body bucked upward, but his arm was still there and he pinned me down as wave after wave of ecstasy obliterated me.

When my body came down from its crest, Tarek didn't lift his head. He turned it, pressing a moist, hot kiss to the inside of my thigh. Every part of my core throbbed, like aftershocks shaking the ground. It was almost like my clit had its own heartbeat and every time it pumped, tingles of pleasure would race over my skin.

Tarek released the hold on my hips and pushed both hands between my knees, slipping up so he could cup my breasts through my shirt.

My breathing was just returning to normal and every cell in my body was lethargic and satisfied.

His hands didn't linger on my chest, but instead moved downward to delve beneath the hem of my top. I thought he was angling for better access to my breasts.

I was wrong.

His large hands spanned my entire middle, almost as if he were cradling my stomach.

Oh.

Oh my.

He was. He was cradling the child he placed there, the little being that was half him and half me. It was the most tender moment I'd ever experienced, and it was at the hands of a man who admittedly was raised not to feel.

"Tarek," I whispered, staring up at the softly lit ceiling.

"Yes?"

"We need to talk."

Up until just a little while ago, I was single, unattached, and had no plans to become a mother anytime soon. But now here I was, pregnant, still single… but maybe not so unattached.

I had no idea what any of this meant. I barely had time to process it all. All I really knew was that my life was likely about to change completely.

the dark

I didn't get many answers.

Maybe he didn't have them. Maybe he didn't think I needed to know. Maybe the glimpse of the man with feelings had been fleeting and he really just didn't care.

I learned that Sapien pregnancy lasted eight months and not nine. I was already over a month along, so that meant in less than seven months, I was going be a mother. To a baby spawned by a man from another planet.

I should expect to feel dehydrated, tired, and my appetite would likely change. But even as he said those things, he seemed doubtful. His doubt was the scariest thing of all. Up until now, Tarek was nothing but calm and self-assured. The thing was I was the first human to conceive a baby with a Sapien. Tarek could tell me what pregnancies were like on his planet, but since I wasn't like him, it might not be the same.

I asked more questions, the most important being what was going to happen to me. My questions went unanswered. Tarek had a canny ability to only answer what he wanted to and seemingly not hear what he didn't.

Before I knew what was happening, he was handing me another bottle of the water from his planet and preparing to usher me home.

"I'm not ready to go," I told him, feeling like I couldn't possibly go back to my life as it was because everything was changed.

He turned from the cabinet, two large clear jugs of water in each hand. Without a word, he walked to me, my eyes fastened to his face like it was the only thing in the room. Would I ever get use to the color of his eyes?

He walked so close that I had to tilt back my head to hold his stare. I had an incredible urge to lay my cheek against his chest, to close my eyes and fall asleep against him. I searched his gaze, trying to look into him the way he did me. But Tarek was very good at shuttering his emotions, at keeping a door firmly latched between whatever went on inside him and what I was able to see.

"Hold on to me," he instructed. His voice was whisper soft and his enunciation of each word, the lyrical tone to his voice, caused me to sway against him.

My cheek slid against his shoulder while my arms wound around his middle, linking together behind his back. The water bottle in my hand annoyed me because it meant less of me was able to touch him.

He didn't wind his arms around me. His hands were full with the jugs. He stood still, not leaning into me, not sighing like he enjoyed the touch. I didn't care. I enjoyed it enough for both of us. My eyes fluttered closed as the sound of his beating heart filled my ear. It beat insistently, like he was running a marathon and should be out of breath.

"Your heart is racing," I mumbled, dipping my head lower and pressing my ear just a little bit closer.

"My heart rate is much faster than yours," he answered.

Disappointment washed over me. Part of me was hoping it was just the effect I had on him.

"Hold on tight," he said.

We began to move, to descend out of the hovercraft, the floor falling away as if it hadn't been there at all. I didn't feel the cool rush of night air. I didn't feel frightened and alarmed like I was plummeting to my death.

All I felt was Tarek.

Even though I was the one holding on to him, I still felt safe. I knew he wouldn't let me fall. It occurred to me I should open my eyes, take in the view below us.

Keeping my cheek pressed against him, I lifted my lids.

The familiar surroundings of my apartment were not what I expected to see. My gaze touched upon my furniture, the white walls, the magazines scattered across the coffee table.

The solidness of the floor beneath my feet intruded upon the lightness I had felt. "We're back," I murmured, feeling a little sad. I wasn't ready for him to go.

Without thought, I snuggled into him a little closer, ducking my face into his robe and inhaling the scent that only he carried.

He probably wanted me to let go now. He was probably about to order me away. A soft thud broke into my thoughts. Briefly, I thought to pull back to see what it was.

Tarek's long arms wrapped around me. He might not have wings, but I felt completed folded into him. Surprise washed over me, seeping into my bones just like the heat of his touch.

He was holding me.

It was the most *human* kind of contact we'd shared. It was almost as devastating as seeing him for the first time.

He held me tightly, like I might float away, like holding me was the most serious thing he'd ever done. He kept me tucked thoroughly against him, and then his chin settled atop my head. He didn't relax into the embrace, and it made me smile. He was nervous. He wasn't sure if what he was doing was right, if he should be doing it at all.

I made a little sound in the back of my throat, hoping to convey how right this was, and flexed my hand against his back, kneading my fingers into him.

If possible, he stilled even more, and really, I think he held his breath.

"I'm pretty sure you need to breathe," I said, repeating the same thing he told me earlier.

His chest expanded, pushing against me, causing little flutters of excitement in my belly. Tarek pulled away, picked up the water jugs beside us on the floor, and carried them into the kitchen as if he'd been in here a million times before.

"The water will help with your thirst," he said, coming back into the living room.

I nodded. "When will I see you again?" I asked, knowing he was seconds away from leaving. I hated looking up at the night sky and not knowing if and when I'd see him again.

"I'll be back to get you when it's time."

"Time?" I said, not understanding.

"For the birth."

My eyes about popped right out of my head. "You mean you aren't coming back?"

"I just said I'd be back for the birth." He stared at me curiously, like my reaction confused him.

"So you implant a baby in me, hand me a couple of waters, and then tell me you'll be back in seven months?"

"My part is over," he said simply.

I laughed. "You're an idiot."

He scowled, and damned if it wasn't an awesome look for him. "Excuse me?"

I threw my hands up in the air. "Just like a man," I muttered. I pinned him with a stare. "Just because you donated sperm to my uterus does *not* mean your job is done."

"It is until the baby is born."

"For someone so intent on saving their race, you're a lot less interested in this pregnancy than I thought," I snapped. Weariness began to seep in around me and I glanced at the sofa longingly. "What will I say when I start showing? People will want to know who the father is."

"Don't tell them," he said casually, like it didn't matter.

"I don't know how it works on Sapia, but here on Earth, when a woman is pregnant, she is usually in a relationship or married. My parents are going to flip."

"Flip?" he asked.

"Be angry. I got pregnant and I don't even have a boyfriend."

"Is it really that big of a deal?" he asked.

"Of course!" I yelled. "Isn't pregnancy a big deal where you live?"

He shrugged. "I've never seen a pregnant Sapien."

I lapsed into silence. We were from two completely different worlds. Trying to make him understand what it meant for me to be pregnant was like trying to speak Spanish to a Frenchman and expecting them to know what I was saying.

"But I'm told that men were not involved in female pregnancy. They did their part and then the children were raised elsewhere," Tarek said.

"Your planet is seriously messed up."

"Messed up?"

"Here, men and women are a team. They raise the baby together. They're a family." Well, for the most part. I wasn't about to get into single parenthood, teen pregnancy, etc. This wasn't an after school special, and frankly, it wasn't the way I'd ever planned on bringing a child into this world.

"Family." Something about the way he said it made me look up.

I nodded emphatically and my hand found my stomach. "Family," I repeated.

Emotion, real and stark, flashed over his features. And then it was gone. “I must go.”

“Wait!” I said, rushing after him as he walked toward the open window.

He stopped but didn’t turn.

“I’m scared.” I admitted, the confession ripping from my throat.

His shoulders tensed, telling me he heard. “Do not be afraid,” he replied after long minutes. “I will be back in seven months to get the child.”

I blinked.

He was gone.

I raced to the window and sagged against the sill, staring up into the empty sky. The meaning behind his words penetrated my overwhelmed mind. He’d be back to get the child…

I gasped.

He planned to take away my baby.

the normal

I could feel his eyes on me.

Even in the crowd, his stare was like a magnet to my ever-moving form. When I would step up to the bar to fill my tray with whatever order needed delivering, I expected him to ask me questions I just didn't have answers for.

Well, yeah, I had answers. Answers I didn't want to give.

For the most part, I'd done a good job avoiding Matt. I managed not to be alone with him and to sneak out after my shift at night when I knew he was too busy to follow me into the parking lot. He tried to call a couple times. I didn't answer; I let it go to voicemail.

I had several excuses ready to give, but he never asked me why I didn't answer.

I knew it wouldn't be much longer until he gave up altogether. Matt wasn't into the whole hard to get thing. He didn't have to be. There were too many willing ladies in his sea for him to have to chase around a piece of bait.

I tried to ignore the feeling of regret that burned the back of my throat when I told myself it wouldn't be long until he forgot about me completely. Even though my life was a crap circus and starting anything with Matt was number one on the list of worst things I could ever do, I couldn't help but feel sad. I couldn't help but mourn the loss of someone I'd wanted for so long.

Why couldn't he have showed interest in me six months ago? Things were a lot easier back then.

I stood at the bar longer than I intended, wallowing in the mess that was my life, giving him the perfect opportunity.

"Have dinner with me," he said, leaning over the counter to speak low.

My eyes snapped up to meet Matt's. His hair was perfect and his polo unlined.

"Dinner?" I croaked, casually arranging the beers and single martini on the tray.

"You can't avoid me forever. We need to talk," he said, still leaning over the bar top.

"I'm not avoiding you." I lied.

"I know, Sophie," Matt replied. He didn't mean he knew I was lying. His tone suggested he knew something else, something bigger.

Panic chewed its way through my stomach and seeped out into the rest of me, causing the muscles in the back of my neck to tighten. He knew? How could he possibly know I was pregnant? I hadn't told a single soul.

I resisted the urge to look down at my middle, wondering if today was the day someone noticed my clothes were getting too tight.

"You do?" I whispered, leaning a bit closer.

He nodded. "We need to talk." Matt reached down and picked up a couple empty beer glasses and began washing them beneath the counter. Even as he worked, his eyes remained fastened on me.

"I—"

He interrupted me. "Dinner. Tonight. After work. On the deck."

The deck was a large, open, screened-in structure on the side of the bar. There were at least fifteen tables out there that me and the other waitresses took turns waiting on.

"I'm really tired," I said, relieved it wasn't another lie. I was tired, constantly.

"How long did you think you could keep it from me?" Matt asked.

A lot longer than I did, I thought. How was I going to explain this? What if he told other people? He couldn't! I wasn't ready for that. "Okay." I relented. "Dinner."

I spent the rest of my shift trying to come up with some sort of explanation for my current condition. I was afraid of the look I would see in his eyes when I sat down, the look of disappointment—the look of pity.

Because it wasn't a weekend night, the bar cleared out early. Usually this would thrill me, but I dreaded the conversation about to come. I also sort of dreaded the closing of the door between Matt and me. He wasn't going to want me now that I was pregnant with another man's child.

Nerves gathered in my stomach when the last waitress cashed out and stepped out the bar door. Matt was behind the bar on the other end of the room, finishing his closing routine, and I took the moment to stare at him openly.

He really was good-looking. Nearly ideal, just like a Ken doll, but he lacked the whole "fake" aspect of that look. He didn't appear to try and look the way he did. It was effortless. He wasn't overly muscular, but his body was undeniably defined. His hair was combed and styled but didn't give the impression that he spent hours trying to style it (which of course brought my mind right to Tarek and his perfect boy band hair). I knew beneath the white polo, Matt sported various tattoos, some that he himself designed.

I knew his motorcycle sat out in the lot, waiting for him to rev the engine and pull out onto the street—a complete oxymoron as he glided over the pavement through the night.

On the outside, he appeared one way, but underneath the exterior, he was the complete opposite. Kind of like a wolf in sheep's clothing. A bad boy pretending to be good. Only Matt wasn't pretending; he was being exactly who he was.

Women loved it.

Hell, I loved it.

But something had changed these past couple months and it wasn't Matt. It was me.

Matt turned from the register and leaned back against the bar, pinning me with a look. "You hungry?"

"Sure." I lied. I really wasn't. I hardly ever was these days. Well, except for bananas. I ate so many of them it was a wonder my skin hadn't turned yellow. I didn't even like them.

What was weirder?

I never went out and bought bananas. One morning there was a perfectly ripened bunch on my kitchen counter. I hadn't even realized it was odd until I was halfway through the first one and it occurred to me I didn't like them and hadn't bought them.

It didn't stop me from eating, though. They were the first thing in weeks that actually appealed to me. I ate the whole group that day. The next morning, there were more. I ate them too and all the ones that appeared every day after that.

I didn't know who was leaving them.

But I had an idea.

"I asked the guys in the back to cook something up before they left for the night."

"You did?" I said, his voice drawing me away from my banana obsession. His words caught me a little by surprise. I don't know why. He did ask me to have dinner. Maybe it was the fact he thought ahead enough to ask them to make something.

He flashed me a smile I couldn't help but return and pushed away from the counter to prowl across the floor to my side. He was taller than me, so when he stopped, he angled his head down to look me over. "Come on," he said, taking my hand and threading our fingers together.

He led me through the back, past the salad station and coolers with the bottled beer supply. Still keeping my hand in his, Matt pushed open the door leading onto the deck and pulled me through. My feet stuck to the floor when I saw what he'd done.

Off to the left, right next to the screened-in view, sat the round table that was always there. But the plastic green top was covered with a simple white cloth and topped with a white candle in a short, clear glass. The candle wasn't large, but it cast an intimate glow over the table.

Along with the candle and tablecloth were two plates, some silverware, and two bottles of beer.

"It's nothing fancy," Matt said, a little bit of nerves creeping into his usually self-assured tone. "But I mean, this is a bar."

I laughed. "It's perfect," I said, taking in the burgers and fries. I really was surprised he'd put so much thought into this. I expected frowns and a lecture, not a casual candlelit private dinner.

"You like it?" he asked.

I tore my eyes from the table to look at him. "Yeah, I really do."

He smiled, and my heart beat a little bit faster. "That's good." Matt gestured toward the chair closest to me and I sat, once again taking in everything. There was even a bottle of ketchup near my plate. It touched me that he remembered I liked to drown my fries in the stuff.

"How did you do all this? You barely left the bar tonight," I asked, dumping the condiment on my plate.

"So you were keeping your eye on me, huh?" His voice was smug.

I blushed, keeping my attention on my plate. I wished it was for the reason he was thinking and not because I was trying to avoid him. "Seriously, how did you pull this off?" I asked, trying to divert the conversation.

"I have my ways," he said, giving me a wolfish grin. The candlelight cast a glow over his features, making him look even more devilish.

After dunking a fry into the ketchup and twirling it around, I popped it into my mouth. The flavor exploded on my tongue, and for the first time in a long time, something tasted good (besides a banana, of course). I made a sound of appreciation and helped myself to more.

I felt his eyes on me, but I kept my attention on the food, which frankly wasn't hard. God, this was so good.

"Did you think I wouldn't figure it out?" he asked, low.

"Matt," I said. The fry I just swallowed scraped down my throat.

"I'm really not that surprised, actually." He continued. "I kind of expected it."

I abandoned the food entirely, looking up at him sharply. What the hell did he mean he expected me to get pregnant randomly? What did he think I was?!

"Excuse me?" I said, lifting an eyebrow.

He took a long pull of the beer in front of him. I wished I could drink the one he set there for me. Hell, at this point I needed more than one.

"You think I'm playing you," he deadpanned.

I blinked. Wait. What?

"I know my reputation. I'm kind of proud of it," he said, a little smirk pulling at his lips.

I could only stare as his words totally seeped in. He didn't know. This whole night I thought he'd figured out my secret when really, he hadn't. He thought I was avoiding him because I was afraid of getting hurt.

"The thought did cross my mind," I said. The relief I felt was incredible.

He sat back, gripping the long neck of his bottle, and studied me through the dim lighting. Beyond us, the evening crickets were out full force, filling the darkness with their song as a night breeze stirred the air and wrapped around the deck.

"Not with you, Soph," he intoned. "Never with you."

His words and the way he delivered them affected me. For so long I thought the way I felt was one-sided. I thought he was too busy playing the field, chasing skirts, to give me more than a single thought. I thought the easy chemistry we had between us was more a sign of friendship than anything else.

"I backed off when I noticed how leery you'd become. I thought giving you space and showing you I wasn't going to chase you and try to charm my way into your pants would finally show you it was different with you."

It was why he never seemed to question the distance I put between us. "I figured you would lose interest," I replied honestly. I really thought he would just move on.

He sat forward, resting his forearms on the table. "That's not going to happen." He pushed his chair back and stood, making his way around the table to where I sat. His hand wrapped around the back of my chair and he slid it around to face him with ease. The rough texture of his jeans brushed against my legs as he crouched down so we were eye level.

Part of me was shocked. Part of me was scared… and part of me was freaking thrilled.

"I'm done giving you your space. I'm telling you I'm not playing a game. I'm not going to hurt you. I want you. Only you."

I stared down at where his hands touched the outside of my legs. It was a gentle touch, yet it was possessive. *Matt is touching me. Matt wants me.*

I'd imagined this moment a million times.

"Matt, I—"

I didn't get to say anything else because he pulled me to my feet, sweeping me against his chest and locking his arms around me. His mouth descended upon mine and his tongue slipped over my lips, coaxing me open so he could take my mouth completely.

I melted against him, allowing him in, my tongue reaching out to meet his, to gently entwine them together. He groaned and pulled me a little bit closer so my front was pressed firmly against his. Matt tilted his head and increased the pressure in the kiss, delving his tongue deeper into my mouth.

I grabbed onto his shoulders and held on as the reality of being kissed by Matt washed over me. He was a skilled kisser. He knew exactly how much pressure to apply, when to groan into my mouth, and the exact right moment to tug my lower lip between his and suckle it until it was the only thing I could feel.

Matt's hands slid up the back of my neck and tugged at the ponytail that hung down, groping for the band that kept my strands contained. He yanked away his lips and looked at me, his pupils dilating with passion. "Do you know what it does to me watching this thing bounce around the bar all night long?"

I shook my head, unable to speak.

He growled and tossed the hair band so my dark hair cascaded down my back and over his hands. "You're fucking gorgeous."

I leaned up and kissed him again, wanting to get just a little bit closer. Feeling him against me was so good. I hadn't realized how lonely I'd felt… how abandoned.

The thought pricked at my consciousness, trying to loosen the hold Matt was gaining. I pushed it away, my body's needs eclipsing my mind.

One of his hands slid down my back and cupped my ass, taking a big handful and kneading the flesh.

Something inside me wobbled. It was an odd feeling, like nothing I ever quite felt before. I paused in the middle of the kiss. Matt squeezed my ass again and came back for more, licking at my bottom lip.

The feeling came over me again.

I yanked my mouth away and rested my forehead on his shoulder, trying to compose myself. It sort of felt like there was an actual butterfly in my middle, and it was confused and trying to break free.

Oh.

Oh my.

It wasn't a butterfly. It wasn't the effects of Matt's skilled kiss.

It was my baby.

It was mine and Tarek's baby.

He was moving.

Reality tumbled over me like a world record Tsunami. What the hell was I doing? I couldn't get involved with Matt! I couldn't get involved with anyone.

I jerked back out of his arms and pressed a hand to my swollen lips. My skin felt flushed and my breathing erratic. The little fluttering inside me shook my middle once more, and without thinking, I pressed my hand to my belly.

My baby was moving.

I glanced up at Matt, pure joy filtering through me.

He smiled, likely thinking my joy was for another reason.

I giggled. I didn't know feeling him would incite such a reaction, that I would feel so much at such a tiny little movement.

"Are you laughing at my kisses?" Matt said, curling a hand around my waist.

I jerked back. I didn't want him to touch me there. This baby wasn't his to be near.

"Sophie?" he said, giving me a puzzled look.

"I can't," I whispered, taking another more deliberate step back.

"You can't what?" he asked.

"I can't be with you."

A look of hurt crossed his face but was quickly replaced with confusion. "I think that kiss proves there are feelings between us."

"You don't understand," I said, my hand still pressed to my stomach. I glanced up, looking into his eyes, not wanting to hurt him, but needing him to realize.

A wary look overcame his eyes. "Sophie…" He glanced at my hand, the hand that refused to leave my child.

"I'm pregnant," I blurted out.

Matt would have poked holes in any other excuse I gave him. He would have worn me down, and my loneliness for Tarek would have made me cave. I couldn't cave, and I didn't want to hurt Matt. The truth was my only option.

"What?" he said, shock lacing his tone. His hands fell at his sides.

"I'm sorry." I rushed past him, wanting to leave, to be alone, to think.

"Sophie," Matt said, catching my hand and pulling around. "What…?" The single word hung in the air and I watched him grapple for something else to say. "Who's the father?" he said finally.

The mere mention of Tarek sent a sharp pain through my chest. I tried not to think about him. Usually, I wasn't successful, but I managed to bury the way he made me feel the times I'd been with him deep inside me. But it seemed kissing Matt unearthed those feelings, brought them rushing toward the surface with a fierceness that wouldn't be denied.

"He's not in the picture," I whispered, a slight sting of fear pricking at my consciousness.

"What the hell kind of man gets a girl pregnant then bails?" he demanded, a dark look crossing his face.

The kind who says he's going to come back and take your baby.

A sound ripped from my throat as pure terror overtook me. "I have to go," I said, tearing my hand from Matt's and racing out of the bar.

I couldn't deny it anymore. I couldn't pretend Tarek hadn't intoned he was coming back for my child. I couldn't pretend this was some bizarre dream. Up until this point, I'd been confused, scared, shell-shocked.

And then I felt him move. I felt the first fluttering of life inside me. My body was nourishing this child, giving another being life.

My baby.

My son.

I knew right then this baby was a boy.

I wasn't confused anymore. The way I felt was crystal clear.

I loved him.

I loved this baby with every ounce of life inside me.

And no one—not even Tarek—was going to take him from me.

the offer

I was exhausted.

Being kissed by someone you crushed on for years, then blurting out you were pregnant after feeling your baby move for the first time was enough to emotionally drain any girl.

I could only imagine what Matt was thinking. Likely, he was patting himself on the back for dodging the bullet that was me. I shouldn't have run out like that. I should have stayed, talked to him, asked him not to tell anyone until I knew what I was going to do.

Who was I kidding?

I had no fucking clue what to do or where to even start trying to figure it out.

It was better if I didn't drag Matt into this anyway.

What I did know was that I couldn't keep living in denial. Pretending I wasn't pregnant didn't mean I wasn't. I was, and the clock was ticking. I was going to start showing anytime now. My pants were already too tight, and I wouldn't be able to hide it forever.

I needed a plan. I didn't have to know everything right now, but I needed some kind of path to follow at least for the near future. Maybe if I seemed more confident in my situation, people wouldn't be so shocked (mainly my parents) when I started telling them.

Tarek's words about coming back for the baby haunted me.

I could leave town. Pack a bag and just drive until I liked the scenery out the windshield. But he would find me. I didn't know much about Tarek, but I did know that. And I didn't want to leave. I had parents, friends, school… a life. A life I needed now more than ever.

Maybe he wouldn't come back. Maybe his emotionless state of mind would keep him away. He wouldn't come back for a baby he didn't love. Right?

My stomach twisted and I yawned so wide my jaw made a popping sound. I could figure out my plan tomorrow. But before I would let myself crawl under the covers, I dragged my ass into the bathroom to shower and wash away my shift at the bar.

My hair smelled like smoke and beer. I hated it.

I paused beside the sink after stripping off my top and bra. Should I be working in a place like that in my condition? People weren't allowed to smoke in the bar, but they did outside and then came in, dragging some of that second-hand smoke with them. Could that hurt the baby?

I worried over it as I pulled off my black shorts and panties and turned on the shower, switching the water to hot. As the water heated, I stepped in front of the mirror to stare at my naked reflection.

My long dark hair was a complete disaster mostly because Matt's hands had been tangled in it. My skin was flushed, but there were dark circles beneath my eyes. My full lips were still slightly puffy from the kissing and my dark eyes appeared confused.

Basically, I'd looked better.

Abandoning the judgment of my face, my eyes dropped down to my achy breasts, which were already larger than they'd been before. They were sensitive to the touch, felt swollen, and screamed for some kind of relief. At least they were still perky, and the normally blush pink nipples had turned darker, more of a ripened peach shade.

My eyes moved on, down toward my bare stomach. It was definitely thicker. No longer was it willowy and lean. Instead, there were soft curves developing.

Chewing the bottom of my lip, I turned sideways, glancing at the side view of my waist. It was rounding outward, no longer flat. I brushed my palm over it, fascinated with the way my body was changing, a little in awe that there was a baby growing beneath that little bump.

Another yawn stole over me, and I stepped away from the mirror and beneath the warm, gentle spray of the shower. I wished the water pressure were better. The knots in my neck were tight and the massaging hot spray would have been nice.

But this was an old rental in Frostburg; great water pressure wasn't a normal amenity. Hell, I was just thankful the water heater provided enough warm water for a quick shower.

After scrubbing clean and rinsing the conditioner from my hair, I shut off the spray and dried, wrapping the damp towel around me.

I was tired and it was an effort to pull the comb through the tangles in my hair. When I was done, I sighed in relief. Leaving my work clothes in a heap on the floor, I exited the bathroom, shivering a little at the cooler air in the hallway. On my way to the bedroom, I heard knocking at the front door.

My heart rate spiked and fear scrambled through me. Who could be pounding on my door this late at night? Clutching the towel around me, I crept toward the door as the pounding intensified.

"I know you're in there, Sophie," Matt said from the other side.

"Matt?"

"Yeah. Can I come in?"

Surprised, I turned the lock and opened the door. He was standing there in his jeans and polo, his hair finally looking less than perfect, like he'd been running his hands through it.

"What are you doing here?" I asked.

His eyes widened and he completely forgot I had a head. I might as well have been naked the way he was staring.

Well, okay. I *was* practically naked.

"I was in the shower," I said, as if it wasn't totally obvious.

"Here I thought you were just avoiding me," he drawled, still staring at the hollow space between my breasts and the towel.

I waved my hand in front of his face. "Yoo-hoo, up here!" I called, gesturing toward my face.

He smirked and glanced up. "Can I come in?"

I stepped back and he walked in. I locked the door behind him.

"I'll go get dressed."

He reached out and splayed a palm over my towel-covered hip. "I like ya the way you are."

I rolled my eyes. "You didn't know I was gonna be in a towel when you came over, so I figure you have something to say."

I tried not to think too much about his hand on my hip and the way his fingers moved slightly, rubbing against the softness of the towel.

"You're pregnant," he said. It wasn't a question.

"I'd appreciate it if you didn't tell anyone just yet."

He pulled away from me and paced into the living room, jamming his hand through his hair. "How the hell did this happen, Soph?"

"It's a long story," I said, weary. I realized I needed to come up with some kind of story as to how I ended up pregnant and alone.

Matt's hands fisted at his sides and he avoided my gaze. The muscle in his jaw jumped a few times, and I just stood there, allowing everything to sink in.

I was surprised to see him here. Of course, maybe he just wanted answers to explain the bomb I dropped before running.

"Who is he?" Matt asked, his voice pained.

"You don't know him."

"Does he know?"

"Yeah, he knows." At least I could tell the truth about that much.

A low curse slipped into the silence that followed my reply. "Where is he?"

"Not here." And Lord help me, I missed him.

His jaw clenched again. I really didn't have it in me for some fight with a pissed-off guy. Even if the guy was Matt.

"I'm really tired. Can we talk later?" Water dripped from the ends of my hair and trailed down my shoulder blade, making me shiver. I pulled the towel more closely around me.

He didn't say anything. He just stood in the center of my living room. Completely silent. The silence that emanated from him was so thick it made it hard to breathe.

When he finally spoke, his words cut through the substantial quiet with unwavering ease.

"I'll claim the baby."

I heard his words. There was no mistaking what he just said. But my brain was so shocked that it took me a while to process them, to make sense of them.

"Matt." I meant to gasp, but I couldn't put the force behind the word. Instead, his name sounded like a leak. Like I was a balloon that had been punctured by the sharp end of a needle and it was his name that came out in lieu of air.

He looked up at me. His brooding eyes were clear, intent… sincere.

"You don't know what you're saying," I told him, even though it appeared he did.

"I do," he replied. "I know exactly what I'm saying."

My knees wobbled, causing my body to teeter over the floor. Matt was there, taking my bare arm gently and anchoring me to the ground.

"This isn't your responsibility. This isn't the time to make some romantic gesture because you want to feel like the hero," I told him. "I don't need a hero right now. I need a friend."

He released my arm, dragging his fingers up the bare skin to brush away the wet strands of hair clinging to my shoulder and collarbone. "I'm nobody's hero," he murmured. "Hell, I'm probably not a very good friend either. I don't know the first thing about kids. But I'm willing to try."

His words created an ache in my heart, a raw kind of hurt. His words were so incredible, so genuine, it actually caused me pain. "You are a good friend," I whispered. He'd always been a good friend to me. Always. But being a friend didn't mean having to also be a father. "I already had one man walk out on me. I'm not doing that again."

"I'm not going anywhere."

I looked straight into his eyes. "Yeah? And what happens tomorrow night when a hot, willing blonde sits down at the bar? And the night after that and after that? Are you gonna point to me and my growing belly and tell them your days of playing the field are over?"

"Yes."

My eyes shut. I hadn't expected this. I always knew Matt was a good guy, but I had no idea he would make this kind of offer.

"You'll resent me. You'll resent my son."

"It's a boy?" he asked sharply, his body shifting just a little bit closer to mine.

"I don't know," I murmured, embarrassed. "It's just a feeling I have."

"A boy needs a father," he said, his voice low.

"He'll have my dad. His grandpa."

"What will people say, Sophie? Your parents? Everyone in this backward ass town?"

"It doesn't matter," I said, lifting my chin defiantly.

"You say that now, but when people start talking. When the rumors fly, you're going to feel it. That baby is going to feel it."

I swallowed. Why was he saying those things? Didn't he know how hard this already was?

"I can shield you from that," he said, splaying a hand across my lower back. "No one but us will ever have to know he's not really mine. I'll raise him as my own, Sophie."

"Why?" I asked, tears welling in my eyes. I looked up, trying to find the answer in his face. "Why would you do this? Why would you want to?"

His hazel irises swept over me, a tender light leaking into his gaze. "Ahh, Soph," he whispered, brushing at my hair once more. "I—"

His words were cut off by movement on the other side of the room. I stiffened, glancing up as soon as I sensed we weren't alone.

Matt moved quickly, putting his body in front of mine, acting as my own personal shield. "Who are you? How the hell did you get in here?" he demanded, staring across the room at the figure in a silver, hooded robe.

Tarek.

He came across the room with the grace only he contained. The hood stayed low on his head, completely hiding him from sight. My eyes stared into the shadow of the hood, desperate for a glimpse of his face. It felt like forever since I'd seen him last.

He acted as if I wasn't here. His sole attention was focused on Matt.

"Call the cops, Sophie," Matt ordered, his body rigid as he anticipated some sort of violent threat.

I took a step back, unsure what Tarek was going to do or why he was even here. Before I could reach for the phone, Tarek's long, ultra-pale fingers reached out and took hold of Matt's head on either side.

"What the fuck?" Matt said, fear creeping into his voice.

A soft glow emanated from Tarek's fingers and seemed to drift around Matt's head. "Forget the last few hours. The last thing you remember is leaving work and going home."

"What are you doing!" I demanded, worried for Matt.

I'd never been frightened of Tarek before, but this was changing my mind.

"Making him forget," Tarek said, releasing his gentle hold on Matt.

The next thing I knew, Matt was letting himself out of my apartment without another word. The lock on the front door latched behind him without any help from me.

I gaped at the space Matt just vacated before swinging around to stare at Tarek.

"What the hell is going on!" I demanded.

Tarek pushed back the hood, revealing his radiant amethyst eyes, faultless skin, and face. His wide stare drank me in with a desperation I found jarring.

"Tarek?" I asked.

"I don't like him," he replied as if that explained everything.

If I didn't know any better, I would have sworn he was jealous.

the promise

"I thought you weren't coming back," I said.

"I didn't say that," he answered, his eyes sweeping over my entire body with one lingering stare.

"No, you just said you were going to come back for my baby," I snapped, placing a hand protectively over my stomach.

His eyes followed my movement. "You aren't dressed."

"I was taking a shower."

"With the human?" His eyes narrowed into slits and again I got the hint of jealousy from his tone. Part of me drew pleasure from that. Part of me wanted him to be jealous, to know what he was missing.

And yeah, the other part of me knew he likely wasn't jealous at all. He was, after all, a man who was raised not to feel anything.

"Does it matter?" I asked, not giving him a direct answer.

His eyes flashed, a lightning storm of neon violet taking over his glare. "Yes."

Satisfaction burned through my middle and I hid my smile. "Matt wasn't in the shower with me."

Tarek pushed a hand through his totally touchable hair and shut his eyes briefly. When he refocused on me, they had returned to the deep purple I found so stunning. Looking at him was so easy. It was like he was his own personal force of gravity I could not resist.

I knew it was wrong that his presence somehow energized me. Like he was a giant Red Bull coursing through my veins. The baby must have felt his presence too because that fluttery sensation of him moving took over my middle.

My fingers flexed over my abdomen and a feeling of awe washed over me.

"What is it?" Tarek said. He was at my side instantly, before I even realized he had moved.

"I can feel him moving," I whispered.

His eyes widened, the awe that I was feeling reflected back at me.

"Would you like to feel?" I asked tentatively.

He hesitated only a moment, then reached out his pale hand, hovering just above where mine rested. I reached out to guide his touch, but he brushed me away gently and grasped the end of the towel, yanking it away.

A sound of protest rumbled in the back of my throat, but he ignored it. The only thing covering my nakedness dropped around my feet. I stood there before him completely naked, slightly damp, with goose bumps rising along my flesh.

His eyes studied me, taking in every last detail of my body. Strangely, I didn't feel uncomfortable. He didn't leer at me like I was some kind of plaything. He gazed upon me like I was some kind of exquisite creature, like the most beautiful thing he'd ever seen.

"You're beginning to show," he said, his eyes flicking up to mine. The unmistakable emotion there caused my breath to catch.

I nodded.

"Here," I said, taking his hand and placing it over the area where I last felt the baby move.

Tarek's hand was large and so long it almost covered my entire abdomen. I groaned a little without thinking because his skin was so warm he was like a giant heating pad that gave off delicious rays of relaxing warmth. Not wanting to pull away, I settled my hand atop his and hoped the baby would move again.

Several seconds went by and then the light flurry of movement took place. I gasped, pressing his hand harder against me. "Can you feel that?" I asked excitedly.

A smile unlike any other I'd ever seen broke over his face. It was like the beginning of a new day breaking over the darkened horizon and illuminating everything in its path with the first blush of dawn. His eyes shined with pride and his fingers spasmed over my skin like there was just too much inside him to hold still. "I feel it," he said, rubbing slow circles over my belly.

The baby moved again the minute he spoke. Tarek gasped and looked at me. "Was that…?"

I nodded. "He must know you."

"He?" He glanced at me, puzzled.

I nodded. "I think it's a boy."

"A son," he whispered, looking down at where our fingers rested over the baby. His hand tightened over my skin possessively. It caught me off guard because up until this point, Tarek had always touched me carefully.

I stiffened and he glanced at me. "He's mine."

I pulled away, wary. The promise he made before about coming back for this baby reared up in my mind. "I'm his mother."

If he heard me, Tarek gave no indication. He paced over near the couch, and I bent to pick up the towel. Just as I was lifting it around me, he turned abruptly. "You're mine as well," he said, his voice hard.

Heat curled in my belly at his declaration. I lifted my chin. "You do not own me." I sniffed. Even if the idea of being possessed by him excited me, I wasn't about to show it. A woman had to have a backbone. I wasn't about to let him think he could just boss me around.

He moved in a flash, bringing his body right up against mine with such force we hit the nearby wall. Tarek's arms were around me, and his palms flattened against the wall, keeping me from feeling the collision.

I dropped the towel with our movement and the entire front of my naked body pressed up against his and that damn silky robe. "Don't you own a pair of jeans?" I asked.

Slowly, he withdrew his arms from behind me, leaning his forearms against the wall, caging me in, making no attempt to give me any kind of personal space.

"I didn't like seeing him with you," he growled. The accent he carried seemed to punctuate every single word.

I shivered. "I thought you didn't feel emotion. I thought caring about people wasn't something you did."

His eyes roamed my face, not settling on one feature, but taking them all in, like he was committing exactly the way I looked to his memory. "I don't."

"Then why are you here?" I challenged.

The chemistry between us was palpable, crackling around us like tangible electricity. While he might say he didn't feel, that he didn't care, he so totally did.

Maybe he just didn't know it. Maybe he didn't know how to express it.

He shifted closer, dipping his head just a little bit. "I…" He stuttered, trying to come up with a reason.

I didn't wait for him to figure it out. I was impatient and needy. Plunging forward, I crushed my lips to his. The second we made contact, I felt a jolt of energy coursing through my veins. It was almost like I shot some huge gun and the force of the bullet exploding from the chamber threw me backward. My hands fisted in the front of his robe, keeping me against him, unwilling to break contact for even just a second.

Tarek's reaction was immediate. I felt the ripple of surprise at my bold action, but it was quickly snuffed out by desire.

Emotionless my ass.

A guttural sound ripped from the back of his throat, and I swallowed it as Tarek opened his mouth and deepened the kiss. Both his arms came around me like vises, pinning me against him as he slanted his lips over mine again and again.

My knees went weak, my entire body turning boneless. He kissed with the kind of fervor that made everything else around me go completely black. It was only him and his mouth, the moist heat of his lips, the way his silky smooth tongue glided over the inside of my mouth like cool water.

My lungs burned with the need for oxygen, but I'd rather die than break the kiss just for air. His lips wrapped around my tongue and tugged, pulling it into his mouth and sucking it as I tumbled against him, totally unable to keep myself upright.

Just when I felt like my chest might burst from lack of air, Tarek released my tongue and covered my mouth with his. In one deep rush of air, he breathed out, pushing the oxygen from his lungs into my body, flooding my system with the wind right from inside him.

My chest expanded. A lightheaded feeling swept over me as every cell in my body drank in the very air that kept him alive.

He wasn't just kissing me; he was now literally giving me what I needed to live.

My hands wound up around the back of his head, delving into the hair that was so very enticing. It was whisper soft. How something this silky and yielding could have so much body I didn't know. I pushed my fingers through it even more, reveling in the way it felt between my fingers and groaning with the new breath he'd given me.

I'd never felt so alive in my entire life. My body was on fire, burning with passion and need. The air he gave me mingled in my lungs as his tongue swept over the roof of my mouth. He was literally filling me up from the inside out.

When he pulled back his head, my fingers tightened against his scalp, refusing to let him pull too far away. "You make me…" He gasped, pressing his lips on mine again before pulling back to look at me once more. "You make me *feel*."

I untangled my hand to slide the zipper down on the robe. The minute I caught a glimpse of his marble-like skin, I pushed my hand over it, gliding my palm against him.

"I will own you," he demanded.

"Yes," I begged. "Own me."

He picked me up, my legs wrapped around his waist and his lips fastened over my already puckered and throbbing nipple.

I groaned and thrust out my chest so he would have better access. He laved at my nipple as he walked. I was so far gone I didn't even wonder how he seemed to walk without trouble while he was so focused on my breast.

Tarek brought me into the bedroom, where he gave my nipple one last long suck and then laid me across the bed. He towered over me, staring down with flashing purple eyes and kiss-swollen lips.

He peeled off the robe slowly, his eyes never leaving mine, and I desperately wanted to stare at his perfect body, but I couldn't look away. I was hypnotized by the look in his eyes, the awe, the carnal desire.

Tarek came over me, his wide chest causing me to lick my lips with anticipation. He'd barely touched me, but I was so wet and ready I'd probably die if he tried to prolong with foreplay what I really wanted.

I wanted him. I wanted his long, thick cock inside me. I wanted to feel him pound into me. I wanted to be consumed by him.

I reached up and grabbed his biceps and spread my legs, sending a clear invitation.

"Look at me," he ordered.

My eyes latched onto his at the exact moment he plunged into me.

My entire body stiffened and an exaggerated groan rumbled through my chest and filled the air around us.

His eyes burned with purple heat and beneath my palms, I felt his muscles tremble.

He slid out and speared me once more. I dragged in a ragged breath as my eyes slid closed.

"No," he said, his voice hoarse and low. "Look. At. Me."

I obeyed.

We stared at each other as he moved inside me. Long strokes of pleasure rippled through me. I swear if I didn't know any better, I would say his dick was a magic wand.

He kept his hands planted on either side of me. He didn't lean down to kiss me. He didn't fondle my body. He didn't whisper dirty words or even words of love.

He didn't have to.

I could see it all play out over his face, in the depths of his eyes.

It's amazing how much I saw and felt just staring into him as his rigid length moved within me. It was beyond erotic; it was all-consuming. Not only that, but it was something I would never experience with anyone but him.

I saw the shift in his eyes when he was close to release, the way his body seemed to stiffen and his cock seemed to swell inside me. I gave him a little knowing smile and spread my legs just a little bit more. I wanted every ounce of his release.

"Together," he said, the word rushing past his lips like he'd just run a marathon.

Tension was definitely coiled inside me. My body wanted the release, but I'd been holding it off because I wanted this moment to last. Tarek wasn't having it, though. Planting his hands a little more firmly on the bed, he rocked upward, pressing his hard pelvic bone down into me and thrusting deep.

I moaned as ripples of bliss shot over my body and my head tipped back in surrender.

"Hey," he murmured.

I tilted my chin back down, meeting his eyes again.

"Stay with me."

I nodded.

Tarek rocked his hips. His twitching cock deep inside me rubbed against my inner walls and be bore down with his hips, pushing against the swollen lips of my entrance.

And intense orgasm ripped through me, causing my back to arch up into him even farther. He held my stare, watching the pleasure he'd just delivered play out over my features.

The veins in his neck stood out and a low shout ripped from his throat. He rocked upward one last time as hot seed poured into me. The throbbing of his penis vibrated my insides and another orgasm snuck up on me and crested over my body.

Little mewling sounds of pleasure filled the room, and I could no longer hold his stare. My head fell to the side, damp strands of hair clinging to my cheek as I panted out the pleasure and stretched against him like a satisfied cat.

Tarek scooped his arms beneath me, bringing his body down against mine, his weight pressing me into the mattress. He buried his face in the side of my neck where I heard him inhale, taking in my scent.

Thank God I took a shower!

He was heavy, but I didn't complain about his weight. I could likely be crushed by him and I would die without regret. I don't think he wanted to crush me, though, because a few moments later, he rolled off, settling against the comforter beside me.

I looked at him, giving him a small smile. Suddenly, I felt a little self-conscious. He pretty much rocked my world, delivered the highest standard of sex that any woman would ever know… and I'd pretty much done little more than lie there and enjoy it.

He probably thought I was the world's worst lover.

But how in the hell was I supposed to knock his socks off with my sexual prowess when he literally paralyzed my entire body with passion?

Okay. Maybe I didn't have any sexual prowess.

"You're mine now," he said simply, smug satisfaction in his tone. "He will not touch you again."

I felt my brow wrinkle. "Who?"

"That bartender."

"Matt?"

Tarek got a look on his face like he smelled something bad. Then a cold expression seeped into his eyes. "And he most certainly will not be claiming my child."

I felt my eyes widen. "You heard that?"

"Of course I did."

"Are you, like, stalking me?"

"Stalking?" he asked, frowning.

"Like watching me?" I explained.

"Of course," he replied like it was a silly question.

"That's just creepy," I said, pushing up into a sitting position and bringing my knees into my chest.

Gently, he grabbed my ankle and pulled my leg to straighten it. "Do not hide yourself from me."

"I'm not hiding," I said. "I'm cold." His body heat was incredible and my skin missed it now that he wasn't on top of me.

Tarek grasped the end of the blanket at the top of the bed and pulled it back, motioning for me to get beneath it. I did, and he tucked it around me with care.

How could a man be so… alpha one moment yet so tender another?

"Better?"

I shivered a little between the icy sheets. "A little." I lied.

"Say what you really mean," he scolded.

"You're much warmer than any blanket."

He seemed taken aback by my words. He stared at me for long moments before joining me beneath the covers and sliding over. Like I was metal and he was a magnet, I went to him, fitting my body against him and laying my cheek on his shoulder.

In my middle, the baby moved around, making me think once again he could sense his father close by.

"This is what you wanted?" he asked, his voice seductively low.

"Mm-hmm."

"I like the way you feel against me," he said.

I smiled. "Me too."

Then I remembered I was supposed to be totally irked that he'd been stalking me. I rested my chin on the top of my hand and glanced up. "Now, about you being creepy."

The corner of his mouth lifted with an amused smile. "Yes?"

"You can't just follow me around and eavesdrop on all my conversations."

"Why not?"

I stuttered. "Because it's invasion of privacy."

"How else am I to keep watch over you and the child?"

"I have this thing called a door. You could knock on it. Come visit."

He turned thoughtful, like the idea of actually just spending time with me never occurred to him.

"Tarek?" I asked softly.

"Yes?"

"How is it that every woman on Sapia isn't pregnant?" I glanced away shyly. "I mean, sex like that… You'd think there would be tons of kids running around."

"Did I please you?" he asked, like he genuinely didn't know.

I gaped at him, a little hollow hole forming inside me. If he had to ask, he clearly did not enjoy it as much as I did.

"I'm pretty sure you've ruined me for anyone else ever again," I replied honestly.

"No one else is to ever touch you," he said, hard, his eyes glittering like dark diamonds.

I drew back, slightly intimidated.

He tightened the arm around my waist. "The thought of it…" he said, looking at me intently. "It makes the center of my chest feel as if it's on fire."

I smiled. "You're jealous."

A light of understanding came into his eyes. "Yes.

Jealous."

I giggled.

He looked at me sharply. "I don't like it," he growled. "It's not pleasant."

I couldn't really disagree with him. Jealousy wasn't the most pleasant of emotions.

"Promise me," he demanded, his fingers tightening on my hip.

"I promise." It wasn't hard to say it. The thought of anyone else touching me after what we just shared was repulsive.

He blew out a breath, relaxing into the bed.

"The women?" I reminded him, genuinely wanting an answer to my question.

"We don't have sex like that on my planet."

"Then how?" Shock washed over me.

"Sex on Sapia is for procreation only. It's very… unfeeling."

"I don't understand how something like that could be *unfeeling*."

"Yes, after this with you, I have a hard time understanding it myself."

"So you liked it?" I asked, uncertainty in my tone.

He smiled, a quick, smug smile. Instead of replying, he took my hand and pressed it against his cock. I gasped and looked down. He was rock hard and creating a tent under the blankets.

"You're ready *again*?"

"Is that unusual?" he asked.

I laughed. "Most guys would either be ordering pizza right about now or snoring into the pillow."

"I'm not most guys. I'm a Sapien."

"So I see," I said, rubbing my palm into his stiffness.

He made a low sound. I felt powerful in that moment. Like I had the ability to take him places he'd never been. I could show him sensations and feelings he'd never known.

"Have you had many women?" I asked, some of that jealousy he was talking about now affecting me. The thought of any other woman touching him this way made me want to claw her eyes out.

"A few," he answered, rolling his hips toward me as I stroked him boldly atop the blankets. "But it was never like this."

I released my hold on his cock and slid all the way beneath the blankets, positioning myself between his legs. Before taking him in my mouth, I dragged my fingernails down the inside of his thighs and enjoyed the sharp intake of breath that reached my ears.

After cupping his balls in my palm and kneading them for long moments, I couldn't keep my lips from reaching toward his straining member.

I took him in with a long, wet stroke of my lips. The sound he made spurred me on, and I put everything I had into sucking him.

When his thigh muscles started to quiver, I pulled back and climbed up his body, straddling his waist. He stared up at me through unfocused eyes.

I took his hand, directing those long, magical fingers down to my opening where it was leaking with silky juices. "Feel that?" I murmured boldly.

He made a sound of agreement. "That means I'm ready for you too."

He put a hand on my hip as if to roll me over. I caught it and shook my head.

"It's your turn to lie back and feel me."

Dragging my already swollen clit over his solid abs, I lowered myself until his head poked at my center. I lifted up, holding his cock straight up and down, and then lowered myself onto him one delicious inch at a time.

Tarek groaned and I grabbed his hands, placing them over my full breasts and instructing him to squeeze them. He did so, never applying too much pressure to cause me pain.

I rotated my hips, enjoying the play of satisfaction over his face, and then I began rocking back and forth, riding his cock like I was a cowgirl and he was a wild bull.

God, he was so incredible. It felt so good. My inner walls tightened around him, squeezing his shaft until I cried out with delight.

Even after I collapsed across his chest, I kept moving, determined to give him everything he gave me. As I moved, I trailed my lips across his jaw and tugged his earlobe into my mouth to suck it gently.

He made a sound of pleasure and rocked against me. I kissed down his neck and up his jaw. Tarek took me by surprise when his hand fisted in my hair and he pulled my head down to invade my mouth with his tongue.

He licked into my mouth with determination and drive, tangling us together so every moan I made disappeared into the back of his throat.

His free hand grabbed my breast and squeezed, so I bore down on him and rocked hard, creating friction between our bodies. He ripped his lips free of mine and shouted with release, pulling me down so I was completely against him.

He thrust into me for long moments spilling his seed, milking every last drop and releasing it into my welcoming body. Tarek stayed inside me even after his hard-on went soft. My juices mingled with his released seed, but neither of us moved or seemed to care. I lay on top of him, his arms around me, my core pressed against his as both of us fell asleep.

the confusion

I was standing at the bar when he walked in.

I'm not sure if everyone else in the place felt the rush of energy when he entered, but I sure as hell did. My body knew it was him before I even turned to look. It's amazing how in tune I felt with him, how my energy played off his. The baby knew it too. He fluttered around anxiously in my tummy, causing me to turn.

At first, I looked in the shadows of the room and around the corner near the walk-in cooler where we kept the beer.

He wasn't anywhere to be seen. Part of me grew anxious because he had to be here. I felt him, yet I couldn't see him.

"Hey, man," Matt said from behind me. "Can I get ya a beer?"

"Thanks," he replied.

I knew that accent anywhere. I spun quickly, almost losing my balance and reaching out to steady myself on the edge of the counter. Tarek was poised on the edge of the stool, not quite sitting down, like he was about to jump up and catch me if I fell.

Once he saw I wasn't, he settled more firmly into the seat.

I blinked, trying to process what I was seeing because I was so surprised.

He gave me a half smile and just watched me as I gaped.

When I woke up this morning, still naked and in his arms, he penetrated me again. Yeah, I could say we "made love," but it sort of went beyond that. It was odd to say I supposed because making love was pretty much the epitome of closeness between a woman and a man. But it wasn't like that with Tarek. It was more profound somehow. He truly did penetrate me, not in some smarmy eighties porn kind of way, but in a way that went beyond the physical. It was like he climbed deep into a part of me that no one had ever been before. I felt him to my very core, branded in a way that only I could see.

The amount of passion between us was like a titanium chain. Unbreakable. Solid to the core. Unyielding.

He told me I would see him again. He told me he'd stop with the creepy stalker shit.

I hadn't expected him to come back this soon.

I hadn't expected him to walk into this bar.

In a leather jacket.

It was black, collarless, and had chrome-like buckles on the sides. It hugged his perfectly straight shoulders, tapered in with his long narrow waist, and the buttery black color accentuated the pale coloring of his face.

One would think that dark of a jacket would completely wash out someone with his coloring, but it didn't. His hair was once again artfully arranged, messy on top with dark sideburns playing off his angular features.

Beneath the jacket, he wore a gray T-shirt and a pair of jeans. Jeans that hugged his thighs to perfection and were slightly scuffed up, making it appear he'd worn them a thousand times when really I knew better.

I peaked around the bar, unable to stop myself from looking at his shoes. Black Converse. I smiled.

Matt returned with a bottle of Bud and set it in front of him. I watched aptly as Tarek's long fingers wrapped around the neck of the bottle and dragged the glass bottom across the table right in front of his chest. "Thanks, man," he said.

His accent combined with that damn leather jacket was going to give me an orgasm right here.

I didn't hear what Matt said because I was too intent on Tarek. He was… for lack of a better term… sex on a stick.

I mean, seriously.

It was so incredibly wrong that he looked so good.

Yet it was so damn right.

As if he knew the effect he was having on me, he lifted the dark bottle to his lips and wrapped them around the rim. The way his upper lip slid down into the opening at the top made me whimper a little, and he tipped it back to swallow some of the liquid.

His Adam's apple worked beneath the ultra-smooth skin of his neck, and all I could think about was early this morning when his lips had been on me.

He set down the beer and leaned over the counter toward me. "I think you're the one being a little creepy now."

My eyes widened and I looked away, slightly embarrassed that I was that entranced by him. But to be fair, it was the first time I'd seen him in clothes. In public… among other humans.

Aside from his light skin and amethyst eyes, he blended in almost seamlessly. I say almost because someone as spectacularly good-looking as Tarek could only blend in so much. I could feel the stares of some of the women in the bar, wondering where he came from and if he was unattached.

It made me feel slightly murderous. Them bitches better keep their distance.

"You can't walk in here and sit down…" I said, reaching out to finger the top of the leather jacket, the part just below his jaw. It was smooth just like his skin. "And expect me not to be surprised."

"I told you, you would see me again," he said. "Did you not believe me?"

I don't know what I believed. I was having a little trouble processing everything. I was pregnant with an alien's baby. And the idea just didn't freak me out like it probably should. Not to mention, he was an alien who was like the freaking hottest thing I'd ever seen. I was a pretty girl, but next to him, I was downright homely.

He pursed his lips. "You're more beautiful than any woman I've ever seen," he whispered, leaning across the bar once more.

My lips parted. "How did you…?" Could he read my mind?

"Your emotions are so easy to read, love. They constantly play in the depths of your eyes."

"No one's ever said that to me before," I murmured, feeling like he was feeding me some lame-ass line. What was worse? I was totally falling for it.

"Then no one's ever bothered to look deep enough into them."

Okay. If that was a line, then consider me caught.

A sharp sound beside me caused me to jump and turn. Matt was standing there frowning at me. "These orders have been up for like five minutes," he said.

"Sorry!" I said, moving the drinks onto my tray. There went my good tips tonight.

"You know him?" he said, gesturing with his chin toward Tarek.

"No," I said at the same time Tarek said, "Yes."

Both Matt and Tarek pinned me with stares. "I better get this to the table," I said, making a hasty exit.

I took my time delivering the drinks and checking on my other tables. I refilled a couple of waters, a couple baskets of popcorn, and took an order for a burger and fries.

Ooh. Fries.

I needed to get some.

Before heading back to the bar, I slipped into the bathroom and untied the short apron around my waist and set it on the bathroom counter. After I did my business (side note: pregnant women have to pee like every five seconds), I washed my hands and glanced in the mirror at myself.

I felt better than I had in weeks. Well rested, my energy was back, and my skin was glowing. Maybe it was all the bananas I'd been eating.

Maybe it was Tarek.

Tarek, who I left out at the bar with Matt. I hadn't thought about the fact that he'd made his dislike of Matt very clear last night. I also hadn't thought about the fact that he'd wiped Matt's memory so Matt still thought I was avoiding him after our kiss.

Who knew what Matt might say to Tarek and what Tarek might do if he didn't like it. Tarek seemed like a reasonable man, but there were times his cold, emotionless persona made me think he could do some damage if really pushed to the limit.

I had no idea what that limit was, but considering he was experiencing jealousy for the first time, I needed to get back out there.

After retying my apron around my ever-growing tummy, I stepped back out into the bar, my eyes going directly to the bar. Matt was at the other end, making drinks, and Tarek was still in the same spot I'd left him.

Except he wasn't alone. There was a skinny blonde with big boobs standing right beside him.

I marched right up to the end of the bar and plastered a fake smile to my face. "Can I help you?" I asked her.

What I really wanted to say was *get the hell away from him you extension-wearing, fake eyelash, no good dirty ho.*

See the self-restraint I showed there?

I should get an award.

Like French fries.

Blondie flicked a glance in my direction. "No."

Sucking in a deep breath, I pulled a beer out of the cooler below me and snapped it down in front of her. "Here. On the house. Buh-bye."

She turned to me with a nasty expression on her face. "I don't drink beer. Besides, handsome here was about to buy me a drink."

I went from pissy to murderous in about five point two seconds. Just as I was about to unleash all the hormones of a French fry hungry pregnant woman, Tarek spoke up.

"I suggest you take the free beer and go," he said, his accent making his words sound pretty. "Because it's the nicest offer you're going to get tonight. I'm not interested."

He dismissed her without another glance, effectively turning all his attention away from her and bestowing it onto me.

Score for him.

Matt set some drinks in front of me. "Order up."

I smiled at him. If my smile was a little brighter than usual, it was because Tarek just totally made my night. Unfortunately, Matt seemed to think it was because of him.

"Did I tell you you look great tonight?" he said, leaning in close. I could feel his breath against my ear.

"Thanks," I said, trying to shift away.

He grabbed onto my upper arm. "Hey, how about we talk tonight? After work?"

I glanced at Tarek. A dark look was hanging over his features.

"I can't."

"I know you're avoiding me, Soph," Matt said. It was like a replay of the last conversation we had. The one Tarek took from him.

I started to make an excuse, but Tarek spoke first. "Let go of her arm."

Matt glanced up. I felt stubborn male pride rear its ugly head. "Do you mind? Me and my girl here are having a conversation."

Oh shit.

Tarek's eyes flashed neon purple. "She is not yours," he growled. As if to punctuate the words, several bottles of liquor on the glass shelves behind the bar shattered with loud popping sounds.

Several women screeched in surprise, and I jerked. Matt shouted and shoved me away from the flying glass and alcohol. I stumbled, my shoulder catching the corner of the bar as I fell forward, toward the floor.

Tarek caught me, lifting me away from the floor and darting back the little hallway to get away from the chaos.

"Was that you?" I demanded in a harsh whisper when he stopped beside the large silver walk-in cooler door.

"He touched you."

"We're friends, Tarek."

"No."

"Umm, yes," I said, knowing I should make him put me down, but damn, the feel of him and his leather jacket was really nice. "I'm allowed to have friends. And if you hadn't taken away his memory," I whispered, "I could have just told Matt you were the baby's father and this wouldn't have happened."

He pursed his cupid-shaped lips and I forgot I was supposed to be irritated with him. I reached up and fingered the hair swept upward away from his face and said, "I really like your new look."

"I saw it in a magazine," he answered.

Matt came around the corner. "Shit, Sophie, are you okay?" He stopped when he saw I was in Tarek's arms. A confused and hurt look flashed across his face. It made my stomach hurt.

"Put me down," I told him, patting him on the arm. He set me on my feet but stayed firmly at my side.

Matt disregarded him and came forward, his eyes studying me. "Are you cut?" he asked. "I think one of the bulbs above the liquor got too hot and exploded, and it cause a few bottles to shatter."

Or maybe a pissed-off alien did it with his mind.

I think I'd just let Matt believe his theory.

"I'm fine, thanks."

Matt looked at Tarek again, then at me questioningly.

"We should talk," I told him.

He nodded, looking a little relieved. It made me feel bad for having to tell him I was with Tarek. I paused in thought.

Was I with Tarek?

I had no idea. I was just as confused as Matt.

"After work?"

I nodded ignoring the angry glares I was getting from Tarek.

"Cool," Matt said. "Hey, don't come behind the bar until I get the glass cleaned up. I don't want you to cut yourself."

"Okay, yeah."

Matt walked off without another glance at Tarek.

"He shouldn't concern himself with your safety."

"You're not the only person who cares about me, you know," I said, irritated. Then I paused, feeling totally awkward. I spun toward him. "I mean, I don't know if you care about me."

Maybe he just wanted to own me. Maybe I was just his possession until his baby was born and he could take him.

"Soph, burger's up!" One of the cook's in the back yelled down the hall.

"Coming," I called over my shoulder, incredibly thankful for a reason to get the hell out of this conversation. "I have to work," I said and then hurried back into the kitchen.

I left quickly, not even glancing at Tarek before I ran off. Yes, he and I were tangled together, and yes, he literally made my head spin with passion and turned me on in ways I never knew possible, but beyond that, I really didn't know anything about him.

He literally came for me in the middle of the night, took me up into his hovercraft, and impregnated me with his baby. I thought I was done freaking out about this. I mean, the entire first month after it happened, I pretty much walked around as a spaced-out mess.

Apparently, the panic was coming back because as I stood in the kitchen, it became increasingly harder to breathe.

"Sophie?" Jess, one of the other waitresses, called my name. Her voice sounded a million miles away.

The face of Josh, one of the cooks behind the line, swam into my blurred vision. He was frowning. "What's the matter?" he said, his lips spelling out the words even though I couldn't hear them.

I swayed. Jess grabbed me so I wouldn't fall.

The next thing I knew, I was being carried out onto the empty, dark deck. Cool air brought a little clarity back to my fuzzy mind, yet I still struggled. I still felt lightheaded and on the verge of passing out.

I felt something warm and familiar cover my mouth. Breath rushed past my lips, and I felt it traveling down my windpipe and swirling into my lungs.

I took a great gulp, sitting up like I was coming out of some weird coma.

"I've never met anyone so prone to not breathing than you," Tarek said. His rhythmic voice floated over my frayed nerves and, damn him, it soothed me.

Just like the oxygen he just gave me.

He was sitting at one of the green tables in a plastic chair. I was cradled in his lap, his body supporting my weight with ease.

I glanced up at him. "I've never met anyone who breathed for another person before," I muttered.

His lips lifted in a smile.

"I need to get back to work." I tried to get down from his lap.

An arm came around my waist, anchoring me against him. "We need to talk, Sophie," he whispered against my ear. He made my name sound exotic. I shivered.

"I can't talk right now."

"You're angry with me."

I didn't say anything because it was true. I was angry. I was also hurt and confused.

A few moments of silence passed. "I don't like it." He admitted. He seemed thoroughly amused by that.

"So me being angry is amusing to you?" I snapped.

"No, but me being so upset by it is."

"Oh." Well, what did a girl say to something like that? I sighed. Suddenly, I felt exhausted. It was sort of depressing because I'd been so energetic earlier.

Damn hormones.

"Come on," he said. "I'll drive you home."

I glanced at him. "You have a car?"

"No, but you do."

"You know how to drive?" I said dubiously.

He sighed. "I drive a hovercraft. The technology on that craft far outweighs that of your Jeep Wrangler."

"Hey." I sniffed. "I like my car."

He chuckled and set me down. "I'll wait outside."

"I can't just leave," I said. "I'm working."

"Tell them you're sick."

It really wouldn't be that big of a stretch considering I almost passed out in there. Matt was behind the bar, making some pink martini, and he smiled when I stopped at the counter. His smile faded a bit when I didn't return it. "I'm not feeling that great. Would it be okay if I went home early?"

I didn't feel too bad because we weren't that busy. If it was a weekend night, I never would have left, but the girls here could definitely handle the crowd we had tonight.

"Did you get cut and not tell me?" he asked, stepping closer.

"No, I just don't feel well."

"She almost passed out back in the kitchen," Jess said, coming up behind me.

Matt's eyes widened. "Yeah, of course."

I turned to Jess. "Are you sure you don't mind?"

She waved her hand at me. "I got it. Go."

"Thanks," I said, meaning it. "Just keep my tips."

She flashed me a smile. "Thanks!"

I pulled off my apron and flung it on the shelf and picked up my bag.

"What about our plans for later?" Matt said.

"You can come by my house if you want."

He nodded, looking relieved I hadn't called the whole thing off. "Yeah, I'll come by."

Tarek wasn't going to like it, but he would just have to deal.

"I'll see you later, then."

On my way out the back, I grabbed a stray basket of fries and dumped half a bottle of ketchup on it. I picked up a couple and shoved them into my mouth with a satisfied sigh. One of the line cooks looked at me like I suddenly had a tail.

I shrugged. "Low blood sugar," I explained, then left, walking down the deck stairs to where my Jeep was already running with the lights on. The top was down. Tarek was sitting confidently behind the wheel.

Little butterflies curled around in my stomach just seeing him sitting there. I climbed up into the passenger seat, slinging my bag on the floor and fastening the seatbelt. He wrinkled his nose at the basket of fries in my lap.

"What is that?"

"Fries," I said, shoving another huge bite into my mouth.

"That is not healthy for the baby," he said, taking them away.

I snatched at the basket, only managing to grasp air. "I need them!" I shouted.

"You humans put garbage in your bodies."

"Give. Me. The. Fries," I growled.

He produced a banana from God knows where.

"You've been leaving these, haven't you?" I said, glaring daggers at it.

"They are healthy. My son likes them."

"I want fries."

"No."

I gasped. "What did you just say to me?"

He must have realized his grave mistake because he glanced at me warily.

I thought of a hundred really badass things to say.

Then I burst into tears.

The look of alarm on his face didn't even cover it. He was genuinely horrified by my display of blubbering.

"Sophie," he said, leaning forward.

"I'm hungry," I said pitifully.

He sighed dramatically. The fries appeared before me. I sniffled. Then I took them and put one in my mouth.

Heaven.

Tarek shook his head. I ignored him. Before driving away, he shrugged out of his jacket and draped it around me. "If you're going to eat garbage, at least let me keep you warm."

I snuggled into the leather, which was insanely warm from his body heat. Just as he was pulling back his hand, I caught it and pressed a kiss to his palm.

His face softened and he smiled.

He drove expertly, of course. Really, was there anything he couldn't do with ease?

I ate my fries as the wind whipped through my hair and I stared up at the stars in the night sky. Just because he gave me my "garbage" and drove like a professional did not mean I wasn't still angry with him. My emotions and my hormones were all over the place, and I really needed to know where I stood with Tarek… and with Matt.

He pulled in close to the building and turned off the engine. I was still gazing up at the glittering sky when I softly asked him, "Do you miss it?"

"Miss what?" he answered.

"Home."

"I used to." He gazed up at the sky, a feeling of

peace washing over his features.

"But not anymore?" I asked, only able to look at him.

He shook his head. "Not anymore."

"What changed?"

He pulled his gaze from overhead and looked at me intently.

"You."

the summons

Inside my apartment, Tarek pinned me against the wall, covering my body with his and kissing me senseless. His lips, *oh goodness*, his lips were like velvet rubbing over mine. They were full and warm, soft and yielding, yet they claimed me in a way only he'd ever been able to do.

His hands came up and cupped my face, holding it up to give him unbidden access. Longing filled my body as he coaxed even more desire within me.

Our tongues stroked each other, and I made a sound of gratification when he increased the pressure. My crotch began to throb and my panties dampened with moisture. I arched closer to him, pushing my hips outward to meet his. His throbbing cock strained against his jeans, begging for release.

I pulled my mouth away, denying my body what it was screaming for. I was supposed to be mad at him. I was supposed to be getting answers, not confusing myself more by falling into bed with again.

“I’m going to go change,” I said, slipping around him. He didn’t try to stop me, and I was glad because frankly, I was weak when it came to him.

In my bedroom, I took a few deep breaths, trying to calm the raging need boiling my blood. After tossing my work clothes in the nearby hamper, I pulled out a pair of jeans and stared at them wistfully. They were just too tight now. I could probably wear them unbuttoned, but that wasn’t very appealing, and it seemed kind of uncomfortable.

I was going to need to make a visit to my parents this weekend. It was time to tell them because the next time they saw me, they would probably guess anyway. With a sigh, I put back the jeans and reached for a pair of black leggings instead. The stretchy material was much more comfortable. I added a white V-neck T-shirt over top and stepped in front of the mirror. Surprise greeted me because I was totally showing. When did my belly pop out like that?

I thought about the date… I was roughly four months along. Since I was a thin person, I guess it seemed logical that my belly would be noticeable at this stage. I rubbed a hand over the bump and smiled a little.

I was scared. I was shell-shocked. I was confused. But I really did love this baby.

That was a good sign, right?

Because Matt was coming over later, I reached into my closet and pulled out an oversized hoodie and carried it out to the living room with me. I didn't think answering the door with my baby bump on full display was a good way to start the conversation.

Tarek's eyes went directly to my stomach the second I stepped into the room. He watched me possessively but also like he too was just realizing just how much I was showing.

"My being here is good for you," he said, a little bit of surprise in his tone.

I tossed the sweatshirt on the couch and turned to him. "What do you mean?"

"I mean you've been exhausted for weeks. Looking a little sickly and tired. It was one of the reasons I watched you so carefully. I thought perhaps you wouldn't be able to carry my child."

Denial swift and strong cut through me. "I can carry him," I said, putting a hand on my stomach.

The corner of his mouth lifted briefly. “So I see.”

“If you thought I couldn’t carry him, why did you get me pregnant?” I asked suspiciously.

“I told you, our race is unable to procreate. This was pretty much a last effort.”

“So you’ve tried this with other human women before?”

He nodded.

A sick feeling came over me. The thought of any other woman carrying his baby made me ill. I sank on the sofa, trying not to think about it.

He came to stand before me, looking down.

“I have not,” he said quietly. “But others have tried. No pregnancies have taken.”

Relief was like a cooling rainstorm on a dry, summer day. “Really?”

“I think I see some jealousy in your eyes,” he teased.

“Maybe,” I said, ducking my head.

“About what you said.” He began, sitting down on the coffee table in front of me. “About me caring for you.”

"I know you don't. I know you're only here for the baby," I said quickly.

Long, pale fingers covered mine, linking with my hand resting in my lap. I studied them, the way they curled around mine gently. I felt the radiant heat his skin gave off, and I experienced the usual surge of energy I always did when he touched me.

"I'm not only here for the baby," he spoke.

I stopped breathing, still staring at our hands.

"At first, yes. But now… now I'm here for you too."

I lifted my chin. His amethyst gaze was sincere when he searched my face.

"The way you responded when I touched you. The way your emotion is so raw that it radiates out of your skin and I can feel it in the air. You make me feel things too. The way your eyes tell me exactly what you're thinking and the way you make me *want* things…" His voice trailed off.

"What things?" I whispered. Butterflies took flight beneath my ribcage and my heart rate increased with his words.

"I never realized how singular we were, how isolated Sapiens made themselves. Even in a room full of others, we were still always alone. After being with you just a few times and then going back up in my hovercraft alone… it was so silent. I missed you. Once a person begins to feel something, it's hard to go back to nothing."

Tarek always had a way of getting beneath my skin, from that first moment he pulled me into his ship. Even scared and bewildered, I'd been drawn to him. Even when he was cold and distant, I was drawn to him. Even before I'd seen his face, I was drawn to him.

He wasn't being cold and distant now. He was saying things that literally made my heart bleed.

I wasn't just drawn to him now.

I was irrevocably in love with him.

"In my world, people don't care, people don't belong to other people," he said. "But you have me," he whispered. "I belong to you."

Automatically, I pressed a hand against my chest and took a deep breath. So much emotion, so much overwhelming feeling, overcame me it felt as if my heart might burst right out of me. If I hadn't just admitted to myself that I loved him, it would be painfully obvious in this moment.

"Tarek," I whispered, tears welling in my eyes.

He frowned, pulling his hand away to brush at the wetness trailing down my cheeks. "I upset you."

"No," I said. "You made me very happy."

"Then why are you crying?"

"Because you filled me up with emotion and it's leaking out," I said, turning my cheek into his palm when he stroked my face. "And because pregnant women cry a lot," I added.

"I want to stay here," he said instantly. "With you. You need me and I'm good for the baby."

I smiled. "You think so?"

He nodded seriously. "You've been nothing but drained. I've noticed the nights I've sat in your room, watching you sleep, you are more rested the next day. And after you slept in my arms last night, you…"

"I felt better than I have in weeks," I answered for him. I glanced up suddenly. "You sit in my room at night?" How had I not known?

"Not always. But sometimes after I leave the bananas, I watch you. Some days you seemed wearier than others. It… it worried me."

"How did you know I would like the bananas?" I asked abruptly.

"All women on my planet eat them." He shrugged.

Alrighty, then. Next question. "So you think your presence gives me energy?" I said, trying to understand.

He nodded. "I think the baby drains you. Sapiens have higher energy levels and higher metabolisms than humans. It's been a concern of mine that the baby would take too much from you. It seems when I am around, he is able to somehow pull from my energy as well, thus making it easier to carry him."

"You didn't think I needed to know that?" I said, annoyed.

He shrugged. "It didn't seem important."

"If it's about me or this baby, it's important and you need to tell me."

He nodded.

"Can I ask you something else?" I asked, tilting my head to the side.

"Of course."

"Why haven't any other pregnancies with humans taken?" It made me nervous. What if there was something incompatible between me and Tarek? What if this baby wouldn't make it? Nerves scattered through me, making my foot tap insistently on the floor.

Tarek reached out and placed a steadying hand on my knee, effectively stopping my rapid movement. His fingers caressed the area and the warmth of his hand seeped through the leggings and into my skin.

"I'm not sure. But the more I'm around you, the more I watch humans, I think it might have something to do with emotion."

"How in the world can emotion have any impact on carrying a child?"

"You've taught me that emotion is very strong. It can tether you to a person."

My heart tripped a little as he spoke because it was the exact same as I felt about him. Tethered.

"Our bond strengthens our baby. And in a sense, your body knew what was happening even before your mind did," he explained, releasing my knee and standing up to pace the room.

I watched him, entranced by the graceful beauty of the way he moved.

"Do you remember when you asked me not to take away your memory?" he said, looking over his shoulder at me.

I nodded. "I thought you were going to strip it away."

"I was. It's common practice of the Sapiens. Humans aren't the most accepting of others."

"By others you mean an alien race who beams us up into ships to experiment on us?" I pointed out, trying to make him see why humans might not be so tolerant.

His teeth flashed with his easy smile. Have I mentioned how beautiful his smile was? It literally lit up his face and made his eyes even more incredible. "When you put it that way…" he said.

I laughed.

"But you wanted to remember," he said, giving me a searching look.

"You're too amazing to want to forget," I replied softly.

The look he gave me melted my heart just a little. Tarek paced to the window and looked out into the night sky. "It was wrong. Taking women, checking their health, their ability to carry a child. Then implanting them with Sapien sperm once we knew they were healthy. We took their memory of it. The mind-body connection was disrupted," he said. It was almost like he was talking to himself now, working it out in his own mind. Even still, I found what he was saying fascinating.

"Their bodies were different. Changed by pregnancy, but they didn't understand. Their mind didn't even go to that possibility, didn't allow for it. And so their bodies rejected what was happening. They rejected the child."

"You really think that's what happened?" I asked.

He seemed to remember I was there and turned to look at me. "I wouldn't say it's out of the realm of possibility."

He studied me quietly for a moment. "Even if the pregnancy took, it's very possible the woman just didn't have the energy levels to maintain and give to a Sapien child."

"But that's not going to happen to me." I worried, jumping up from the couch and holding my stomach. "This baby will be okay."

I felt him watching me. I didn't like the lack of expression in his eyes. "Tarek?" I questioned.

He closed the distance between us in the passing of a single second. "You love this baby, don't you?"

"Of course!" I said as if it were obvious. "I'm his mother. All mothers love their children."

"Not all mothers," he said softly, gently brushing his fingertips down my cheek.

"Your mother?" I asked, sorrow draping over me.

"I don't remember my mother. Most Sapiens are not raised by the woman who gave birth to them."

I drew back and met his eyes. "That's terrible. Did you ever think that taking a baby away from a mother time and again might be the reason the women on your planet aren't getting pregnant? I don't care how you are raised; that has to be emotionally damaging."

He tilted his head to the side, considering my words.

"I haven't even had this baby yet." I continued. "Technically, I'm not a mother yet, but I already love him so much. I can't imagine someone trying to take him away from me."

A look drifted behind Tarek's eyes and then a frown weighed down the corners of his mouth.

The words he spoke to me not so very long ago chose that moment to sneak in and totally chase away the ease Tarek was making me feel.

I will be back in seven months to get the child.

I backed away from him, all the beautiful words he'd just filled my head and my heart with evaporating like smoke. "You're going to take this baby from me, aren't you?"

His body language stiffened like he'd been caught with an ugly secret.

I gasped. "Everything you just said… you only said to make me compliant. You don't want me to fight you."

The backs of my legs came up against the couch and I began to skirt around it.

He flashed forward, taking my shoulders in his hands and staring down at me intently. "Everything I just said to you is the truth. I care about you."

"And when the baby is born?" I asked. My heart felt like it was shattering in a million pieces. "Will you still care about me then?"

His fingers tightened around me. I could see his mind spinning.

He was *not* going to take this baby. I would never allow it.

"Sophie…" He began, and my heart pounded.

This was it. Whatever he was going to say, the words he chose to speak next would have so much power over my future that my skin actually broke out in a fine sheen of sweat. Maybe he did care about me. Maybe he was only here for the sake of his child. From this point on, he was either with me—*with us*—or against us.

His eyes glittered like polished amethyst, and I found myself wanting to make a wish on those silver specs in their depths, wanting desperately to wish he would love me, that he would understand how much I wanted him.

But there weren't really stars in his eyes.

Wishing something wouldn't make it true.

He opened his mouth to deliver the words that would determine my next moves in life.

Bright neon light flooded the living room. It was so intense I actually flinched away, shutting my eyes against it.

"What is that?" I asked.

Tarek pulled me into his chest, hiding my eyes from the intrusive light.

"They're here," he said, his voice seeming far away.

I glanced up. He was looking over his shoulder at the window where the light poured in.

"Who?"

"The Sapiens."

Fear clawed the back of my throat. Intuition told me not all Sapiens were like Tarek. I gripped the front of his T-shirt, crushing the cotton between my fingers.

"Tarek?"

He palmed the back of my head and looked down at me, his eyes softening. "They just want to talk to me."

I shook my head. "Don't go."

He smiled softly. "It's okay. I'll be back."

"What if you aren't?" Suddenly, all the bad things that could happen to me when he *wasn't* here far outweighed the things that could happen when he was here. It seemed that intuition also told me Tarek wouldn't hurt me.

He cupped my face; the gesture was so intimate and gentle that my chest actually tightened, even amongst this moment of severe anxiety. "Remember what I told you." He reminded me softly. "I belong to you."

He pressed a gentle kiss to my forehead and then looked into me with his gem-colored eyes one last time.

And then he was gone.

Just like that.

The neon light disappeared with him.

I was alone.

The baby fluttered in my belly, reminding me I wasn't as alone as I thought. Even though I was still confused, even though I didn't get to hear whatever Tarek was going to say, even though I wanted to break down right there and cry… I wouldn't.

I was going to be strong for me. For this baby. For whatever the hell was going to happen next.

There was a muffled knock on the door, and I spun around to look at it.

"Soph?" Matt said. "It's me."

After everything, I completely forgot he was coming by. Now, not only did I have to worry about

Tarek and if he was coming back *and* what would happen with him if he did, but I also had to essentially break up with a guy that I wasn't really dating and had no idea the otherworldly crap he'd indirectly become involved in.

I glanced out the darkened window one last time, seeing the stars so distant in the sky, and wondered if Tarek was up there among them.

I glanced at the hoodie I'd brought out to cover up my pregnancy. Then I turned away and straightened my shoulders.

Screw that.

I wasn't hiding anymore.

Matt knocked a little louder this time. "Sophie?"

"Coming!"

Part Three

the conclusion

the talk

I opened the door, preparing myself for whatever was about to happen. It was hard to prepare for this kind of conversation, especially knowing the kind of reaction Matt had the first time I told him I was pregnant.

I sorely wished Tarek hadn't taken his memory.

Of course, maybe it was better this way.

Better for Matt, because I could handle the conversation better this time. Now that he had seen Tarek and I knew Tarek was somewhat in the picture, I could say so. It would save Matt from offering to claim this baby and save me from having to tell him no.

"Hey," Matt said from the other side of the door. His eyes searched mine and swept over my face. His hazel irises were green tonight, reminding me of moss growing up the side of a mature tree. "Are you feeling any better?"

"Yeah," I said, feeling the weight of his stare in the center of my chest. Part of me was sad, so incredibly sad. I'd crushed after Matt for a long time, so long he was the one I wanted, the guy I thought I'd never have.

And now he wanted me.

Only it was too late.

I stepped back and he came inside with the familiar swagger that made all the ladies stare. It was startling when I realized he wasn't wearing his usual preppy attire. He was wearing a white ribbed tank and a pair of loose gym shorts.

It was totally distracting. Tattoos covered the majority of his arms, winding around his strong biceps and climbing up over his shoulders. The tattoo on his right shoulder stretched out near his chest.

"You changed clothes," was all I could manage, still unable to pull my eyes away from the tattoos he kept covered at work.

"I spilled beer all over my clothes before I left so I just threw on what I had in my gym bag," he explained, looking at me. I knew instantly when he saw the baby bump.

His eyes dropped down, moved back up, then swiftly dropped back down to do a double take.

"Sophie." His voice was laced with disbelief and confusion.

"I have been avoiding you lately, Matt," I said, starting out with what I already knew he thought. My hand went to my belly and I took a deep breath. "But it's because I haven't wanted to hurt you."

He didn't say a word, just stared at my rounded stomach.

"I'm pregnant."

He seemed shell-shocked, so much so that he sank down on the sofa, leaning his elbows forward to rest on his knees.

"I know," I said softly, coming to sit beside him. He didn't shy away from my closeness, and that was a good thing. "Trust me, I was just as shocked."

His eyes slid over to mine. "How long have you known?"

"Remember that night you came over? When I was sick and you brought me food?"

Light dawned in the depths of his eyes. "You weren't sick."

"Well, yeah, I was," I said, not wanting him to think I was a total liar (though wasn't I?). "But it was kind of like morning sickness, the kind that lasts all day. I found out the next day."

He rubbed a hand over his face and blew out a breath. "I thought you were avoiding me because you were…" He glanced at me again. "Ah, hell," he muttered, embarrassed.

I didn't want him to feel uncomfortable for the way he felt about me or assuming I had felt the same, because I had.

Before Tarek.

I put a hand on his arm. He looked down at it. "For what it's worth, I wouldn't avoid you because I was scared to be with you. You don't scare me."

The corner of his mouth tilted up. "Even with my rep?"

"Well, you are a ladies' man." I teased.

He fell silent. "I waited too long," he whispered and lifted his eyes to mine. "With you."

"Matt," I said, pulling my hand back as this achy feeling encompassed my chest. Almost like on a day so cold and windy it made it hard to breathe.

"How far along are you?" he asked, dropping his hands down between his legs and clasping his fingers. I wanted to lay my head on his shoulder. I felt like we needed to comfort each other about what would never be.

"A little over four months."

"The guy from the bar tonight," he said.

I nodded. "He's the father. His name is Tarek."

"What the hell kind of name is that?" he grumbled.

"It's unique, just like him," I said, wondering where he was right now and what kind of talk he was having with the other Sapiens that came for him.

"Is he British or something?" he asked. "What's up with that accent?"

I stifled a laugh. "Something," I said vaguely.

"So is he…?" He paused and cleared his throat. "Is he gonna be around for you? For the kid?" Matt sneaked a glance at my stomach.

"Yes," I answered, my stomach twisting just a bit as I thought of before when he offered to be there for me and the baby. "He's a good guy." I finished, praying to God Tarek wouldn't prove me wrong.

It didn't escape my consciousness that he never answered the question I'd asked—if he was going to try and take my son from me.

"Why am I just hearing about this guy?" Matt asked and stood up to pace around the other side of the coffee table.

I had to think a second. I wasn't sure what to say. "Well, we were sort of casual at first. Off and on," I said. "But since I told him about the baby, he's been there for me."

Matt stopped his pacing and stood before me, looking down. "Sophie, if you don't want to be with him…" Vulnerability shone in his stare. "If you don't have feelings for him—"

I held up my hand, not wanting him to say it. "I do."

Matt was silent for long moments, like the fact I had feelings for another man bothered him. "My timing sucks," he said somewhat sheepishly. He started to walk away, across the room.

I couldn't take the pain in my chest anymore. I stood up and grabbed his hand. "*Your* timing was perfect," I said. "It's just that *our* timing isn't very good."

"I should have kissed you sooner," he rasped, his fingers tightening around my hand. "Then this guy wouldn't have had a chance with you."

My, he was confident.

And before Tarek, I would have agreed. No guy would have had a chance against Matt. But Tarek was different.

I belong to you. I heard his words like an echo in my head, like a vibration in my heart.

“I don’t want to hurt you,” I whispered to Matt, turning away.

Still holding my hand, he yanked me back. I stumbled a bit and fell into his chest. His arms came around me. In between us was my baby.

His lips swooped down on mine, capturing them in an aggressive kiss. An angry and passionate kiss. I was caught off guard at the amount of emotion I felt in that brief touch of our lips.

I say brief because one moment he was crushing me against him, and the next he was flying across the room and hitting the wall. Beside him a picture fell to the floor, the glass making a sharp cracking sound.

I shrieked and watched him slide down the wall, slightly disoriented.

“Matt!” I said, starting to move toward him when a rush of warm energy stopped me.

I swung around at the familiar feeling. Tarek was standing in the open front doorway, his eyes flashing, looking like an angry stormy sky.

the choice

I was caught. Standing between two men, knowing Tarek would take it wrong if I rushed to Matt's side, but wanting to be sure he was okay.

I stared at Tarek for a few moments. His eyes were hard when he stared back. It kind of made me angry. I wasn't doing anything wrong, not really.

Maybe I shouldn't have been kissing Matt, but technically, he kissed me. Tarek told me not to let him touch me, but who was he to boss me around? We weren't together; there was no promise between us.

Matt made a sound and I made a split second decision and rushed across the room to him and grabbed his arm, helping him stand. "Are you okay?" I worried.

"Geez, man," Matt said, looking at Tarek, who had moved farther into the room. Then his eyes narrowed. "How the hell did you do that?"

Great. The last thing I needed was Matt being all suspicious of Tarek.

"Why are you here?" Tarek asked, offering no explanation. He acted as if he didn't owe one.

"He came to talk," I answered for him, trying to will Tarek to understand with my eyes. "I told him about the baby, about *our* baby."

"After what just happened, I wonder what the hell kind of father he's going to be," Matt said, his voice taking on a hard edge as he straightened and drew up to his full height.

"So you accept that this is my child?" Tarek asked, completely ignoring the insult.

"Sophie doesn't lie," Matt replied.

"Then you must know there is no room in her life for you."

I gasped and stepped forward. "Tarek!"

Matt shook his head. "Possessive and jealous."

I crossed the room to stand before Tarek. "Matt is my friend. We've been friends for years. Just because you and I…" I faltered. I didn't know what to say. I decided to skip that part. "Me being pregnant doesn't change the fact that Matt and I are friends."

Tarek's eyes narrowed. "I don't like him."

Behind me, Matt snorted. "I don't have warm and fuzzy feelings about you either."

I sighed. Men are idiots.

"You don't have to like him. I do. End of story."

Tarek regarded me for a long moment. "Okay."

I wasn't really prepared for him to just give in. "Okay?" I asked.

He nodded and reached for my hand. I wasn't sure if it was some kind of ploy to show Matt that I was his or if he genuinely wanted to touch me. Before giving over my hand to him, I studied his face, searching for the answer, looking to see some kind of motive behind his action.

I didn't see anything there. There was no gleam of spite, no hard edge of jealousy. And he stared at me openly. His eyes weren't shuttered in the least.

He waited for me to make up my mind about him, leaving his arm outstretched and his hand in an open invitation. I couldn't say no. I wasn't able to deny myself the pleasure of his touch, the simple act of holding hands. I wanted him too much for that. I *felt* too much for him for that.

When my fingers slid between his, closing around him and linking us together, I thought I saw the merest sigh of relief behind the purple depths of his gaze. Even after I surrendered my touch, he didn't look at Matt. He didn't smile in victory. His eyes stayed with me.

Like I was the only person in the room.

Perhaps to him, I was.

Warmth and energy flowed through me, making me feel full inside.

Behind us, Matt cleared his throat. "I should probably go."

I turned, not letting go of Tarek. "Matt," I began, not sure what else to say. I was standing here in the middle of them, and it occurred to me that I had just made a choice. Maybe it hadn't been intentional, and maybe it had.

But, either way, I'd chosen.

I was with Tarek, whatever that meant for me. He wasn't the safe choice. Hell, he probably wasn't the right choice, but he was *my* choice.

"It's okay, Soph," Matt said, his eyes sweeping over me in a way that soothed the worst of my guilt. "You have a baby to think about now."

I pulled my hand free and trailed after him as Matt went to the door. He stopped and turned before leaving and gave me a little smile. "If you need anything, you know where to call," he said softly.

My eyes watered with unexpected tears. "I do," I replied with a nod. I didn't want to give him the whole "can we still be friends" speech because I didn't feel like I had the right to ask. It seemed like the rest of our relationship—whatever that may be—was going to be up to him.

"I'm still here for ya, Soph," he said, brushing some hair back behind my ear. It made my breath catch. Behind us, Tarek said nothing, and I was grateful he was letting me have this moment. "Still friends, right?" Matt asked, a hint of vulnerability in his voice.

I sniffled. "Definitely."

He gave me a quick grin and yanked open the door. Matt didn't glance back at Tarek as he left the apartment. I just stood there near the empty doorway, wondering if I made the right choice.

In front of me, the door slowly swung shut, latching fully, and then the echo of a turning lock brought me out of my turbulent thoughts.

I spun and looked at Tarek. "You're telekinetic, right?"

Either that or I was freaking insane.

He nodded.

I placed a hand over my stomach, wondering if this baby would be too.

"I didn't expect you to come back so soon," I said.

"This is where I belong now," he answered simply.

"Tell me what happened while you were gone," I implored. *Tell me what the others like you wanted.*

"After," he replied.

There was a clear question in my eyes at his word.

"There's something I need to do first," Tarek said and then closed the distance between us.

the sex

I knew we needed to talk. But as Tarek reached out and pulled me close, I realized something about him.

Tarek was a less talk, more action kind of guy.

Who was I to complain?

His touch was like one of those giant pink erasers I had in kindergarten; it totally erased everything on the page. He made me feel like nothing else mattered when we touched, that he was the only person in my entire universe.

I liked the feeling; never had I ever known such complete bliss.

Tarek's very long, pale, and smooth hands cupped my face, turning it up so he could stare down at me. "When I was gone, I only thought about touching you."

"I thought about you too," I told him, not because it was the correct thing to answer, but because it was true.

He frowned, his thoughts turned inward. I could almost see his concentration leaving my face. But then he refocused and said, "I've never wanted to touch anyone before. I've never missed the presence of someone when they weren't at my side." He swallowed, a pained expression crossing his remarkable features.

One of his hands slid away from my face to reach for mine. He brought it up between us and laid my palm flat against his chest.

"I felt this sort of hollowness," he said, pressing my hand against him. "Right here." He looked up at me, like he was trying to understand, like he wanted me to explain it to him.

How the hell could I explain something like that when I could barely breathe?

His heart was beating rapidly, almost like he should be running and not standing still before me. I wondered how he could appear so calm when his thoughts seemed to be moving so fast. It caused my heart to speed up; it caused a fine tremor beneath my skin. My desire for Tarek went beyond the physical.

Yes, I wanted him and, yes, my body literally craved him.

But my heart, my heart was equally as affected.

How could it not be when he said the most beautiful things to me. And what made them even more beautiful was that he had no idea just how incredible his words were. He didn't say these things because he thought it might endear him to me. He didn't try to spout pretty words so I would fall under his spell.

Tarek spoke with an honesty that he didn't realize. He said exactly what he was thinking without realizing yet that it was words that caused so much feeling.

Words were far, far more powerful than his touch would ever be.

And it was his words that were going to cause me to totally fall for him.

"Sophie?" Tarek questioned, giving my hand a squeeze.

"I feel the same way when you're not here too," I whispered.

"So it's normal, then?"

I shook my head. "No. This isn't normal," I said. "But it's what everybody here on Earth searches for."

He kissed me. Completely captured my mouth and made it his own. For someone who admittedly did little (if no) kissing up until this point, he was a very fast learner. He drank me in like he was starved, like there just wasn't enough of me. His lips devoured mine. The heat of his skin seeped into me, making me melt.

Tarek's tongue glided over my lips, teasing them open and then gently delving into the depths of my mouth, sweeping past my tongue and brushing over the roof of my mouth. My hands slid up the back of his neck and threaded through the silky, thick strands of his hair, trying to pull him even closer.

Tarek lifted me as if I weighed nothing at all, and my legs fastened around his lean waist like Velcro. He made a sound in the back of his throat, and I greedily snatched it from him, sucking it into my throat.

Energy coursed through my body like I'd had way too much coffee, leaving me feeling jittery and out of sorts, but I didn't care.

He was so unbelievably everything.

He was oxygen to my lungs, blood to my veins, and the sun to my sky.

As the kiss stretched into minutes and my body melded even farther against him, I wondered how the hell I had ever lived without him.

"Take me to bed." I gasped, then instantly sealed our lips back together.

Without hesitation, Tarek carried me into the bedroom and laid me in the center of my queen-sized bed. His body came down over mine, and I clutched at the T-shirt he wore, desperately wanting it to be gone.

In one fluid movement, he pulled it up over his head and tossed it aside, covering me with his hard, smooth chest.

I purred, little sounds of satisfaction filling the dark bedroom as he rubbed against me like a cat, pressing lingering kisses across my jawbone and down my neck.

My hands roamed all over him, delving into the waistband of his jeans and kneading the muscles of his butt. He pulled back abruptly, and my hands fell onto the mattress on either side of me.

His eyes, even in the dark, glittered down at me. I was lost when I looked into them, like I was being sucked into a world that didn't scare me at all. I couldn't be scared when he was this close—the way he touched me, the way he looked at me. Tarek wasn't going to hurt me. I didn't think he was capable.

With careful ease, he removed my clothes until I was totally naked and laid out before him. I could see the length of him, contained and pressing against his jeans. He ignored it, like the insistent need of his body would wait until he was done pleasuring me.

On his knees between my legs, Tarek smoothed his palms over my rounded belly. “I don’t understand,” he said, caressing me with long, gentle strokes.

“Understand what?” I murmured, my eyes half closed from the gratification of his hands.

“How the men on my planet could not have been affected seeing their child inside a woman’s womb.”

His eyes lifted from my middle and settled on my face. “How anyone could be so utterly unaffected, so emotionless, about a woman nourishing a seed they planted, literally giving them another piece of themselves.”

“You’re not unaffected?” I asked.

“Oh no,” he said, slipping his hands lower than my belly, delving them between my thighs, and dipping into my silky heat. “I think you’re absolutely amazing.”

I moaned softly as his fingers slid inside me, working me gently. It took a moment for me to reply, but the thought wouldn't disappear. "What about when your baby isn't inside me anymore?" I asked as a sliver of fear worked its way up my spine.

What if what was between us slipped away when I was no longer pregnant? What if the thing that tethered us together was this baby?

His fingers stopped moving within me. Carefully, he pulled out in one long stroke.

"You will always be beautiful to me."

Being beautiful was one thing. Being someone he needed was something else entirely. I wanted Tarek to need me. I wanted him to want me the same way I wanted him.

He stood beside the bed, staring intently as he unfastened the top button on his jeans. All thought left me. Every worry, every fear evaporated. I sat up, reaching to help free his strong, hard cock.

Just the sight of it made excitement tingle in my lower half. My inner muscles flexed and readied for his entrance. As he pushed the jeans down, I stroked him, sliding just a little bit closer to him.

When he straightened, his cock was at the level of my lips. On impulse, I let my tongue loose and licked the tip, enjoying the way his body shuddered.

"Again," he growled.

I licked him again and then sucked him into my mouth, drawing him as deep as my throat would allow.

The way his hips pumped, thrusting into me, was so satisfying because I knew he liked the way I made him feel. I curled my lips around him, holding tight to his dick as he slid it in and out of my mouth.

Abruptly, he pulled out, leaving me to grasp at him for more, but he shook his head and grabbed behind my knees. I fell backward on the mattress as he dragged me closer to him until my legs were off the bed and my hips were at the very edge.

He positioned himself at my entrance, and I whimpered. Just the hint of his round, hard head getting ready to push inside me was enough to make me beg.

Long fingers slid over the front of my legs and inside my thighs, and I linked my ankles behind his back.

He delved into me with one long, hard stroke.

I cried out as he stretched me and complete bliss coursed through my limbs.

Tarek bent, bringing his body over mine, covering me as our naked chests came together. Usually, any sexual encounter with him was all about pleasure. It was all about what kind of reaction he could illicit from me. Or, more recently, it was about what kind of feelings I could withdraw from him.

This time was different.

I was expecting hard and fast.

I was expecting fierce and carnal.

It wasn't any of those things.

His lips found mine in a gentle, almost lazy kiss as he braced his forearms on each side of my shoulders and used his hands to cradle my head.

He moved within me as he rocked over me, connecting with me from the inside out. His thrusts were slow and deep. He pushed inside me and buried himself there, rocking easily with his hips with a smooth and easy motion. His chest stayed in contact with mine and his hands stayed in my hair, cupping me as he kissed me dizzy.

I was in danger of imploding. Emotion built up within me, so intense I was almost frightened. I felt like there was a wire inside me and it was stretched absolutely thin, ready to snap at any moment. The butterfly sensation in my stomach didn't stay there; it spread throughout my limbs until I was shaking noticeably. So much so that it made Tarek pull his lips away and tilt his head as he looked at me through heavy, amethyst eyes.

"Are you all right, Sophie?" His voice was incredibly rich and husky. "Are you not enjoying this?"

He started to pull away, as if the idea of me not enjoying this was unacceptable. I snatched him back, wrapping my arms around his neck and tugging him back down. "Don't stop."

"But you're shaking." He frowned.

"You're not the only one who's new to this emotion stuff," I whispered, running a hand through his tousled hair. "I've been feeling all my life," I said, "but I've never felt like this before."

His hips, which had been still for long moments, moved gently. The hard length inside me moved and caused me to moan.

"So you like this," he whispered, rotating his hips and causing sparks of heat to burn me from within.

"Oh yes," I breathed. "Please don't stop."

He lowered his lips again, this time his tongue tracing the outline of my lips before dipping into my welcoming mouth and dancing with mine. He started to move again, his movements achingly slow, and they built the kind of tension that only this pace could.

I clutched at his shoulders, pulling him deeper, wanting him closer. Every single part of me was somehow touching him, yet I wanted closer. Tarek left my mouth and began trailing kisses across my collarbone and pressing his face between my neck and shoulder.

My body was turning to Jell-O, and soon my legs were no longer able to stay clasped around his hips and they dropped, dangling over the side of the bed.

Without a word, Tarek lifted me, the movement causing him to slip out of my body. I made a sound of despair, and his throaty chuckle had my insides burning again.

"You are a needy little thing," he said as he dragged my body farther onto the bed and climbed back between my legs.

I grasped his biceps and urged him to hurry.

His cock sank back into me one inch at a time, and I bit down on my lip to keep from crying out. This time he braced himself on his hands and rocked into me a little bit harder, and my back arched up off the bed.

One of my erect nipples was tugged into his mouth and he lapped at it as he thrust deeply into my core.

My body was hungry, hungry for release and to feel the pulsing release of his orgasm. But he wouldn't let me go there yet.

He kept the pace slow as he explored my body until I could no longer think or see. All I could do was ask him for more.

When at last it seemed he couldn't take any more, his arms slid around me, pulling me close, and with a soft grunt in my ear, he plunged right into my core.

I splintered apart; my entire body shattered. Wave after wave of ecstasy washed over my body, making me weak. "That's it, love," he murmured, holding me close. "I want all of it. Give it to me."

I did. I gave him everything. By the time I started to come back from the high, a feeling of complete rawness crept over me. I literally did give him everything. I gave him so much of myself that it scared me. I'd never felt anything like this in my entire life.

I might have started freaking out, but the sudden moan that ripped from his chest, the tightening of his arms around me, and the feeling of his hot cock pumping inside me obliterated everything else.

I wrapped my legs around him, pulling him even closer as my body milked every single last drop from him, eating it hungrily. Some of the rawness left me as he filled me up inside. I hugged him close, reveling in each little aftershock that rippled through his body.

Long, blissful minutes of us being connected drifted past, and then Tarek stirred, bracing himself over me on his elbows. He brushed the hair out of my face and stared down at me with emotion swimming in his eyes.

"When emotion slips in," he began, stroking the side of my head, "when a person starts to feel it…"

I nodded as he searched for the words he wanted.

"It all comes at once. It's not something that happens gradually, you know?" It really wasn't a question because he kept talking. "My entire being is bombarded with emotion after emotion. I don't know how you humans walk around every day with so much going on inside you."

I smiled. "It gets easier. Once you know what it's like to feel all the time, the intensity of every emotion will lessen."

"Perhaps," he said, considering my words. "I hope what I feel for you never goes away."

Tears sprang to my eyes. He still had no idea how much his words affected me. The truth that lay between us was beautiful. He was so pure with what he felt.

"I hope not either," I said, my voice tearful.

"Did I say something wrong?" he asked, wiping a rogue tear away from the corner of my eye.

"You did everything exactly right."

"There is something I need to know," he said, slipping off me and onto the bed. Before settling down, he pulled the covers up over us, then wrapped his arms around me.

"Okay," I said, laying a cheek against his chest.

"Can I kiss you whenever I want?"

I smiled. "Yes."

"Even if we are not here? Like out where there are others?"

He wanted to know about PDA. I giggled. "Yes, Tarek, you can kiss me whenever you want."

"And you would like that?"

"I would love that," I replied softly.

"And kissing you…" He began. "People would know you are mine?"

There went his possessive side again. "I think if the kiss doesn't prove that, then my growing belly will," I said ruefully.

"So here on your planet, the fathers, they are involved with the child and the mother?"

"Not all the time, but usually, yes."

"You said it would be hard for you if I wasn't here?"

A sharp pain pierced my heart. I felt my limbs stiffen, no longer able to relax completely into him. I didn't understand why he was asking me this.

He felt the change come over me and whispered my name. Unable to lie there against him with utter joy any longer, I sat up, covering myself with the blanket, and looked down at him.

"You're leaving me, aren't you?"

the relationship

I went from blissful to scared in about three seconds flat. The idea of losing him—of losing the way I felt with him—was so incredibly awful it made me feel physically ill. How had it gotten this way?

I used to be independent. Living on my own, going to college, setting the pace for my life, and happily unattached.

And now.

Now it felt like Tarek was the oxygen I needed to live.

I wanted him desperately. I couldn't imagine not feeling his hands on me every single day. I couldn't imagine a man without a galaxy in his stare. How in the hell did he insert himself beneath my skin so deep, so fast?

True, I had known him for over four months, but most of that time had been spent apart. I wanted the chance to know him, to know everything about him, from what kind of food he liked most to the secret behind his perfect hair.

I didn't see him move, but suddenly, I felt his lips cover mine, his tongue part the entrance to my mouth, and then his oxygen once again filling my lungs.

"You're doing it again," he said, pulling away.

I dragged in a ragged breath. "You're leaving," I said, flat.

"I'm not leaving," he replied, reaching out to finger the ends of my dark, tangled hair.

"You aren't?" Damn the hope I felt rise within me.

He settled back against the pillows and lifted me into his lap, tucking the sheets around me. One of his arms wrapped around my middle so his palm could splay over my belly while the other on rested over the blankets in my lap.

"I was trying to ask you if I could stay."

"You want to stay," I echoed. Yes. I realize I'd pretty much been echoing his words. Clearly, I was having a massive brain fart.

"I wasn't sure if you would have me." He began, nerves creeping into his tone. "So I was going to point out that having the father of your baby around might alleviate some of the stress you spoke about, you know, from people talking."

"I want you to stay." The words rushed out of me like a rocket.

"You do?" he asked.

It struck me then that we were sort of acting like teenagers. Unsure, kind of guarded, but underneath we were totally in lo—totally into each other. It was a large step back from the honesty we had going for us.

I laid my head back against his chest. "I want you, Tarek. Not because I don't want people to talk about me behind my back. Because you make me feel like no one else does. I like having you around. And frankly, you're freaking hot and I like looking at you."

He laughed.

I loved that sound.

"I like looking at you too."

"Remember that when I'm fat," I muttered.

His arms tightened around me. "Good thing I have, as you say, a large wingspan."

I smiled and snuggled closer. "So you're going to stay?" I asked. "Just like that?"

"Just like that."

"Don't you have, like, somewhere else to be?"

"I told you. I belong to you now. The only place I need to be is with you."

"What about them?" I asked, a yawn distorting my words.

"Them?" he asked. His accent didn't help with my sleepiness. Neither did being wrapped up in his warm embrace. Both combined was like my own personal lullaby.

"The other Sapiens. What did they want to talk to you about?" I asked, yawning again.

"I told them I was staying here with you."

"And they were okay with it?" I asked, tipping my chin up to look at him. It didn't seem like they would just say okay and be done with it.

Tarek placed his hand on the back of my head and gently guided it back down against him. "I told them it was best for the child. They agreed."

"So it's because of the baby," I said.

"No," he said decisively. "But that's what they understand. They don't understand… my attachment toward you."

I smiled, my eyes drifting closed. "I'm attached to you, too," I murmured.

I felt him smile against the top of my head. "Go to sleep, Sophie. You're tired." He began dragging his fingers through my hair.

"I'll see you in the morning," I murmured, already slipping into slumber.

"I'll be here." He promised.

I slept so soundly that when I opened my eyes, I was shocked to see sun streaming through the bedroom window. I rolled over and glanced at the clock, my eyes still partially blurred from sleep. But once I noted the time, my eyes shot open when I saw I only had an hour before my class started.

With a groan, I stretched a little. Awareness swept through my body as I remembered exactly how I spent last night. In Tarek's arms. I smiled a little knowing he was the reason I slept so well.

I glanced over my shoulder, peeking through my hair, but the bed was empty. He wasn't here. Before I could think the worst, I heard a muffled noise in the kitchen, and I smiled. His T-shirt was lying at the foot of the bed so I pulled it over my naked body, enjoying the way it smelled just like him, and wandered out into the kitchen.

He was standing there with nothing on but a pair of tight gray boxers. The muscles in his back were well defined and his waist tapered into his tight ass, which I knew from experience was total muscle.

Tarek must have sensed me because he turned from the counter, giving me a full-on view of his incredible body.

Like, seriously. He could be an underwear model. And yes, his hair was still perfect.

"I was going to bring you in some juice and breakfast," he said, a glass of orange juice in his hand.

I wrinkled my nose. "I don't like orange juice. It makes my stomach upset." I didn't even know I had that stuff in my fridge.

Without turning away, he reached behind him and produced an identical clear glass like the one he was holding, only this one didn't have OJ in it. This one was filled with apple juice. "This one is yours," he said with a little smirk.

I didn't ask him how he knew this was the only thing I could tolerate the first few weeks after I found out I was pregnant, because I already knew. He'd been watching me from afar.

I liked him up close much better.

I padded over before him to reach out for the juice. Tarek snatched it away, setting it on the counter, and then pulled me into his arms. He wrapped me in a bear hug, not squeezing too tight, and then pressed a kiss to the top of my head.

Before I could get over the surprise, he lifted me and sat me on the counter, placing the glass in my hand.

"I made you breakfast," he said.

"You can cook?" I marveled, sipping the sweet juice.

"I've been sitting in my hovercraft for a long time. I watched a lot of American TV to get a feel for your kind." He shrugged. "My favorite channel was the one where they cooked all the time."

"If you keep cooking in your boxers, I'll eat anything you make," I quipped.

He flashed me a brilliant smile and then dumped some scrambled egg whites out of a pan and onto a plate that already contained whole wheat toast.

"Where did you get all this food?" I asked. "I know for a fact I didn't have any wheat bread in there."

He grunted. "I went to the store before you got up.

You had nothing but junk in your cupboards."

"Did not," I said, snatching the toast and taking a bite. It was lightly buttered and it melted onto my tongue.

"White bread and Pop-tarts are not healthy for you or my child."

I sighed dramatically. "But they taste good."

"Drink your glass of sugar and be glad I poured it for you," he said, making a plate for himself. His was piled much higher.

"How dare you insult my juice," I said in mock anger.

"You amuse me," he said, a little smirk playing on his lips. "I've never known anyone who talks with such animation."

He made his planet sound absolutely horrible.

"Stick with me," I said, setting aside the juice and reaching for his arm to draw him closer.

He slipped readily between my legs, leaning against the counter, close to me.

"I'll teach you my ways," I purred, running my fingers over his rock-hard abs with a little shiver.

Tarek lowered his head and kissed me. It was a gentle kiss with just enough heat that I sighed and leaned forward, wanting more. My lips parted on a satisfied sigh as I gripped his sides, reveling in the way he felt.

But before I could get carried away, he pulled back. "Your breakfast is getting cold."

I scowled at him as he lifted me off the counter and placed me on the floor, swatting at my bottom so I would move toward the little bistro table in the corner. There was a banana beside my plate, and I picked it up, peeled it, and took a bite.

"Tarek?" I asked around a bite of fruit.

"Yes?" he said, sitting across from me with his plate.

"How long have you been here?" I asked. "Earth, I mean."

"Several years."

"You've been in your hovercraft this entire time?"

"Mostly." He agreed. "I've been around your planet, visiting various places, researching the climate, human nature, and just learning about your kind."

"Have you always been alone?" I asked.

"Rarely." I watched as he took a huge bite of eggs.

"But your hovercraft was always empty when I was there."

"Not that first time. That first time, others were there. They were just in other compartments of the craft."

"But the other times?" I asked, tilting my head.

"The other times I wanted to be alone with you."

I smiled and reached across the table for his hand. At first, he didn't seem to understand what I wanted, but then he slid his hand toward mine and I grasped it, giving him another smile.

"You humans like to touch," he said, not pulling away.

"Only the people we really like, though."

"I could get used to it."

A fluttery sensation filled my middle. At first I thought it was just butterflies, but then I realized it was the baby. "He's moving," I told him, my voice hushed, as if the baby might stop if I spoke too loud.

Tarek abandoned his plate and my hand and came around the table. Carefully, he slid out my chair and sank down before me. His hand trembled out over my middle and he looked at me for permission.

"You don't have to ask to touch me," I said.

His palm covered my belly and then stilled. Tarek sat there waiting, a veil of concentration over his features. I willed the baby to move, wanting Tarek to be able to feel what he clearly was hoping for.

A few moments later, there was a soft kick to the center of his palm.

His eyes widened and he glanced up at me. "Did you feel that?" he asked, wonder in his tone.

I nodded.

My cell phone began to ring from over on the kitchen counter. Tarek stiffened and glanced in its direction. I patted the hand resting on my middle. "It's just my phone."

After unhooking it from the charger, I answered. "Hey, Mom," I said into the receiver. I felt a little pang of guilt because I hadn't been to see them in several weeks. I hadn't been ready to tell them about the baby.

I felt Tarek's eyes on me as Mom and I talked for a moment, and I turned to stare at him.

"Shouldn't you be on your way to class?" Mom asked, snapping me out of it.

I had completely forgotten about class. I'd been too wrapped up in Tarek and his underwear-clad, egg-making self. "I'm sort of skipping," I said into the line.

"Sophie." Mom warned.

"It's just this one time." I lied. I wasn't a constant skipper, but this wasn't my first time either. "Hey," I said, changing the subject quickly. "I was wondering if you and Dad would be home later. I thought I might come by. I wanted to talk."

"Is everything okay?" she asked, suspicion in her tone.

"Yes," I said, my gaze still lingering on Tarek. He seemed to be able to hear my conversation with her and was listening intently.

"How about you come for dinner, then?" she suggested.

I pulled the phone away from my chin and gazed at Tarek, a question in my eyes.

Slowly, he nodded.

"That would be great, Mom," I said, lifting the phone back to my ear. "Would it be okay if I bring someone? I'd like to introduce you."

"Is that why you've been scarce lately?" Mom asked, her voice taking on a new tone. "Do you have a new boyfriend?"

Tarek stiffened a little, proving he could hear the entire conversation.

"I'll be by about five," I said quickly. "I'm getting another call! See you then." I clicked the phone off and dropped it on the counter.

"If you aren't comfortable going to my parents' tonight, I can go alone," I said, letting him off the hook. I imagined he had to be overwhelmed with basically becoming a part of the human world. I knew he'd been here for years, but I didn't think he'd actually interacted with many humans.

"Do they know about the baby?" he asked.

"No," I said. "I'm going to tell them. I'm showing. I can't hide it anymore."

"And it will be easier if I am there?"

I thought for a moment. "I don't think it will be easy at all. But…" I began, not wanting to sound like I was demanding anything, but not knowing how else to say it. I shook my head, unable to finish my sentence.

"Sophie?" Tarek asked.

"I don't know what we're doing." The words rushed out quietly. I stared at the floor, not wanting to see the look on his face.

"Eating?" he questioned.

I laughed, the worst of my tension evaporating. I looked at him, new confidence finding its way inside me. "This," I said, motioning between us. "I know you don't really have relationships where you're from. That you all are, like, singular or whatever."

"But that isn't how it is here," he supplied.

"No." I shook my head. "It isn't." I sighed. "You said you want to stay here. You want to be here with me. What does that mean, Tarek? If you come with me tonight, my parents will assume we are involved, that you're my boyfriend. They might even want to know if we're getting married."

His eyes widened a bit.

"Do you know what marriage is?" I asked, flustered.

He nodded. "I've been here long enough to know your customs."

"People at the bar are going to want to know about us." I lifted my eyes. "*I* want to know about us."

"You're upset," he said, getting up from the table and standing before me. "I don't like it."

I smiled a little. I loved how literal he was.

"What do you want, Sophie?" he whispered, taking my hand.

"I want to call you my boyfriend. I want to be in a relationship with you. The kind where everyone knows we're together."

"I want that too," he said simply.

"You do?"

He nodded. "Yes."

My elation was short-lived because part of me whispered that he had no idea what he was saying.

He grasped my face and held it so he could look straight into my eyes. I had to struggle to listen because being this close to his hypnotic amethyst glance was distracting. "I understand what I'm saying," he murmured. "I've been here long enough to know."

Knowing and being were two different things.

I didn't say it out loud. I couldn't bring myself to. Tarek was basically giving me everything I wanted. I wasn't going to doubt it all to death.

"'Kay," I said.

He kissed me, then pulled back. "You're missing class today?"

I nodded. "I wanna be with you. But after today, I have to go to school and work."

He brushed the hair back away from my face. "Did you sleep well last night?" he asked.

I nodded.

"You aren't tired today?" Tarek stepped a little closer to me, pressing his body up against mine. I realized then what he was really asking. The hardness jutting from beneath his boxer briefs made it quite clear.

I smiled. "I'm not too tired for you."

"I like touching you, Sophie," he whispered.

I took his hand and led him back to the bedroom. "Lucky for you, I like it too."

the visitor

THREE MONTHS LATER

I don't know how it happened. How Tarek seamlessly fit into my life. How could someone who was literally not of this Earth belong here so completely? I thought it would be a difficult adjustment for him, and for me. I thought we would get strange looks out in public, that my parents would boycott my relationship with him

It wasn't. We didn't. My parents loved him.

Of course, there was the initial shock that people always displayed when I announced I was pregnant and showed off the baby bump with more fitted shirts. And sure, some people did whisper behind me, but I hadn't expected less because this was a small town and up until this point, I'd been single and not seen with anyone.

But not anymore.

Tarek was like a permanent fixture at my side. His pale skin, purple eyes, and accent were not regarded as freaky or even unnerving. Women drooled over him, followed him with their eyes, and tried to flirt when I wasn't looking.

I was always looking, though. Not because I was insecure. Frankly, I wasn't. Tarek never once gave me a single reason to think his devotion to me and his baby was anything but one hundred percent. In fact, I'd heard him tell women he wasn't interested more than once. No, I looked because his body was like a magnet for my eyes. His voice was like a siren in the middle of a darkened sea. Not only that, but I loved to see people react to him, to be taken in the same way I always was.

His accent was panty melting. And the smile he flashed more and more frequently was enough to rob everyone of their voice.

Even men liked him. Tarek wasn't a fake person. I don't think he knew how to be. Even in a place where one would think he would do everything humanly possible to fit in, he didn't. He was himself. Always. He gave his opinion when asked for it, he didn't sugarcoat his words, and he treated everyone with respect.

Frankly, I was beginning to wish more humans acted like him.

Of course, he didn't use his telekinesis around others, he certainly didn't tell people where he was from, and if he didn't understand something about our culture, he waited to ask me about it when we were alone.

Three months passed. Three months of holding hands at the movie theater, of waking up in his warm embrace, and three months of falling deeper and deeper in love with him.

I couldn't deny it. The way I felt about Tarek literally leaked from every pore on my body. I loved him fiercely, like I never thought I'd love anyone.

It was the kind of love that scared me.

It didn't matter how often he smiled at me, touched me, or made love to me (like a ton), there was always this little nagging fear deep inside me that once this baby came, things would change.

I knew Tarek cared about me because emotion was so new to him he couldn't hide it. But did he care enough? I had to remind myself that Tarek wasn't human. He was a Sapien. He'd been a Sapien his entire life, and I knew the Sapiens wanted this baby.

I worried that after the baby was born, his people would put his loyalty to them to the test. That they would force him to choose between them and me.

I was afraid I would lose.

I was afraid he would try and take my son.

I couldn't imagine my life without my son and Tarek.

I didn't bring it up. I never asked him about it. I never pressured him. I simply tried to love him enough. Enough to make him stay. I know, that sounded whacked. In any other situation, I would tell myself I was ridiculous and if he didn't want to stay, then I didn't need him anyway.

But this was different.

Tarek was different.

He still saw the other Sapiens that were here. He met with them when I was at work or at school. He never told me what they talked about; he didn't act like it was a big deal. But sometimes… sometimes he would get this look in his eyes. The purple would darken to an almost black shade, and I knew there was more going on beneath the surface.

What did he talk about with them? What did they want?

Tarek told me he just passed along information about this planet and its people. That he was acting as sort of an informant since he was immersing himself in our way of life. But I knew there was more to it.

The closer I got to my due date, the more concerned I grew. There was going to come a day when I was going to have to ask him. When he was going to have to choose. Sometimes I told myself I was just being paranoid. That there was no underlying struggle going on and the other Sapiens were fine with the fact Tarek was here and staying with me and the baby.

It was hard to lie to myself.

It was Friday night. The bar was busy. I was exhausted.

Tarek wasn't happy I came to work tonight. He seemed to think my place was on the couch or in bed. I didn't admit (out loud) that either of those places sounded heavenly after a day of college classes. Usually, I didn't take classes in the summer, but I was super close to finishing my graphic design degree, and I wanted to get done before the baby arrived. In just a couple short weeks, I would be finished with my bachelor's and I could hopefully get a better job that didn't involve serving beer to a bunch of guys.

Did I mention it was hot?

Yeah, it was like an oven inside the bar. One would think that going back and forth from the deck outside might give me a little bit of a break. It didn't. Summer was in full swing here in Maryland, and the last week or so had felt unbearably hot. Especially to a woman who felt like she was going to burst at any moment. At seven months pregnant, I knew I had a month left (according to my doctor here, I had two months left and I didn't bother to inform him that non-human babies came early), but even knowing my son wasn't making an appearance for several weeks, I still felt restless and uncomfortable.

Basically, I was a watermelon with legs.

So waddling out into the sticky heat and back into the crowded stifling bar only seemed to make me more irritated. Matt and another bartender were behind the bar, serving up drinks as fast as they could as me and the rest of the waitresses hurried through the loud, rowdy weekend group.

"Hey," Matt said, catching my arm as I stepped around the waitress station beside the bar to steal a quick drink of my water. I lifted my eyebrows in response as I poured the cool water down my throat. "You doing okay?"

I nodded, setting down the water. "Yeah, Matt, I'm good."

"You look flushed," he observed.

"It's hot in here."

"Maybe you should sit down." He worried.

"I'm pregnant, not an invalid," I pointed out.

"Where is Tarek?" he asked, looking over my head toward the bar.

"It isn't his job to babysit me, you know."

"I realize that. But the guy is good at making sure you don't overdo it," he said, looking back at me. "At least he's good for that." His lopsided smile made me grin.

I smacked him in the stomach. "Admit it. You like Tarek."

He shrugged. "He's not as bad as I first thought." He allowed. "You seem really happy, Soph." Matt reached up and tugged on the end of my ponytail.

In the three months that Tarek and I had been officially together, with him living at my apartment, Matt seemed to gradually accept him. Tarek spent a lot of weekend nights at the bar, mostly watching me and hanging out. During that time, he and Matt had developed a sort of relationship. I wouldn't really call it a friendship because they definitely wouldn't be hanging out anytime soon. It was more like mutual respect.

"I am happy." Just saying those three words made me realize how far we'd all come in three short months. Before, I wouldn't have been able to say that to Matt. I would have gotten a stomach ache just imagining it.

I never wanted to hurt Matt, but Tarek was it for me.

Matt seemed to accept that, and after a few awkward weeks, we settled back into our friendship with ease.

Matt started to turn away, but I caught his arm. "Matt?"

"Hmm?" he asked, turning back.

"Are you happy?" I wanted Matt to be happy.

"You know me." He grinned. "I'm always happy."

I did know Matt, and that's why I didn't really

believe him. True, he went back to his player ways, but something seemed a little different. He seemed less into it than before. Something whispered inside me that maybe Matt was ready to focus all his charm onto one lady.

I felt a light, warm tingle of energy race over my arms and little butterflies erupted beneath my ribcage. *Tarek must be here.* I always knew when he was nearby because I felt him before I saw him.

I picked up the tray of drinks waiting for me as my eyes searched the bar, but I didn't see him. Figuring he hadn't made his way through the crowd yet, I went around and delivered the drinks and checked on all my tables. After taking a few more orders and putting them into the computer, I glanced back at the bar.

Still, he wasn't there.

I felt a little disappointed and focused inward, looking for that rush of energy he always gave me. It wasn't there anymore. I was feeling as tired as ever.

Odd.

My eyes swept the crowd on the way out to the deck, but he wasn't anywhere to be seen. I thought about texting him but decided to wait until I had a short break.

A few minutes later, Matt waved to me from the bar, and I hurried over to get the drink order he set out for me. As I was loading it on the tray, a strange feeling of being watch slithered over me. I looked up.

My eyes met a pair of purple ones.

My lips parted on a gasp as I tried not to show too much reaction.

It wasn't Tarek.

But I would bet all of my money it was another Sapien.

It was a woman, sitting at the bar alone. She was tall and lean. She almost looked like a graceful ballerina. Her hair was very dark, thick, and long. It cascaded well down to the center of her back. Just like Tarek, her skin was very pale, her lips full, and her eyes the shade of amethyst.

But her eyes weren't like Tarek's.

They lacked the warmth of feelings.

Wariness prickled the back of my neck. The longer she watched me, the more uncomfortable I felt. She was here for me; I knew it by the way she stared. As I moved around, her eyes followed my swollen belly, like she was hungry and awed at the same time.

After I delivered all my orders, I returned to the bar. She was still watching me. God, didn't she know how rude it was to stare?

"I'm going to take five," I told Matt.

He nodded. "Take ten if you need it."

I didn't look back at the woman. Instead, I hurried toward the back into a little corner where the wait staff kept their coats and bags. It was empty except for a couple extra aprons lying around, so I sat on the little bench and pulled out my phone.

Where are you? I texted Tarek.

Seconds later, my phone buzzed with his reply.

Are you okay?

I felt a little bad that I probably worried him. I never texted when I was at work. But then I thought maybe he should be worried.

There is someone here, at the bar. I typed out.

Who? he replied.

She's like you.

I waited, but he didn't text back. I started to wonder if maybe my text hadn't gone through when I felt that familiar rush of energy over my skin again. This time it was stronger. I knew it was him. He was here.

I told myself I shouldn't be freaked that he rushed over here. Maybe he was just curious. Or maybe I should have asked more questions about the meetings he had with the other Sapiens.

Maybe the time I thought I had to ask him those things had just run out.

the unexpected

I was stupid.

Stupid to have lived in blinded bliss for the past three months. I should have asked more questions. I should have pinned him down about what would happen after the baby came.

I shouldn't have trusted him so completely.

And the fact was I did trust him.

I trusted him almost as much as I loved him.

But…

I shouldn't have let my overwhelming feelings overshadow the doubts I buried deep inside of me. The fact there was another Sapien here, and she was clearly interested in me, proved they were still very interested in my son.

(In case you are wondering, I had an ultrasound and it confirmed I was having a boy. Score for mommy spidey senses!)

As soon as I felt Tarek, I went back out into the bar, but the woman and Tarek were not there. I glanced at the door and caught a glimpse of him out on the sidewalk, and I knew she was out there with him.

It took everything in me not to storm out there and demand answers.

Instead, I kept working. Causing a scene wouldn't do any good, and the woman might talk more openly to just Tarek without me standing there glaring at her.

It seemed like forever had passed when the door finally opened and Tarek and the woman came inside. His posture was stiffer than usual, but it wasn't unfamiliar. I realized he was carrying himself the way he did when I first met him. More controlled. More rigid.

Our eyes collided and for a quick moment, stark emotion passed through them. It was almost like he was trying to say he was sorry but at the same time telling me it was going to be okay. When the woman turned toward him, all the emotion was wiped clean, and I was looking at a colder version of the man I loved.

Following his lead, I straightened my back and continued to the bar where he and the woman were sitting down.

"Hey," I said, stepping up to the corner of the bar. "Your usual?" I asked casually, and he nodded. I felt the woman's stare so I looked at her and smiled. She didn't smile back, but she didn't give me an angry look so I figured that was progress.

I stepped behind the bar and grabbed a bottle of beer out of the cooler and popped the lid before handing it across to Tarek. He took a long pull, which surprised me, but I pretended like it was normal.

Usually, he was a sipper, not a chugger.

This did not bode well.

My belly started to churn.

"You look tired," Tarek observed, setting down the bottle and studying me.

"Busy night," I answered, wanting to shout at him for an explanation.

"Come here," he said, his lilting accent calming my frayed nerves.

Not caring about our audience, I stepped around the bar and up against Tarek's side. His arm slid around me, causing a sigh to slip through my lips.

I closed my eyes and leaned into him a little farther. It never ceased to amaze me how my body seemed to absorb some of his energy, like I was a phone and he was my docking station. The further along I got with this baby, the more of his energy I seemed to need.

I understood now why pregnancy between a Sapien and a human was so unsuccessful. If Tarek wasn't here to recharge me, then my body might not be able to handle this.

I wasn't able to stay in his arms as long as I would have liked because I was at work and because I couldn't help but feel nervous about our unexpected visitor.

"So it's true," murmured the woman sitting beside Tarek.

I pulled back, about to fire a million questions, not caring in the least we were in public, but Matt sidled up beside us.

"Hey, Tarek," Matt said, holding out his fist for Tarek to give him a pound.

Tarek returned the gesture with ease because they'd been doing the same greeting for months. I noticed our little guest's eyes finally left me (thank God) and were latched onto Matt.

Apparently, Matt's good looks were just as effective on Sapien females as humans.

"I was wondering where you were tonight," Matt was saying, his eyes pulling away from Tarek and toward the woman.

"I was with my sister," Tarek said smoothly. I stiffened, but no one noticed. "This is Teagan," he said in way of introduction.

"Well, you definitely got the looks in the family," Matt said, leaning over the bar toward Tarek's "sister." "Can I get you a drink?"

Her wide purple eyes flared a little with everyone's attention fully directed on her. I waited to see what she would do. I wondered if she was surprised by Tarek's introduction, or maybe she really was his sister.

I thought he didn't have any family.

"Thank you," Teagan said to Matt, curving her lips up in a smile that I frankly thought looked like she never used it before.

Matt didn't seem to notice. He was a guy after all.

"She's a lightweight," Tarek cautioned Matt, sounding exactly like an overprotective brother. "Nothing too strong." For some reason, a pang of jealousy stirred within me.

"I need to check my tables," I said and left without another glance at any of them. My head was reeling, trying to make sense of it all.

Why was she here? What did she want? Tarek hadn't seemed pleased by her appearance, and I wanted to know why.

After making a few rounds, I reluctantly went back to the bar. Teagan was sitting there with some blue concoction with a little umbrella in it. I wanted to roll my eyes.

Matt was watching her from the other end of the bar, and Tarek was focused on his beer.

"So…" I began, drawing both Teagan's and Tarek's eyes. "How long will your sister be visiting?"

"Not long," Tarek said.

At the same time, Teagan replied, "A while."

At that moment, I wished I could drink.

The rest of the night passed like a lazy turtle. So basically, it was the longest night of my life.

I kept busy, which wasn't hard because we were slammed, but even still, I watched Teagan and Tarek together.

The blue drink Matt poured her seemed to warm up that chilly aura around her, and her smiles seemed to become a little more real. I caught them talking intensely a time or two, their heads bowed together as they whispered, and then a look or two would cut in my direction and cause my nerves to fray just a little bit more.

As the night wore on, I slowly began to unravel like a poorly knitted sweater.

When the bar finally was empty enough for some of the waitresses to be cut, I wanted to cry from the relief. I must not have done such a great job of looking like I wasn't a nervous wreck because I was the first one they told to go home.

I'd take it. I didn't even bother trying to tell them I wasn't completely exhausted. I couldn't lie that well.

Besides, I desperately wanted to talk to Tarek. Alone.

Tarek saw me walking toward him and pushed off the stool and stood. His eyes swept over me as concern darkened his features. "I'm ready to go," I said wearily.

He pulled some cash out of his pocket and laid it on the bar and turned to Teagan. "Ready?"

I slumped with disappointment. Was she coming with us? I wasn't up to dealing with her right now. I wanted to get all the info out of Tarek before I talked to her.

"I'm not done with my drink," she said, surprising me.

"Sophie is tired," Tarek said. I heard a slight chill in his tone.

"You staying at their place?" Matt said, interrupting the conversation to talk to Teagan. She glanced at Tarek and me.

"Yes."

"I'll bring her home," Matt said, waving us off. I wanted to kiss him.

"I'm not leaving her here alone," Tarek said, his eyes narrowed.

I wasn't sure if it was because he was concerned for her or if he was worried about what she would do.

Matt made a scoffing sound. "I'll make sure she gets home. We won't be that long."

Tarek hesitated. I reached out and wrapped my fingers around his and squeezed, silently asking him to go.

Matt leaned across the bar toward Tarek. "Before you came around, I'd been looking out for Soph for years. Your sister will be fine."

I didn't bother to point out that while I was apparently on Matt's watch, I got pregnant with an alien's baby.

That probably wouldn't encourage Tarek to leave Teagan.

"I'll be home shortly," Teagan said, her eyes flicking right to me. It was almost a warning. "Better get her home. She looks like she might fall over."

Tarek's attention focused fully on me, and he wrapped an arm around my shoulders. "Let's go," he said. "Thanks, Matt."

Matt waved and we left, Tarek helping me up into the passenger side of my Jeep. "This really isn't the best kind of car for a baby," I grumped, settling into the seat.

Tarek leaned down and kissed me, silencing every complaint I likely would have made next. His lips glided over mine like a cool summer breeze. His tongue caressed the juncture of my lips until I opened and he slid inside. Our tongues tangled together, and I moaned lightly as his hand came up to knead my swollen, sore breast. I pushed my chest farther into his hand because it felt so good.

After kissing me a few more moments, he pulled back and looked into my eyes. "I'm worried about you," he whispered. The pad of his thumb brushed beneath my eyes. "You look exhausted."

"Nothing a little time with you won't fix." I smiled.

He frowned and pulled away, going around to get into the driver's seat. He didn't say anything as we drove through the dark and quiet streets. I let the wind blow through my hair and make a mess of it. I pretended the worst of my worries blew up into the sky and disappeared.

When we turned onto the long road that led to my apartment, I rolled my head toward Tarek and studied his strong features in the light of the dashboard. My heart hurt a little looking at him. I never understood the saying of "loving someone so much it hurt" until I met him.

It was almost physically painful to love him.

Added to the fact I wasn't sure what the future held for us, it seemed to make me hurt worse.

"What's happening, Tarek?" I asked. My words were soft, but I knew he heard me.

He didn't answer as he parked the Jeep and came around to help me out. His hands lingered on my waist a little longer than needed, but I didn't pull away. I started for the stairs, but he caught me, swept me up into his arms, and carried me all the way up to the apartment.

Instead of stopping to reach for the keys, he used his telekinesis to turn the lock and open the door. The door closed quietly behind us, and I thought he would put me down.

He didn't.

Instead, he carried me toward the bedroom. "I want a shower," I said. I felt so sticky and gross from work that I desperately wanted to stand under the cool spray of water. I could question him while I washed.

He veered into the bathroom, the door closing behind us as he set me on my feet and reached around me to turn on the water.

I started to strip my clothes away, and I felt the heat of Tarek's stare. He was watching me with this hungry, naked expression in his eyes.

There was a sort of desperation that rolled off him, filling up the tiny bathroom. I reached around behind me for the clasp of my bra and unhooked it. My breasts spilled out, and I sighed in relief as I chucked the bra onto the floor. I couldn't help but reach out and grab them, rolling my fingers around and kneading the swollen flesh.

Tarek watched me, his eyes not once leaving my skin.

When I reached for the waistband of my shorts, he pushed off the wall and came forward, replacing my hands with his and gently peeling away the fabric and bending to take them off my legs. His fingers skimmed up my bare legs, leaving a trail of tingles in his wake as he hooked two fingers in the waistband of my panties and slid those down as well.

Once I kicked away the fabric, he looked up at me as his fingers reached for the area between my thighs I could no longer see. Anticipation singed through my blood as his fingers probed my folds, delicately dipping between them. I moaned just a little and spread my feet out on the floor to give him greater access.

Tarek shifted closer and positioned himself just under me. His tongue came out to stroke across my slit, and I grabbed onto the nearby counter for support.

Using his hand, he parted my folds and then began licking and sucking the most tender flesh on my body. Arousal dampened my opening, and he lapped it up like it was the best thing he'd ever tasted. His thumb found my clit and pressed down on it, gyrating it around and creating a delicious friction that caused my knees to wobble.

I moaned as two fingers slid into my entrance and scissored open, stretching my inner walls and causing my lower abdominals to spasm.

"Tarek," I whispered, shoving my hands into his hair as he grabbed a hold of my hips and began eating me out with a ferocity that made it hard to breathe.

His tongue was everywhere, sliding over every inch of me and swirling into my juice-slickened hole as he groaned his pleasure.

Just as I was about to beg for sweet release, he stood and lifted me into the shower. The cool spray was jolting compared to the way my blood boiled, but it was a welcome feeling.

Tarek disappeared on the other side of the curtain and then appeared just seconds later, completely naked.

His incredible thick rod jutted out from his body, pointing at me like it knew exactly what it wanted. His ab muscles contracted with the deep breaths he pulled in as he reached around me for the bar of soap. After his hands were completely sudsy, he began washing me.

My breasts must have been very dirty because he concentrated the most on them, rubbing the soap around and flicking his fingers over my nipples until they tightened in delight. When I was panting and leaning toward him, he reached around my back and cupped my butt, spreading my cheeks open just a little and sliding his fingers down my crack. His forefinger circled around my anus and then moved on, delving into my wet depths from behind. As he fingered me, his other hand went down the front of my body and met my clit. He rolled the swollen bud between his fingers, and I moaned loudly.

My orgasm ripped over me with blinding ferocity. Even as my body shook with pleasure, I collapsed against him. His solid body supported me with ease as he continued to work my opening like an expert.

My teeth sank into his chest as the orgasm rolled on and on, until finally I started to come back to reality.

Very slowly, Tarek pulled his fingers out of me and grabbed me by the hips. He pulled back and looked at me, water cascading down his face and rolling over his lips.

I leaned up and sucked off a large droplet, swallowing it down as he kissed me with intensity. Once again, I felt desperation flowing off him in waves, and I opened myself up to him, giving him what he seemed to need.

"If I hurt you at all, tell me immediately," he said, reaching up to fondle my breasts once more.

I nodded and then he turned me around and bent me over so the water sprayed over my lower back. I braced my hands on the wall of the shower and spread my legs as Tarek moved behind me.

In a gentle, protective move, he ran his hand over my stomach, making sure I wasn't hunched over too far.

I wiggled my butt, and he moaned. The head of his penis probed my entrance, and I jutted my butt out just a little bit more to give him greater access.

Tarek plunged his cock inside me with one long stroke. I felt every inch of him slide inside me. He reached up and grabbed my breast, filling his hand with it as he began to thrust his hips. His cock slid in and out of me with perfect ease as water from the shower ran over our bodies and the thick juices from inside me coated him.

He took me hard and fast without being rough. I felt his heavy balls slapping against me, and I cried out because the sensation was just so good.

I felt his thigh muscles stiffen, and I knew he was close to release. I braced my arms against the wall and rocked my hips back, taking him even deeper.

He made this sound, a cross between a growl and a moan. It bubbled up out of his chest, and I ground my hips down onto his cock.

He began to pulsate inside me. I felt his seed spill, shooting deep within me and filling me up. He thrust in me over and over as his cock quivered with his release and small gasps of breath filled the shower stall.

When he was at last sated, he drew me up so my back was pressed against his chest and his semi-erect cock was pressing against my backside. Tarek wrapped one strong arm around the top of my belly, anchoring me into his chest, and then his other hand skirted low, between my thighs.

His entire hand slid into my core and rubbed with great friction, causing delicious little ripples of pleasure to shoot through my body.

His two center fingers thrust inside me, and his thumb began working my slit.

I rocked my hips back and forth frantically, my body craving release.

I called out his name when I started to come. Everything but the feel of his hand and fingers working me fell away.

When I was okay to stand on my own, Tarek finished washing me as I stood there completely limber and totally sated.

Then next thing I knew, I was being wrapped in a fluffy towel and lifted out of the shower. In a tender display, he brushed through my washed hair before bending to dry my legs so I wouldn't have to.

When I was totally dry, I watched him dry himself (using the same towel) and then toss it over the shower curtain rod.

After making sure we were still alone, he took my hand and led me into the bedroom, where he shut the door behind us.

Since he'd moved in, I'd taken a liking to wearing his shirts, but only the ones that he'd worn and smelled just like him. Tarek knew this and would put his shirts on a nearby chair after he'd worn them so I could slip them on when we were home.

He snatched one up, a dark-gray one that felt like combed cotton, and slid it over my head. Even seven months pregnant, the shirt was roomy on me. I sighed a little as his scent wrapped around me.

Since I knew Teagan was going to be coming over, I pulled on a pair of panties and cotton sleep shorts.

Tarek dressed in a white T-shirt and a pair of worn-looking jeans.

"She's going to be here soon," I told him.

He nodded.

"Tell me, Tarek." I began, sitting down on the edge of the bed. "Who is Teagan and why is she really here?"

the lie

I prepared myself for whatever was coming.

Okay, that's a lie. I wasn't prepared for any of this. I had no idea what he was going to say. But judging from the look on his face, I knew it wasn't good.

"You've never lied to me before," I told him. "Don't start now."

"I will not lie to you," he vowed.

I sat farther back on the bed, resting my back against the pillows. I felt better now that I was home, showered, and had a mind-blowing orgasm, but I was still exhausted.

Tarek seemed to realize this, and he sat down beside me and picked up my hand to gently fold it in his.

"The other Sapiens are not too happy that I am living here with you."

"Why?" I asked, swallowing the knot in my throat.

"Because we didn't come here to cohabitate. We didn't even come here to interact with humans. We came to repopulate our race."

"And you are," I said, rubbing a hand over my belly.

"We always meant to take the child, Sophie. To raise it as a Sapien. To take the new children back to our planet."

I stiffened and ripped my hand away from him. "You said you wouldn't take him."

He frowned.

"You said you were going to stay here with me."

"Calm down." He cautioned as my voice became shrill.

"I will not!" I yelled, trying to roll away from him.

I was still moving like a watermelon with legs, and I didn't get away fast enough. Tarek snaked an arm around me and pulled me back onto the bed and up against him.

"I don't want you to touch me," I said, struggling against him.

"Hush," he said, not letting go. "Listen to me. I do plan to stay here," he said quickly, and my struggles died away. "In the beginning, I planned to take the child, but you changed all that."

"What do you mean?" I said, glancing over my shoulder at him. I desperately wanted him to reassure me.

"I love you," he said.

I sucked in a breath. "What?"

"It's the most powerful emotion I've ever felt," he said, brushing a finger down the side of my cheek. "I didn't know a person could feel so… connected to someone else."

"Tarek," I whispered.

"I love you, Sophie. I'm not taking this baby from you. I want to raise him. Here. With you."

I started to cry. Big, fat silent tears rolled over my cheeks, dipping into my lips. They were salty when I licked at them.

Tarek wiped them away, his eyes never once leaving my face.

"I love you, too," I whispered.

His eyes shut briefly, like the words overwhelmed him. Then he leaned in and kissed me softly, murmuring words in some language I'd never heard before.

"What does it mean?" I asked him.

"It means you're my heart."

I laid my head against his shoulder as he wrapped his arms around me.

"They don't want you to stay here, do they?" I asked, feeling a little less afraid now that I knew he loved me.

"No. All the meetings I have had with them… They are growing increasingly angry. They say they can see the way I've changed, and they don't trust I will take the baby when the time comes."

"Did you tell them you won't?"

"No. I lie. I tell them I am going to, but they are beginning to doubt me."

"She's here to take him, isn't she?" I said, hating Teagan even more.

"She's here to watch us. To make sure I don't try to run off with you and our son. She's to report back to the others about you and me."

"And when he's born?" I prodded.

"When he's born, they expect me to bring him to them."

"And if you don't?"

He was silent a long time, and my stomach twisted at all the possibilities. I really had no defense. I was up against an alien race, for goodness sakes. The only thing that stood between me and them was Tarek.

Was he strong enough to protect us from everyone?

"They'll come get him themselves."

His words cut me like a sharpened blade. The protective instincts in me roared. The thought of anyone coming to take my child from me made me sick with rage.

I pulled away from Tarek, suddenly very angry.

"This is your fault," I told him quietly, turning my back and throwing my feet over the edge of the bed. "If you hadn't taken me onto your ship, if you had just left me alone, I wouldn't be pregnant with freaking aliens after my child."

"Yes," he said solemnly.

At least he didn't try to make excuses for himself.

"They can't have my son," I said, standing. I felt like I'd said this a thousand times. It was a constant echo through my body.

"I won't let them take him," Tarek said, his tone even.

I swung around, angry. "Yeah? And what are you going to do, Tarek? How are you going to stop them? There is one of you and many of them."

He stared at me, his eyes vacant. I knew I wasn't being nice, but everything I said was the truth. I loved Tarek, but I wouldn't let my love for him cost me my child.

And it dawned on me then.

I realized Tarek wasn't the only one caught in the middle. He was caught between me and his people.

And I…

I was caught between him and our child.

Even more startling than that was the realization that it really wasn't a contest. My child would win. I would choose my baby over Tarek. I would do it without thought.

And so…

Why wouldn't he do the same?

Why wouldn't he just take his child and go back to his people? He would have what he came here for and the admiration of all the others because he was the only

Sapien to manage an heir.

"All this time, I thought you never lied to me," I whispered.

His eyes widened when the sorrow of my voice hit him. "Sophie." He slid off the bed to come closer, but I backed away, not wanting to feel his touch. Feeling him would only make it harder.

"You still plan to take him."

"I don't want to take him, Sophie. I want to stay here with you."

"You might not want to take him," I said, my heart breaking, "but you will. If faced with the choice of me or this child."

"I won't let that happen."

He didn't deny it.

"Maybe it wasn't me you've been lying to all this time," I whispered, "but yourself."

The look in his eyes, the naked pain that radiated down to the core of his purple stare, made a sob rip from deep within me.

I turned and fled the room, knowing I couldn't outrun the conversation we just had, knowing no amount of distance would ever erase that look in his eyes from my memory. I stopped in the living room, my rushed steps coming to a halt.

Running was kind of stupid.

Where was I going to go?

Besides, I knew I needed to stay near Tarek, due to the high energy demands of this baby. He was my supply. Running was out, but that didn't mean I couldn't get a little space. Maybe clear my head, try and shove some of the pain and confusion I was feeling deep inside me.

I heard Tarek behind me, and I stiffened. At the same time, there was a knock on the door.

"It's Matt," he said from the other side.

I rushed toward it, grateful for the interruption, and pulled it wide.

Distaste coated my mouth when I saw Teagan standing there beside Matt. My fingers curled into my palm with the intense urge to claw out her perfectly shaped and uniquely colored eyes.

I flicked a cold glance at her, then completely turned away to address Matt. He saw the unshed tears in my eyes before I even opened my mouth.

His eyes narrowed and he stared behind me to where I was sure Tarek was standing.

"What the fuck did you do?" he said, low.

"Matt," I whispered, not wanting an argument.

Matt ignored me and stepped into the apartment, moving toward Tarek. "Why does she look like someone just kicked her puppy? What did you say to her?"

"I don't really think this is your business," Tarek said calmly.

Matt laughed. It really wasn't the humorous kind.

Teagan moved into my apartment, looking around curiously, like she was taking in every detail.

I couldn't deal with her right now. "Matt," I said, drawing his attention away from Tarek. "Can we talk?"

"Sure thing," he said, glancing back at Tarek before turning his back and coming to my side. He draped an arm across my shoulders and I resisted the urge to lean into him.

I felt alone.

Lonely in a room full of people.

In a sense, I was alone. No one knew what was really going on. No one but Tarek and Teagan. I couldn't talk to them because they were part of the problem. I couldn't call my mom and get her advice. I couldn't call anyone.

But Matt was here. Through everything, he'd been constant. A friend when I needed one most. Yeah, maybe in a different world, we would have been more than friends, and maybe that was better. Maybe that connection made me feel like I could turn to him to feel just a little less alone.

I could feel Tarek's displeasure, but I ignored it. This wasn't about him. It was about me and getting what I needed.

We started toward the door when Teagan stepped close. "Where are you going?" She leveled an intense stare on me.

"Out." I sniffed.

"Sophie," Tarek said from behind.

I stiffened beneath Matt's arm and he tightened his grip. "I'll keep an eye on her," Matt told Teagan, giving her a half smile. "Your nephew will be fine."

I felt all the blood rush from my head as Teagan's gaze sharpened. "It's a boy?"

She hadn't known.

I looked at Tarek. His expression was hooded. I couldn't tell what he was thinking. What did it mean that he had withheld the sex of the baby from the others?

"Oops," Matt said sheepishly. "Was it supposed to be a surprise?"

"Not at all." I lied. "We just hadn't told Teagan yet."

Now seemed like a pretty good time to get the hell out of the room. "Can we go?" I asked Matt.

"Yeah, come on." He led me out the door, and when I stepped into the hallway, Tarek called my name.

The emotion I heard in his voice was almost my undoing. "I'll be back," I told him. Then I shut the door behind us.

the friendship

I wasn't sure what to say or where to start when we were alone. I knew I couldn't tell him everything. Hell, I couldn't even tell him half. But I needed to tell him something. Anything that might help ease the terrible weight sitting on my chest.

We were outside, and the summer air turned cooler in the late-night hour. The sky above us was inky black and only a few stars shone through. We walked down the stairs, and I sat down on a cement retaining wall, one that held various landscaping.

Matt dropped down beside me, his arm and shoulder brushing against mine.

"What's up, Soph?" he asked, his tone light.

"I'm scared, Matt," I admitted, staring out into the darkness.

"Did he hurt you…?" he asked, his voice trailing away. "By the way he looks at you, I wouldn't have thought—" He began, but I cut him off.

"He hasn't hurt me," I hurried to say. "He would never lay a hand on me."

"Then what are you scared of?" he asked, shifting a little closer. His closeness made me feel better, made me feel like it was okay to open up a little.

"Did you ever feel like you thought you knew where your life was headed, like you knew the people in your life, but then suddenly, it's like you know nothing at all?"

"I think being confused is a part of life," he whispered. "And sometimes even knowing who you are and choosing to hide it is just as confusing."

I titled my head. "Is that why you dress like a preppy boy even though I know underneath it is all rocker dude?"

He smiled. "Something like that."

I opened my mouth to ask him more, but he put his arm around me. "We're talking about you."

Talking about him was easier. I sighed.

"Tarek's family doesn't like me," I said.

"How could anyone not like you?" he asked.

I giggled. "Right? I'm totally lovable."

His arm tightened around me. "You totally are."

My stomach flipped. Maybe I shouldn't be talking to him about this. Maybe our history wouldn't make him easier to confide in, but harder.

As if he read my mind, he added. "It's okay, Soph. We're friends before anything."

"I need a friend right now, Matt."

"Good thing I'm here."

I rested my head against his shoulder.

"His family doesn't like me. They want him to take the baby when he's born back to… back to his country so it can be raised there, with them."

"That's ridiculous."

"Yeah," I said. "We've been fighting about it." Okay, Tarek and I hadn't really been fighting about it until now, but it'd been an ongoing worry for me. "Then Teagan shows up out of the blue. I feel like she came here to spy on me."

"Well, that would explain why she asked me a hundred questions about you."

I glanced up. "Really? What did she say?"

He shrugged. "I thought it was just sisterly concern," he said. "She wanted to know how you've been with your pregnancy, how you and Tarek get along, how he is with you… stuff like that."

"What did you say?"

"I said you're great and Tarek takes really good care of you."

"You did?" Emotion welled up in my throat. Tarek did take good care of me. Just thinking about it hurt.

"I can't imagine she would want to take your son," he said.

"Well, she does."

"What the hell kind of country do they live in?" he muttered.

I ignored him because I didn't know how to answer.

"I'm very afraid Tarek will do what they want. That he will take away my baby."

Matt was silent for long moments. Then he sighed. "Look, you know Tarek isn't my favorite person. When he first showed up, the urge to punch him in the face every time I looked at him was pretty strong."

I laughed.

"But," he said, giving me a squeeze, "as much as I hate to say this, I don't think he's a bad guy. I see the way he looks at you, Soph. It's like you hung the moon or something. You're his entire world."

"You really think that?" I whispered, desperately wanting it to be true.

"I really do. It's kind of odd because when he looks at everyone else, he seems kind of… empty. It'd be creepy if I didn't see the way he was when you were around. He loves you, Soph."

If I wasn't so scared and overwhelmed, I would be overjoyed. "What if it's not enough?" I said, the words ripping from deep inside me.

Matt fell silent. I felt his thoughts turn inward, and I wanted to ask what he was thinking, but I didn't want to pry. Instead, I rested my head against him and stared out into the dark yard, breathing in the cool summer air and trying to calm my tattered nerves.

After a long time, Matt said, "If it's not enough, I'll be here."

My chest constricted. Did Matt still care about me? Like, as more than just friends? I knew it was probably terribly selfish, but his words made me feel better. Just knowing that he would be here made me less scared.

"Matt, I can't ask you to put your life on hold for me."

"You didn't ask," he rumbled. "I offered. And my life isn't on hold. I'm still living it."

"With Teagan?" I teased, even though the thought of Matt with her made me sick.

He chuckled. "She is smoking hot," he said. "And I kind of like watching her reactions to my flirting."

"You've been *flirting* with her?" I said.

"Jealous?" He grinned.

I sputtered, not sure what to say. I wasn't jealous, not really. I knew eventually Matt would find someone, but I didn't want it to be *her.*

"Relax," he said, kissing me on the side of my head. "I'm just teasing."

I made a sound in the back of my throat.

"Maybe I was interested. But if she's seriously giving you problems, I'm going to steer clear. There's no way I'd get involved with someone who was trying to hurt you."

Tears pricked the backs of my eyes. I wrapped my arms around his waist and hugged him hard. "Thank you for being here, Matt. You mean a lot to me."

"Yeah," he said, returning the hug. "Ditto."

The sound of someone clearing his throat behind us had me pulling away from Matt and looking over my shoulder.

"Tarek," I said.

His eyes glittered in the dark, and his pale skin stood out in the moonlit night. "I do not like when you touch her," he said, cold.

"Chill, man," Matt said, getting up from his seat beside me. "We were just talking."

"Looked like more than talking to me," he said curtly.

I sighed.

"Why don't I give you guys a minute?" Matt offered. "I'll go see what Teagan is doing up there all by herself."

My back stiffened.

Matt laughed. "She's probably snooping through all your stuff."

"That's not funny," I growled.

"Relax," he replied, laying a hand on my shoulder. "I'll go keep her occupied."

He didn't sound the least put out by the job.

"Thanks," I said as he walked away.

I knew Tarek was still there, but I didn't look at him. Instead, I stared straight forward, searching for the right words to say.

He walked around to stand in front of me so all I could see was him. Slowly, he crouched down before me, bringing us face to face. "You turned to him," he said, not angrily. Not even accusingly. It was more like it hurt him.

"I didn't turn to him," I whispered. "We were just talking. I needed to talk to someone."

"You have me."

"Do I?" I asked, my voice cracking. I looked right into his eyes.

"I'll choose you," he said.

"You would choose me over an entire race of people? Your own people?"

"You're my people now," he whispered, reaching out and hovering his hand above my stomach. I knew he wanted to touch me, but he wasn't sure if I wanted him to. "You and my son are the only people that matter to me."

I made a sound and grabbed his hand, pressing it against the spot where our baby lay within me.

"I'm really scared, Tarek." The words tumbled out of me like rain from a storm cloud.

"I'm going to make this right," he vowed. "I'm going to protect you. And him." He caressed my stomach.

I believed him.

God help me, I believed he would choose me and this baby.

"They aren't going to accept this." I worried. "Right this second, Teagan is in our home, plotting against us."

"They won't have a choice." His voice reminded me of the way it was when I first met him. Cold, uncaring… lacking any kind of emotion.

I shivered. What kind of fight was I bringing this baby into?

"I'd like to touch you now," Tarek said softly. "To hold you."

Before I could even finish nodding, he scooped me up and sat down with me in his lap. He held me close, his arms like steel bands around me. "It… hurt when you walked out with Matt," he said, like he was trying to make sense of the emotion. "Like something inside my chest had broken."

"Does it still hurt?" I whispered, not lifting my head from his chest.

"Not anymore," he said, his lips brushing the top of my head. "I don't ever want to feel that way again," he murmured. "I won't let them take you from me."

I wondered if he would have a choice.

the bacon

I woke to gentle, affectionate hands caressing my skin. He started at the small of my back, gliding his fingertips over my spine and into the dip of my hipbone. Slowly, he dragged them upward over the side of my ribs and over my arm.

Little tingles of pleasure invaded my still half-asleep brain and made me settle more closely against the sheets. Tarek walked his fingers downward, across the side of my rounded, enlarged breast, and my body arched into his touch, demanding more.

He palmed the heaviness of my breast, massaging the flesh and making me moan low in my throat. Immediately, my nipple responded, puckering into a hard pebble and aching for more.

As he massaged me, I reached around behind me to grasp the thick, hard length of him. Tarek was so hard it excited me. I knew all too well what it felt like for him to drive his steely rod into me. To massage me from the inside out.

Moisture dampened between my legs, and I rolled onto my back, forgoing the foreplay, wanting him inside me now.

Tarek nuzzled the side of my neck. His breath fluttered the wisps of hair away from my skin as his lips nipped at the sensitive flesh. I rolled my head to give him greater access as he kissed his way down across my collarbone. He drew my aching nipple into his mouth and rolled it around on his tongue. He sucked it harder into his mouth, applying wanted pressure and making my toes curl into the sheets.

I grabbed his bicep and pulled on him, impatient.

His throaty chuckle only served to make me want him more.

I spread my legs eagerly as he moved over me and settled between my legs. "Is this okay, my love?" he whispered as two fingers tested my entrance. Tarek never entered my body without knowing I was ready for him.

"Yes," I moaned. I wanted him inside me. I knew he was only concerned about me and the fact I was merely weeks away from delivering, but I needed him. Now.

He slid into me with ease. I moaned loudly and gripped his arms. God, he felt so good. My entire body was a giant sensitized nerve, and he knew exactly how to touch me.

He held himself over me. I wanted to feel his weight push me into the bed, but I didn't bother to ask. I knew he wouldn't. Ever since my belly grew like I was smuggling a basketball, Tarek wouldn't let me support his weight.

As if he knew where my thoughts were headed, he began to move within me, and thoughts of everything else fled my brain.

All I could do was feel.

Feel the rigid length of him spear me, feel his smooth cock glide against my inner walls and bury deep within me. He moved slowly until I panted his name and grabbed at the pillow nearby. Only then did he whisper my name and begin to move faster.

I groaned and dug my nails into his forearms as he took me on a ride. Sensation after sensation rolled over me, and I began to meet his thrusts with my own, pushing my body against his, grinding my pelvis against his hard lower body.

The orgasm came swift and hard, but it pulsated through me thoroughly and lingered even as he continued to move. My body fell spent against the mattress as I widened my legs so he could delve into me one last time before his entire body turned rigid and I felt him pump into me.

I flexed my inner walls around him, and he shuddered anew.

Moments later, he rolled away and settled back beside me. I rolled onto my side and tucked my hand under my cheek, studying his sculpted, marble-like features in the very dim lighting of the early day.

His galactic gaze swept over me, and he pushed some dampened strands of hair away from my face. He whispered a string of words in the language of his planet, the most poetic, languid speech I had ever heard. He did that a lot these days. Ever since he told me loved me just over a week ago.

He spoke to me in his native tongue, whispering the most beautiful things I didn't understand. But I didn't have to understand the exact meaning of every word he spoke because I knew the intent behind every single syllable.

I understood he was sharing something about himself, showing me a part of who he was before he came here.

Frankly, even if he hadn't said I love you, I would have known.

I felt it.

I tasted it.

I lived it.

His love was tangible. It was authentic, and it was entirely mine.

"I love you," I whispered, knowing my words didn't compare to his. But the look on his face every time I told him was like watching a full moon rise in his gaze and reflect off the stars that lived in the amethyst of his stare.

I liked to hope my words affected him as much as his did me.

He grasped my hand and pulled up to his lips, brushing a feather-light kiss across the tops of my knuckles.

"Morning is my favorite time of day," he murmured.

I smiled. "Because every morning we have sex?"

He shook his head and kissed the back of my hand again. "No. Because every morning when I open my eyes, I see you, and I realize it hadn't all been a dream, that you, my love, are my reality. You're more than I ever thought possible."

Well, damn.

Those were some pretty English words.

"You're more than I ever thought possible, too," I whispered.

He grinned. "I like the sex, too."

I laughed. It was moments like these that gave me hope. Moments where we were so blindly in love that I didn't think it was possible it could all be ripped away. It was times like this that made me believe Tarek and I would beat all odds, that whatever divine force brought us together would never have done so if we were to be ripped so violently apart.

I closed my eyes as I did every single morning and tried to memorize the way I felt in the moment. It was a feeling that would carry me through the times of doubt. The times when Teagan was watching me like a hawk and it was all I could do to not stab her with anything in reach.

Please. Like you didn't expect that? I was fat, hormonal, I felt threatened, and I wanted some bacon.

That's like a recipe for murder.

"You're hungry," Tarek said.

He wasn't reading my mind. I was always hungry. "I want bacon," I announced.

He rolled his eyes. "You ate it all yesterday."

I help up my hand. "If you so much as suggest I eat a banana instead, I might bite you."

"I might like it." He grinned.

His grin was sexy as hell.

"Bacon." I reminded him.

He rolled swiftly and gracefully out of bed. I momentarily forgot about my craving for bacon as I stared at his naked butt.

Too soon, he pulled on a pair of jeans and turned to me. He wasn't wearing underwear—he rarely ever did—and the fly and button were still undone.

The V-shaped muscle on either side of his hips cut deep and delved down into the open waistband of his jeans.

"I don't need bacon," I said. "Come back to bed."

He chuckled. "I will not let you and my son

starve," he said, buttoning the jeans and earning a dirty look from me.

"But after you have him, we are going to work on your eating habits."

It was like a switch flipped inside me.

After.

I tried to never think about after I had this baby. It was far too much uncertainty. Everything was still safe, still happy when he was inside me.

It was the after that scared me most.

Tarek talked like nothing would change, but I couldn't help but be scared nothing would be the same.

"Hey," he said, leaning back onto the bed, bringing his face close to mine. "None of that." He kissed the tip of my nose. "I've got everything under control."

"You really think Teagan is going to abandon everything she was sent here to do and side with us?" I asked doubtfully.

She'd been here a little over a week. She watched our every move. She was like a permanent fixture in this house. I tolerated her because Tarek asked me to. Mostly, I tried to pretend she wasn't there.

Tarek was convinced if we exposed her enough to human life, to our relationship, to emotion, that she would come to realize that taking this baby was the wrong thing to do. Tarek seemed to think her siding with him would go a long way in convincing the other Sapiens they were wrong.

I wasn't as convinced as he was. But I'd try anything.

So far, I didn't seem to notice she was affected at all by our life, the way were together, nor did she show any signs of support for us.

She was, however, keen on Matt.

Big surprise there.

Not.

"I think it's definitely a possibility. I know what it's like to be surrounded by emotion for the first time. She can't be unaffected. She'll come around." He gave me a hopeful, boyish look, and I couldn't help but smile.

"I'm going to the store to get some more of that animal fat you like."

I gasped. "How dare you demoralize my bacon!" I threw a pillow at him and he caught it.

"I'll be sure and bring you some fruit, too." Tarek grinned and tossed the pillow beside me. "I'll be back, love."

"I'll miss you!" I called after him.

I heard his answering chuckle echo back through the hall.

I wallowed in bed for long moments, inhaling his scent off the sheets and, pretty much, craving bacon. A sound from out in the kitchen caught my attention, and I listened harder. It sounded like the microwave was running and someone was rummaging in the cupboard.

Tarek only left minutes ago; I knew it wasn't him.

I got out of bed and pulled on some necessary undergarments and a black cotton sundress. I loved the way the soft, roomy fabric didn't constrict my ever-growing waist.

I didn't bother with a brush for my long, tangled hair, and I walked down the hall, listening as the noise in the kitchen grew louder.

I knew exactly who I'd see when I turned the corner.

I stopped in the doorway and stared, watching as Teagan made herself a cup of hot tea, added a copious amount of honey, and grabbed an orange out of the bowl on the counter. When she turned, her eyes met mine.

We stared at each other for long moments, neither of us saying a word.

Suddenly, I wished I hadn't asked for bacon.

Tarek was gone.

He left me alone.

For the first time.

With the woman who wanted to kidnap my baby.

the confrontation

I thought about cautiously backing away like one might in a room full of angry snakes. But then I remembered this was my house. I'd been doing nothing but tiptoeing around, avoiding her, and trying to be as inconspicuous as I could.

Screw that shit.

She was on my turf.

Tarek had been trying to show her what it was to be among humans, and I hadn't exactly been helpful. I hadn't given her a reason, or even a chance, to get to know me or like me.

She couldn't sympathize with someone she didn't know.

I walked into the room as she lowered herself onto one of the two bistro chairs in the corner. I was aware of her watching me, her wide eyes almost catlike. So I turned and smiled.

"Morning," I chirped as I reached for a small glass, then turned to the fridge for juice.

"Morning," she echoed. She had the same accent as Tarek, yet it didn't affect me like his did.

Teagan looked beautiful, as always. Her long, dark hair was glossy and straight. She probably got out of bed looking like that—just like Tarek. Her purple eyes were almond-shaped, exotic, and rimmed with dark lashes. I knew she wasn't wearing makeup, but she didn't need any. She was just that pretty.

Her posture was rigid, her body reed thin, and she was dressed in a pair of skinny white jeans (yes, white, and they looked perfect) and a flowy-looking blue, sleeveless blouse. Beneath the table, her small feet were a contradiction to her height and long limbs, and they were bare.

Maybe I should have attempted to comb my hair.

On second thought, maybe my looks would scare her. Ha.

After I poured my juice, I went over to the table and sat across from her. She remained stoic, but I knew she was surprised by the way her lips flattened.

"I realized we haven't really spoken since you, uh, came to visit," I said.

"You mean since I came to watch you?" she said.

"That too." I refused to be intimidated by her any longer.

I sipped the juice while I studied her. She'd spent all this time staring at me, so I figured it was time I returned the favor.

I watched as she skillfully peeled the orange in front of her. She placed long ribbons of the orange skin beside her tea, arranging them in a neat little stack. I watched her fingers move, noticing the long shape of her trimmed, unpolished nails. She wasn't wearing any jewelry either, and it made me wonder if the rest of the women on her planet were as unadorned as her.

"Do women wear jewelry where you're from?" I asked. "Paint their nails, wear makeup?"

She paused in peeling. "We do not place importance on physical possessions or the way we look."

"Must be easy not to care how you look when it's nothing less than beautiful all the time."

She glanced at me. "You think I'm beautiful?"

Her question surprised me because she acted like she had no idea how beautiful she was.

"Of course. Surely everyone does."

She shrugged. I remembered what Tarek told me, about how he was supposedly “average-looking,” and wondered if Teagan was just another example of average where she came from.

“Matt thinks so too,” I said, watching her closely to gauge her reaction.

“He does?” Teagan abandoned the orange completely and looked at me straight on, true interest in her eyes.

I nodded. “Definitely.” I paused. “He’s a good guy.”

“He isn’t like the other males I know,” she replied.

“Matt definitely dances to the beat of his own drum.” I agreed.

The expression clearly confused her so I backpedaled to say, “Matt is a unique guy. That’s what makes him special.”

She nodded and resumed taking apart her orange.

“Do you like it here?” I asked.

She shrugged. “It’s okay.”

“Is it very different from Sapia?”

“I don’t remember Sapia. I haven’t been there for a very long time.”

"Where have you been, then?" I asked.

"Mostly on a hovercraft."

"Sounds lonely," I murmured.

She ignored me and drank her tea.

"I really love him, you know," I said quietly, after several long minutes of silence.

"That's going to be difficult for you when he leaves," Teagan replied. "Your kind is very emotional."

My stomach twisted at her matter-of-fact tone of voice. I raised my chin. "And you think being emotional is a bad thing?"

"I think it makes you weak."

"Says the woman whose planet is dying off." I countered.

I was rewarded with a flare of something in her eyes. But then they went back to that cold, emotionless expression and glanced at my baby bump. "Not for much longer."

"So that's your answer, then?" I prodded, anger creeping into my tone. "To take other women's babies and repopulate your planet?"

"That baby is ours," she replied haughtily.

"Since he's growing inside *my* body, I would have to say he's mostly mine."

That seemed to shut her up.

I drank my juice and continued to stare at her. I hope it made her uncomfortable. While I stared, I wondered how much longer Tarek would be.

"What's it like?" she asked, taking me off guard. "To be pregnant?"

She seemed genuinely interested, almost wistful. Something inside me softened toward her in that moment. Surely, she had tried to conceive. All the women from Sapia had likely been trying, considering the dire situation of their people dying off.

And since she was sitting here before me, completely slim, totally planning to steal my son, I could accurately surmise that she was totally not pregnant.

"I've never felt anything like it," I said honestly. "I was scared at first, you know?" I said, my hands automatically going to my stomach.

She nodded so I would continue.

"But it's hard to be scared of something when you love it so much."

"You love that baby?" she asked, like it wouldn't be obvious.

"Of course I do," I said immediately. "He's been living inside me, growing. I feel him move. He's part of me."

She was watching me aptly, so I kept talking.

"It's hard to explain because even though technically I've never met him, I know him. And he knows me. I've been with him every single second of every single day. I can't wait to hold him. To look into his tiny face. I think he's going to look like Tarek. At least, I hope he does," I said sheepishly.

Sadness washed over her features, and I felt sorry for her. "You want to have a child, don't you?"

"More than anything," she answered, looking away.

"Tarek told me the babies on your planet are taken from their mothers and are not raised by either parent. I think that's incredibly sad."

"It's the way we do things," she answered. It made me think she'd been programmed to think that way. I wondered if she would agree with it if she had a choice.

"If you stayed here, you would be allowed to keep your child. To form a bond with her or him. It might make conceiving a lot easier."

"Are you suggesting I betray my people like Tarek?"

Anger sliced through me. How dare she say he's a traitor? I felt my eyes flash as I stared at her. "Tarek hasn't betrayed anyone. He came here to help ensure the survival of your people. He stayed with me because it was the best way to ensure this child survived. We fell in love. Falling in love is not a crime. If anything, your people could learn something from him. He's being punished for doing what you wanted."

"We didn't want him to fall in love. We didn't want him to become loyal to you."

"I feel sorry for you," I snapped. "You spend all your days plotting ways to take my life from me instead of getting a life of your own."

Her eyes narrowed.

"If you ask me, the reason you can't conceive is because you're coldhearted. You have no idea what it takes to love a child. To love anything."

I got up from the table, unable to sit there another second. Screw trying to make her like me. I would never like her so it was useless.

"I want you gone," I spat. "Tarek is far more tolerant of you, which I guess you consider another weakness." I tossed the words at her with heat. "I'm done. Get out of my house."

"I don't need to conceive to have a child," Teagan said, her words almost taunting.

A little prickle of unease climbed up my spine, but I ignored it. "Well, good luck with that," I said. "Now get the hell out."

"I'm not going anywhere until I get what I came for," she replied, still sitting at the table.

Inside me, the baby kicked out, like he heard her words and was disturbed by them.

Realization dawned.

Absolute horror struck me to my core.

I placed my hands over my stomach protectively and swung to stare at Teagan. "They told you that you could have him," I whispered.

She smiled. "Seems I will have a life of my own very, very soon."

"You can't have him," I told her, backing up. I was completely sickened at the thought of them handing my son over to this uncaring, cold, and emotionless bitch.

He would never know a day of warmth in his life.

"Tarek will never let you have him." I threatened. Maybe she would be more intimidated by the idea of his anger than mine.

She smiled. "Tarek doesn't get a say. He's done his job. He's created an heir. He's of no use to us anymore."

I gasped. "What the hell does that mean?"

"It means once this baby is safely delivered, he will be removed."

They were going to kill Tarek? Panic rose up inside me. This woman was completely insane. What the hell kind of people were these? They were plotting to steal my child, kill Tarek, and… "What about me?" I whispered.

Her cold eyes stared at me as if daring me to figure it out.

So they were going to kill me too.

Like fucking hell.

I continued to back away from her, going farther into the kitchen. My back hit the counter, and I slid a few steps down, bringing my back against the drawer I wanted.

God, she was so sick, just sitting there calmly at my table, sipping her tea like she didn't just announce her plan to kill people.

'There's one problem with your plan," I said, sliding open the drawer behind me.

"Is there?" she asked, lifting a perfectly sculpted brow.

I pulled out the biggest knife I had and wielded it in front of me. "Yeah. You won't be able to kill me if you're already dead."

I rushed her, holding the knife like I was some sicko in a horror movie. Maybe I was sick for doing this, but it was her or me. Eat or be eaten.

I'd do anything to protect this baby.

Teagan's eyes widened as I barreled toward her. I swung the knife down as she leapt away from the table, sending her chair clattering to the floor. I knocked into the tabletop, and her teacup fell onto the floor, shattering everywhere around our feet.

I stepped toward her once more, backing her into the wall, feeling the glass cutting into the bottom of my bare feet, but I ignored the stinging pain.

Teagan threw out her hand, and the knife was ripped out of my mine. It spun around, the glistening blade pointing at me and shaking in midair.

I really should have thought this through. It probably wasn't the best idea to attack someone who was telekinetic.

"There you go," she said. "Thinking with your emotions again." She made a tsking sound, and the knife cut through the air toward me.

I shrieked and backed up, slipping on the wet floor and falling backward onto my butt.

I cried out, gripping my stomach, worried for my son as the knife came closer. I threw out my arm to knock it away, and the blade sliced into my flesh.

I screamed as the knife flung across the room, smacked against the wall, and then clattered to the floor. Dark-red blood welled in the cut, dripping down my arm and onto the floor beneath me.

It stung and burned, but I pushed away the pain as anger and adrenaline flooded me. This bitch was completely insane.

She was like the alien version of that bitch from *The Hand that Rocks the Cradle.*

I pushed up off the floor, keeping my wounded arm against me and my eyes on the crazy.

"Don't worry," she said calmly. "I won't tell your son how pathetic his birth mother really was."

With a scream, I charged her, knocking into her thin frame, and she crashed against the wall. I felt sick pleasure when her skull bounced off the doorframe and her eyes rolled back in her head.

I lunged forward to grab her by the hair and pull her up again, but before I could reach her, she threw out her hand again. The force of her energy smacked into me, and I stumbled, unable to walk a step closer.

I fought against the wall she put up between us, but I wasn't strong enough to break through. My energy was draining quickly. The adrenaline, fear, and pain was taking an extra toll on my already tired form.

I stopped struggling, wanting to conserve what little energy I did have, suddenly terrified I could hurt the baby. Once I stopped struggling, her forceful energy pushed me back, and I hit against the kitchen counter.

My back bowed outward and pain radiated across my middle. The cramp in my lower abdomen caused me to double over.

I cried out with pain. "No!" I said, wrapping my arms around my middle. Another pain ripped through my center, and sheer panic ascended.

It's too early for the baby to come!

I still have weeks left to go!

Blood ran down my arm, dripping onto the floor, as another rush of liquid between my legs splattered at my feet.

"The baby!" I sobbed. "My water just broke."

Teagan was standing nearby, staring at me. Her face was scared, like she hadn't meant to send me into early labor.

"It's too soon," I sobbed again. "Get Tarek," I pleaded with her. "*Please.*"

For a split second, I thought Teagan was going to help me. She looked toward the door, like perhaps she was going to go find Tarek like I asked.

Another intense wave of pain tightened my midsection, and I cried out, hunching over.

"Tarek," I called, wishing he were here.

I looked up at Teagan through tearstained eyes, ready to beg. She stepped toward me, that blank look taking over her features.

"Tarek isn't coming," she said calmly. "It's time."

"No!" I said, pushing away from the counter and stumbling toward the kitchen door. My arm was still bleeding, the cut deep enough that it needed stitches. My feet were cut and bleeding, and all the blood was mixing with the fluid my womb was releasing. If I had been in my right mind, I would have been horrified.

Teagan didn't say anything else as she stepped toward me. Fear blanketed my entire body. She reached out her hand and laid it on my shoulder.

And then both of us disappeared.

the birth

I'd been hijacked by a bat-shit crazy alien who apparently thought once I was out of the picture, my son would be hers for the taking.

I was in pain. On the cusp of early labor, my arm was still bleeding and my feet had bits of glass in them.

And I wanted Tarek. I wanted to feel his hot, smooth touch, I wanted to hear his lyrical voice, and I wanted to see that steely, cold look in his eyes. It was that look that would reassure me everything would be fine. It was that look that would tell me he was fighting, that he was going to do whatever he could to keep us together.

Tarek isn't coming.

Teagan's words echoed through my head, taunting me and delivering unparalleled fear. What if he was dead? What if they attacked him, kidnapped him, or something equally horrifying while he was on the way to the grocery store?

The thought of him dying or being tortured was almost too much to bear.

Another intense contraction ripped through my middle, and I cried out, reminding myself to breathe, that I was in pain because I was supposed to be. Labor hurt. It didn't necessarily mean something was wrong with my son.

It became startlingly clear that I couldn't worry about Tarek and this baby at the same time. It would kill me. I had to focus. I had to focus on getting this baby born. I had to focus on keeping him safe. Tarek was strong; he would be able to take care of himself.

He would come for us.

Until then, I had to be strong.

Sweat dotted my brow as the worst of the contraction faded away. I took advantage and looked around where Teagan had literally dumped me and disappeared. I was on a hovercraft that looked a lot like the one I spent time on with Tarek. But I had no idea if it was the same one. They probably all looked the same. These people didn't like dissimilarity; they wanted everything to be the same.

The lighting was a bit brighter than before. It still had a blue cast to it, but it wasn't as dim. The floors were clean and bare, and the room I was sitting in was empty.

I sat up, looking for a anything I could use as a weapon, for anything I thought might help me. There was nothing. Even if I found a door, I couldn't use it. We were likely floating an unknown distance above the atmosphere, and unless I planned to plunge to my death, I would be staying here.

My clothes were saturated with blood and fluid. I glanced down at the open cut on my forearm and winced. I needed to stop the bleeding. I grabbed the hem of my dress and ripped into it, shredding a scrap of fabric from around the hemline. I used it to wrap around my arm, winding it tightly and using my teeth to help. Once I managed to get it into a terribly tied knot, I sagged against the floor as another contraction ripped through me.

It felt like someone was inside my lower abdomen, twisting my insides into little knots and wringing them out so they were nothing but a bundle of matter. Instead of fighting against the pain, I went with it. I let it carry me. I just breathed and stared up at the ceiling, waiting for the worst of it to subside.

When it did, my body felt like Jell-O. How long was it going to hurt like this? My God, I was exhausted already. I craved the energy Tarek supplied. I always thought he would be at my side when I had this baby. I thought I would be in a hospital, with my doctor and my parents.

I also kind of hoped there would be some pain meds involved.

Instead, I was lying on the floor of an alien hovercraft. I was cut, bleeding, and scared. I was completely alone, and this baby was coming.

Not the best of circumstances.

Another contraction assaulted me, and I marveled at how much faster they were coming now. I groaned a little as the pain tightened my body. Just then, a few figures appeared. They were dressed in silver robes like the one Tarek had worn when I first saw him. The oversized hoods were pulled low, concealing their faces, and the silver fabric draped all the way to the floor, concealing their feet.

Behind them was Teagan, still dressed in her "human" clothes and watching me with that expressionless look on her face.

I hated her. Like, *really* hated her.

So much for showing her what it was like to be human. For hoping she might help us.

The people in robes approached me, and I cringed away, not wanting them close to me. They ignored my obvious reaction and reached down to lift me up. I was carried across the craft to a very sterile table and placed in the center. The metal was cold and unforgiving, just like everyone in this room.

"Please," I said, gritting my teeth through the pain. "Don't do this."

They ignored me, like hearing the pleas of a betrayed woman in pain was nothing at all. One of them attached a monitor to my arm, the other took my temperature, and through it all, I stared at Teagan, hoping my expression chilled her to her core.

"Her temperature is very high, her heart rate erratic." Someone beside me was reporting as he read off various monitors and tools. "Her energy levels are fading. Not sure if she will make it through a natural birth."

My clothes were ripped away, leaving me vulnerable on the table, with my bare belly exposed. I started to cry, not because I was sad, but because I was so incredibly angry.

How could I feel so helpless?

A hand reached out and grabbed my arm. A needle came close to piercing my skin. I shrieked and lashed out, sending the man and his needle onto the floor. Someone else rushed at my side, and I threw out a fist, connecting with his chest. Pain vibrated through my hand, but I didn't care. I wanted these things away from me.

"Stay back!" I shouted. "Don't come near me." More contractions ripped through me, and I curled in on myself, more tears leaking from my eyes. I looked up to see that Teagan had come closer, and there was actually emotion in her eyes.

Guilt.

Sorrow.

Regret.

I latched onto that. "I know you don't care about me, and that's fine," I told her, taking gasping breaths. "But I know you want this baby. Maybe you even care about him."

Her eyes flared, and I knew it was true. Her vulnerable spot was this baby, her ability to become a "mother" when he was born.

"I need Tarek, please," I pleaded. "Please get him."

The hooded figures closed in on me, and I couldn't see if my words had any effect on her at all. They grabbed my hands and strapped me down. Even though I struggled, I was no match for them. I was too incredibly exhausted.

Another one came near me again with another needle, and I started screaming. "No drugs!" I yelled. I had no idea what they were trying to pump into me, and I didn't care. I didn't want anything from them. I'd rather feel the pain of a natural birth than let them take away my consciousness.

"Calm down," the one with the needle said.

I nodded quickly. "I won't fight if you put the needle away."

The needle disappeared, but before I could celebrate the small victory, my ankles were grabbed and my legs were spread wide.

Horror shook my entire body. God, I was not an experiment. I was a person. I was a mother. How could they do this to me?

One of the robed Sapiens shoved two fingers into my vagina and probed around. I tried to snap my legs shut but wasn't allowed. I sobbed, feeling so incredibly violated and grossed out.

"She's not fully dilated," he announced when he was done betraying my body.

"We'll just cut the child out," someone else said.

"No!" I shouted. "No!"

Another syringe appeared and so did a tray of very sharp instruments. I was going to throw up.

The needle approached me, and I started to struggle against all the binds that held me down. My back and midsection hurt so fiercely that I was almost numb with pain.

Just as the needle met my skin, the person holding it flew back and hit the wall. He slumped into a heap on the floor. The other Sapien standing nearby was also tossed away.

Commotion and shouting erupted as I lay there helpless and strapped to a table.

A familiar rush of energy charged the air and flitted across my skin. "Tarek!" I yelled desperately.

He appeared, rushing to my side with wild eyes. His face was unlike I'd ever seen it before. Drawn and flushed, his lips were thin and slashed across his face. His eyes are as dark as onyx, and the stars I usually saw in his stare were gone.

He was absolutely infuriated.

The binds that held my wrists and ankles were ripped away, and I sprang up, moaning at the pain it caused but moving anyway. Tarek wrapped his arms around me as I collapsed against him with great heavy sobs.

My body shook violently with the force of my sobs. His arms wrapped around me. I could feel the way his muscles quivered, yet he was steadfast.

His large palm cupped the back of my head, and he held me against him as I sucked in great gulps of air, trying to calm myself.

"I got home and you weren't there," he whispered. "I saw the broken glass, the water, and the blood all over the floor."

I heard him swallow roughly as his saliva forced its way down his throat.

"I thought you were dead."

The words were barely audible. The rawness in his voice was unlike anything I'd ever heard before. "I had nothing before I met you, Sophie. I didn't even know what it was like to exist. You gave me everything. I have nothing without you."

More pain racked my body. I clutched at him, digging my fingers into his skin. "The baby," I said, "he's coming. They're trying to take him."

As if to prove my point, the Sapiens hidden by robes came closer, invading our space in a menacing way.

"Get back," Tarek growled. "I will kill every last one of you."

"I'm so tired," I said, leaning farther into him. Now that I knew he was here and that he would watch over me, my body was losing its fight with itself.

"Take all the energy you need from me, love," he said, holding me tightly. Above my head, he spoke. "Get me blankets." His voice left no room for argument.

Seconds later, he was lifting me in his arms as Teagan spread a soft blanket over the cold table. He laid me down gently, keeping his hands on me, and nodded to Teagan. Another blanket covered up the rest of me, giving me a modicum of coverage.

This incredible pressure built low in my abdomen, and the urge to push filled my limbs. "I think he's coming," I ground out, gripping Tarek.

He pulled his hands away from me, and I made a sound of protest. "I'm just going to look," he said, lifting the blanket. A person moved up behind him and stared down as well. His hand reached out to examine me again, and I winced. Tarek shoved him away roughly. "Do. Not. Touch. Her."

"She needs to push," the man replied, keeping his distance.

I looked at Tarek through watery eyes. "It's too soon."

"He's coming, love. We can't stop him."

I shook my head as Tarek placed his warm hands on my inner thighs. "It's just me and you right now," he murmured, locking onto my eyes with his purple gaze. It was less wild now, more concentrated, and totally focused on me. "I need you to push," he said.

"I don't want to," I said, looking around at all the kidnappers in the room.

"Look at me," he said, drawing my gaze once more. "It's just me and you. I'm delivering him, no one else. I will protect him."

The urge to push was so great I couldn't deny it. I bore down and began the process of delivering my son.

I don't know how long it took; it felt like I pushed forever. The pain was hot and intense, but I couldn't focus on it because I was too busy focusing on pushing.

And then a tiny cry filled the room.

All the burning pain in my body evaporated as I shoved myself up to look for the person I most wanted to see.

Tarek was standing at the end of the table, holding the baby and staring down at him in complete and utter wonder.

The baby made another wailing sound, and Tarek blinked, a large grin spreading across his face. "My son," he murmured, tucking the little boy against his chest and pressing his lips to his forehead.

Teagan moved closer, and I barely paid her any attention because I was so riveted on seeing my son in the arms of the man I loved. It was the most incredible thing I had ever seen.

I thought I knew love before. I thought I knew what it was like for someone to be your entire universe.

That was nothing compared to what I felt now.

Teagan cut the umbilical cord and stepped away. Tarek finally raised his eyes from our son to stare at me. "You gave me a son," he whispered.

I smiled. "Let me see him." I held out my arms for my son, and Tarek moved to hand him to me.

As he extended the baby toward me, I caught a flash of movement behind Tarek as a robed Sapien swung a needle down toward the back of his neck.

"Tarek!"

He looked over his shoulder but wasn't able to strike out because he was still holding our son. I reached out and took the baby, crooning to him as Tarek spun, trying to deflect the needle.

He managed to keep it from going into his neck.

But it speared his arm instead.

The man in the robe went flying back as the syringe stuck out of Tarek's arm. He turned and looked between me and the needle. The baby began to cry as Tarek yanked it out and threw it across the room.

Just as I was about to breathe a sigh of relief, Tarek's eyes rolled back in his head and he slumped to the ground.

the end

I called out his name until my voice felt like it was going to go hoarse. He was lying in a crumpled heap on the floor, his skin more translucent than white and the tops of his eyelids a purple-ish shade that frankly made my stomach hurt.

His full, usually kissable lips were colorless, and he didn't move once.

I didn't know what the hell was in that syringe, but I was terribly afraid it was deadly.

Tears rained from my eyes continuously, and when I finally looked up from Tarek, it was to see Teagan staring down at him with a bleak expression in her eyes.

"You," I whispered hoarsely. Teagan looked up. "This is your fault."

In my arms, my son started to fuss and wiggle about. I gave her one last hateful stare before turning my eyes down to stare at the tiny bundle wrapped in my arms.

Time stopped for me.

Everything else fell away.

He was absolutely perfect.

"Shh," I whispered to him, rocking him gently in my arms. I reached out to feather my fingers through the full head of incredibly soft, dark hair. "Hi there." I spoke softly, running a fingertip over his little round cheek. The baby's cries softened and his eyes fluttered open and looked up at me, focusing completely on me.

His eyes were purple.

A crystal-clear shade of amethyst that was so incredibly innocent it made me want to weep. He looked just like Tarek, except his skin wasn't quite as pale.

His little arm reached out and five long, perfect fingers waved in the air, and I laughed.

"Tarek," I said, "he looks just like you."

I didn't get a reply.

Reality came crashing back, and the momentary joy of meeting my newborn son was sorely interrupted. "Tarek," I called again, clutching the baby against me and leaning forward. He hadn't moved.

A Sapien moved forward, and I stiffened, but he wasn't coming at me. He leaned down over Tarek. He seemed to be taking his vitals, feeling for a pulse.

A few seconds of nothing at all, and the robed figure stood and bowed his head.

A low moan filled the room. It was a sound I would never forget. It was the sound of deep sorrow and keen horror.

I realized the sound was coming from me.

Once everyone in the room realized Tarek was no longer a threat, things began to happen with great speed.

That moment I had with my son, that single joyful moment when everything was right in my world?

It was all I was going to get.

Three hooded figured approached me. I could feel their silent stares from within the dark confines of the hoods. A sick feeling twisted its way into my guts and worked its way up to settle as a hard rock in the center of my chest.

My heart began to pound rapidly; my breaths came in short gasps.

"Give him to me," one of the Sapiens said.

I would have laughed, but there was nothing remotely funny about this. "No."

"You're mistaken to think you have a choice."

"You cannot take my son from me," I said as he reached out his long, ominous fingers and tried to lift the baby from my arms.

I tightened my grip, and I saw the flash of purple lightning beneath the hood. "Give me the child before he gets hurt."

I debated for long moments, both of us griping his little body, and in the end, I supposed it was a weakness to love him.

Because I was the one who loosened my grip.

I couldn't take the chance that he would harm my son. I knew he would because I'd just watched him do it to Tarek.

He snatched the baby away from me, and I launched up off the table, ignoring the protests of my seemingly battered body, and grabbed the back of the robe, yanking the Sapien back. The baby started fussing again, and I was thrown back into the wall with their stupid telekinetic power.

I really hated that power.

I bounced off the curved hovercraft wall and wobbled on my feet, flat out refusing to fall. I started to run at the man holding my son when he said, "Take care of her."

"No!" I screamed, pushing past the robed figure who was trying to snatch me away.

Teagan appeared with her usual cold, sinister look on her face. Both her hands shot out and grabbed me. Then everything went dark.

The next thing I knew I was standing beside my Jeep as dusk claimed the day. I'd been gone for hours. Hours that forever changed my life.

I shoved away from Teagan and looked up at the sky, desperate for a glimpse of the hovercraft.

"It isn't here," she said.

I reared my fist back and smashed it into her face. Her pretty head snapped back on her shoulders, and she looked at me with pure shock in her eyes.

I reared back to hit her again.

She threw up her hand, and my fist smashed against solid air. I opened my mouth to rage, but she stopped me.

"I just saved your life," she said.

I laughed. "You think you did me a favor?" My voice was incredulous. "You've condemned me to an endless string of nothing!" I raged. "You let them steal my son away, my perfect baby—" My voice caught, but I pressed on. "You watched as they killed the only man I have ever loved."

I slumped against the side of the Jeep, completely defeated. "I would be better off dead."

I felt her stare for long minutes, but I didn't look at her again. She'd won. She'd managed to take everything from me, and I had no hope of getting it back.

She left without another word. Disappeared into the fading light of day.

I leaned against the Jeep for a long time, knowing full well I was totally naked, except for what was left of my dress tied around my arm. I knew someone could happen upon me and think I was likely insane.

Maybe it would be better that way.

Maybe they would lock me up in a tiny room where I would sit forever.

As darkness shrouded the sky, blackening out everything around me, goose bumps rose upon my flesh. My body began to shake uncontrollably, but I couldn't bear to go inside.

If I went inside, I would see him everywhere I looked.

I would remember the times he took me up against the wall because he was too impatient to go to bed. I would remember all the times we "watched" a movie on the couch when really all we did was make out like lovesick teenagers.

I would go in the kitchen and see the bananas he made sure were always waiting for me…

I couldn't go in there, not ever again.

My hand fumbled with the handle of the Jeep, and the door popped open. I reached into the back and grabbed a blanket that we sometimes used when we drove up to the lake. I wrapped it around my shoulders and wandered away from my car and into the field beside my apartment.

There were no stars tonight. The dark was sinister, complete, all-encompassing. My body was so tired and hurt in so many places, but it was nothing compared to the gaping hole that now took up my chest.

I sank down to the ground, sitting in the center of the grass, letting the inky night envelope me. I would just sit here in the night and hope it would swallow me whole.

I didn't know how much time passed, likely hours, but it didn't matter.

I was staring out into nothing, remembering the first and only time I'd seen my baby boy. The little sounds of his fussing still echoed through my head, and I held on to the sound, wanting to never forget it.

And then he began to cough. Little gurgling coughs and gasps that sounded like he was sucking air. I wrinkled my nose. I didn't remember him making those sounds when I was holding him.

He did it again.

It was so close… like it was right beside me.

My entire body stilled as I sensed movement behind me. I leapt up and spun around, clutching the blanket around my shivering shoulders, my tired eyes searching the dark.

He was easy to see.

His pale skin was like a neon light in the shadows.

"Tarek?" I whispered, knowing full well I could be hallucinating.

Hell, I might even be in shock.

The little bundle wrapped up in his arms threw out an angry fist and gave a yell.

"There's your mommy," he whispered. The lyrical quality to his voice washed over my frayed nerves.

A sob caught in my throat as I dared to believe.

Tarek took a step forward, his long legs eating up the distance between us. "You have me," he whispered, his voice carrying through the night like a bedtime lullaby. "I belong to you."

My heart burst, a great waterfall of emotion surging forward inside, and I was propelled forward, tripping over the blanket as I rushed at him. He shifted the baby in his arm and held open his other one, completely enveloping me into his embrace.

A torn sob pressed against his chest as I gripped onto the front of his T-shirt. Tarek clutched me against him so tight I was afraid I might not be able to breathe.

But that was okay.

Because if I ever stopped, he would breathe for me.

Right next to me, my son began to cry with great force, and Tarek let out what sounded like a relieved sigh. "He's very hungry," he whispered.

Overcome with joy, I pushed back and took the baby, cradling him in my arms and cooing all kinds of silly words I hadn't realized I knew. I let the blanket slip down over my shoulder to expose one achingly full breast.

He latched on almost instantly, barely needing any guidance, and ate hungrily. I watched him for long minutes, so thankful he was here, realizing how close I came to never seeing either one of my loves ever again.

Finally, I ripped my eyes away from the baby and up to Tarek. He was staring at me hungrily, tense lines around his eyes.

"What happened?" I whispered as I rocked gently on my feet. "I thought… I thought you were dead."

He cupped the side of my face in his palm, and I pressed into him, marveling in his touch. I swayed on my feet, and he frowned, scooping me up, barely disrupting the baby and his gentle feeding. "You've been through too much." He strode quickly up to the apartment. "Your skin is like ice."

I leaned my head against him as I carried my son, and he carried us both. Inside the apartment, he brought me into the bedroom and sat me on the bed. I tossed aside the blanket and lifted the baby off my breast. He fussed, wanting more, but I rubbed his back gently until he was ready to feed on the other side.

Once he was contentedly suckling away, Tarek crouched down before me and lifted my arm, the one that was hastily wrapped in my ripped dress.

"What the hell happened, Soph?" he asked.

I shook my head. The thought of retelling it all was almost as horrific as going through it.

"Shh," he said. "You can tell me in time. It doesn't matter now. It only matters that we are back together."

Carefully, he unwound the wrapping, exposing an angry red slash that was surprisingly still oozing. The skin around the cut was hot to the touch, and I knew it was probably infected. Tarek's eyes turned very dark as he studied the damage, and without saying a word, he wrapped both hands around my forearm and closed his eyes.

My entire arm began to heat, like it had been submerged in a tub full of hot water. The area tingled and began to itch. After several minutes, he pulled away.

The knife wound was entirely healed.

"Where else?" he asked softly.

I lifted my feet. Anger turned his lips into a hard line as he looked at the various cuts and embedded glass. He went to work quickly, somehow using his telekinesis to pull out all the glass slivers and then healing my wounds with his hands.

"Thank you," I said when he sat back.

The baby had unlatched from my breast and had already fallen into a peaceful-looking sleep. "He looks just like you," I whispered, feeling my heart swell with love.

"The sight of you holding him is the most incredible thing I've ever seen," Tarek replied, moving to sit beside me.

"He needs a name," I said, resting my head on his shoulder.

"Do you have one in mind?"

I nodded. "I'd like to call him Axton."

Tarek repeated the name, trying it out on his tongue. "I like it," he said. "Very different."

I nodded. "It's unusual here too, but I think a unique name suits him."

Tarek kissed the top of my head, and I smiled. "You need a warm shower and rest. Once you're cleaned up, I can heal you from the birth as well."

"I want to hold him just a little bit longer," I whispered.

Tarek chuckled and gently pulled me and Axton up onto the bed, where he arranged the covers around my legs and wrapped an arm around my waist.

"What happened up there?" I asked. I needed to know how he managed to come back to me. Then another thought had my muscles going rigid. "Are they going to come for us? Do we need to run?"

"No," he said, pressing me back against him. "You're safe. All three of us are safe."

"How?"

"Only a small percentage of whatever was in the syringe actually made it into my bloodstream. I managed to get the man away from me before he could depress it all into my body."

"But if he had…?" I asked.

"If he had managed to get it all in me, I would be dead."

I turned my face into his chest, the thought just too horrible to imagine.

"But he didn't. And after a while, I came to. Everyone thought I was dead, so no one was watching me."

"Then what?"

"I heard the baby crying, and in between, he was gasping for air." I tipped my head back so I could watch him while he spoke. "They were already traveling to my planet, a trip that would have taken years to complete."

"But?"

"But as soon as we left Earth's atmosphere, little Axton here couldn't breathe."

I gasped.

"They hadn't expected that. They thought as a Sapien, his lungs would have the capacity to breathe like the rest of us."

"But he isn't all Sapien," I said.

He shook his head. "No. He's also part you." His eyes warmed and the silver specks shone like glittering diamonds. "And you, my love, wouldn't be able to breathe on my planet."

"And they just let you have him?" I asked, surprise coloring my tone.

His jaw tightened. "They put him down on a table and left the room. They were just going to let him die."

Rage set fire to my insides, so much so that I tried to jump off the mattress.

"Easy," he murmured. "As soon as they left, I picked him up and I breathed for him, just like sometimes I do for you."

"You did?" I whispered.

He nodded. "Teagan found me and the baby. I thought I was going to have a fight on my hands, but it wasn't like that at all. She helped me slip into a small emergency craft, and I flew it back here."

"So they don't know you got away?"

He shrugged. "By now, they might suspect." He griped my arm, anticipating my reaction. "But it doesn't matter. They won't come back."

"But why?"

"Because Axton can't live on their planet. He's of no use to them."

"What about revenge?" I worried.

He smiled. "Sapiens are too cold and emotionless for revenge." Tarek tucked me into his side, brushing his thumb over the cheek of our sleeping child.

"You're safe. We're all safe. That's the way it's going to stay."

"You really think so?"

"I know so."

I let the warmth of his body seep into mine and the soft breathing of our child fill my ears. "Tarek?" I asked softly.

"Hmm?"

"Thank you for abducting me."

He chuckled. "Oh, love, the pleasure was all mine."

Want more romance from Cambria Hebert?

Check out her contemporary *Take It Off* series.

For an excerpt from *TORCH* turn the page!

TORCH
novel
"If you can't take the heat...stay away from the flame."
a Take it Off novel
CAMBRIA HEBERT

TORCH

by Cambria Hebert

1

The pungent smell of gasoline stung my nostrils and my head snapped back in repulsion. I opened my eyes and lifted my hands to place them over my mouth and nose to hopefully barricade some of the overwhelming scent.

Except my hands didn't obey.

I tried again.

Panic ripped through my middle when I realized my arms weren't going to obey any kind of command because they were secured behind me.

What the hell?

I looked down over my shoulder, trying to see the thick ropes binding my wrists. The lighting in here was dim.

Wait. Where was I?

My heart started to pound, my breathing coming in shallow, short spurts as I squinted through tearing eyes at the familiar shapes around me. A little bit of calmness washed over me when I realized I was in my home. Home was a place I always felt safe.

But I wasn't safe. Not right now.

I sat in the center of my living room, tied to my dining room chair. I was supposed to be in bed sleeping. The boxers and T-shirt I wore said so.

I started to struggle, to strain against the binds that held me. I didn't know what was going on, but I knew enough to realize whatever was happening was not good.

Movement caught my attention and I went still, my eyes darting toward where someone stood.

"Hello?" I said. "Please help me!"

It was so dark I couldn't make out who it was. They seemed to loom in the distance, standing just inside the entryway, nothing but a dark shadow.

My eyes blinked rapidly, trying to clear the tears flowing down my cheeks. The gasoline smell was so intense. It was like I was sitting in a puddle of the stuff.

"Help me!" I screamed again, wondering why the hell the person just stood there instead of coming to my aid.

The scrape of a match echoed through the darkness, and the catch of a small flame drew my eye. It started out small, reminding me of the fireflies I used to chase when I was a child. But then it grew in intensity, the flame burning brighter, becoming bolder, and it burned down the stick of the match.

The dark shadow held out the matchstick, away from their body, suspending it over the ground for several long seconds.

And then they dropped it.

It fell to the floor like it weighed a thousand pounds and left a small glowing trail in its wake. I watched the flame as it hit the floor, thinking it would fizzle out and the room would be returned to complete blackness.

But the flame didn't fizzle out.

It ignited.

With a great whoosh, fire burst upward, everything around that little match roaring to life with angry orange flames. I screamed. I didn't bother asking for help again because it was clear whoever was in this house wasn't here to help me.

They were here to kill me.

To prove my realization, the dark figure calmly retreated out the front door. The flames on the floor grew rapidly, spreading like a contagious disease up the walls and completely swallowing the front door. The small side table by the door, which I'd lovingly scraped and painted, caught like it was the driest piece of wood in the center of a forest fire.

Smoke began to fill the rooms, curling closer, making me recoil. How long until the flames came for me?

I began to scream, to call for help, praying one of my neighbors would hear and come to my rescue. Except I knew no one was going to rush into this house to save me. They would all stand out on the lawn at the edge of the street and murmur and point. They would click their tongues and shake their heads, mesmerized by the way the fire claimed my home. And my life.

I wasn't going to die like this.

I twisted my arms, straining against the corded rope, feeling it cut into my skin, but I kept at it, just needing an inch to slip free.

I tried to stand, to run into the back of the house. If I couldn't get loose from the chair, I would just take it with me. But my ankles were crossed and tied together.

I called for help again, but the sound was lost in the roaring of the flames. I never realized how loud a fire truly was. I never realized how rapidly it could spread. It was no longer dark in here, the flames lighting up my home like the fourth of July, casting an orange glow over everything. The entire front entryway and stairwell were now engulfed. I could see everything was doused in gasoline; the putrid liquid created a thick trail around the room. Whoever had been here completely drenched this house with the flammable liquid and then set me in the center of it.

I managed to make it to my feet, hunched over with the chair strapped around me. It was difficult to stand with my ankles crossed. But I had to try. I had to get out of here. I took one hobbled step when a cough racked my lungs. I choked and hacked, my lungs searching for clean air to breathe but only filling with more and more pollution.

I made it one step before I fell over, my shoulder taking the brunt of my fall, the chair thumping against the thickness of the carpet. I lay there and coughed, squinting through my moist and blurry vision, staring at the flames… the flames that seemed to stalk me.

They traveled closer, following the path of the gas, snaking through the living room, filling it up and rushing around me until I was completely circled with fire. The heat, God, the heat was so intense that sweat slicked my skin, and it made it that much harder to breathe.

It was the kind of heat that smacked into you, that made you dizzy and completely erased all thought from your brain.

I was going to die.

Even if I were able to make it to my feet, I wouldn't be able to make it through the circle of fire that consumed everything around me.

I pressed my cheek against the carpet, not reveling in its softness, not thinking about the comfort it usually afforded my bare feet. Another round of coughing racked my body. My lungs hurt. God, they hurt so bad. It was like a giant vise squeezed inside my chest, squeezed until all I could think about was oxygen and how much I needed it.

My chin tipped back as I writhed on the floor, making one last attempt at freedom before the flames claimed me completely. I heard the sharp crackling of wood, the banging of something collapsing under the destruction, and I blinked.

This is it.

The last moments of my life.

I'm going to die alone.

I started to hallucinate, the lack of oxygen playing tricks on my fading mind, as a large figure stepped through the flames. Literally walked right through them. He held up his arms, shielding his face and head as he barreled through looking like some hero from an action movie.

My eyes slid closed as my skin began to hurt, like I sat outside in the sun for hours without the protection of sunscreen.

I heard a muffled shout and tried to open my eyes, but they were too heavy. Besides, I preferred the darkness anyway. I didn't want to watch as my body was burned to death by fire.

Pain screamed through me and the feeling of the carpet against my cheek disappeared. My first thought was to struggle, but my body couldn't obey my mind. I felt movement, I felt the solidness of someone's chest, and I could have sworn I heard the sound of a man's voice.

"*Hang on,*" he said.

The shattering of glass and the splintering of wood didn't wake me from the fog that settled over my brain. The scream of pain at my back, the extreme burning and melting that made a cry rip from my throat still wasn't enough to get my eyes to open.

And then I could hear the piercing wail of sirens, the faraway shouts of men, and the muffled yell of one who was much closer.

I really thought heaven would be more peaceful.

And then I was sailing through the air, the solid wall of whatever held me ripped away. I plunged downward, and with a great slap, I hit water, the icy cold droplets a major shock to my overheated system.

My eyes sprang wide; water invaded them as I tried to make sense of what was happening. I thought I was burning. But now I was… drowning.

The water was dark and it pulled me lower and lower into its depths. I looked up. The surface rippled and glowed orange. I almost died up there. But I would die down here now.

I wanted to swim. My arms, they hurt so badly, but they wanted to push upwards, to help me break the surface toward the oxygen my body so desperately needed.

But I was still tied to a chair.

The chair hit the ground—a solid, cold surface—as my hair floated out around me and bubbles discharged from my nose and mouth.

It wasn't hot here.

It wasn't loud, but eerily quiet.

It was a different kind of death, but death all the same.

The ripples in the water grew and the chair began to rock. I heard the plunge of something else coming into the water and I looked up. Through the strands of my wayward hair, I saw him again. My hero. His powerful arms pushed through the water in three great stokes. He reached out and grabbed me beneath the shoulder, towing me upward toward the orange surface.

When my head cleared the water, my lungs automatically sucked in blissful air. It hurt so bad, but it was the kind of pain I had to endure. Another cough racked my body, and as I wheezed, the man towing me and my chair through the water said, "Keep breathing. Just keep breathing."

And then I was being lifted from the water, the chair placed on the cement as I coughed and wheezed and greedily sucked in air.

"Ma'am," someone was saying. "Ma'am, can you hear me? Are you all right?"

I looked up, blinking the water out of my eyes, but my vision was still blurry. I tried to speak, but all I could manage was another cough.

The ropes around my wrists were tugged, and I cried out. The pain was so intense that I thought I would pass out right there.

“Stay with me,” a calm voice said from behind. It was the same voice that instructed me to keep breathing.

When my arms were free, I sagged forward. The pain splintering through me was too much to bear. And then there were hands at my ankles; I heard the knife against the rope. When I was completely untied, my body fell forward, sliding off the chair and toward the ground.

But he was there.

I slid right into his arms, my body completely boneless.

A low curse slipped from his lips as he yelled for a medic. Yeah, a medic. That seemed like a good idea. I hurt. I hurt all over.

I cried out when he shifted me in his arms, bringing me closer to his chest. I pressed my face against him. He was wet, but his clothes were scratchy against my cheek. I tried to look at him; I opened my eyes and tilted back my head. I caught a flash of dark hair and light eyes, but then my vision faded out, pain took over, and I passed out.

ABOUT CAMBRIA HEBERT

Cambria Hebert is the author of the young adult paranormal *Heven and Hell* series, the new adult *Death Escorts* series, and the new adult *Take it Off* series. She loves a caramel latte, hates math, and is afraid of chickens (yes, chickens). She went to college for a bachelor's degree, couldn't pick a major, and ended up with a degree in cosmetology. So rest assured her characters will always have good hair. She currently lives in North Carolina with her husband and children (both human and furry), where she is plotting her next book. You can find out more about Cambria and her work by visiting http://www.cambriahebert.com.

CPSIA information can be obtained
at www.ICGtesting.com
Printed in the USA
FFOW02n2153280415
12943FF